Before Chase could put his phone in his pocket, the doorbell rang.

He opened the door without looking through the peephole. He froze, words sticking in his throat.

Jody stood there.

He hadn't seen her in over a year, and his heart stopped just from looking into her gorgeous eyes. In a green dress and heels, she looked more beautiful than ever, except there were tiny worry lines around her eyes that hadn't been there before.

She had a box in her hands and shoved it toward him. "These are some of the things you gave me, and I don't want them in my house anymore."

He refused to take it, so she set the box on the floor by his feet.

"How did you know I was home?" he asked, ignoring the box.

"I have to go. Just wanted you to have those things back because I know they mean something to you."

"That's why I gave them to you. They're yours."

She turned to leave as if she didn't want to get into an argument. He couldn't let her go. Breathing the same air as Jody was intoxicating, and he wanted to keep her here as long as possible, even if they were arguing. It had always been that way with him. He could be in the dumps about a game or something and the moment he heard her voice, it lifted his spirits.

"What are you doing h[...]
spring training or som[...]

"I just wanted to come[...]

Dear Reader,

It's been a fun, exciting journey writing about the Rebel Family, but it's time to say goodbye. It all started with *The Sheriff of Horseshoe, Texas*, Wyatt Carson and Payton's story, and as the parents of Jody, they play a big part in this book. *A Texan's Christmas Baby* is book eleven of the Texas Rebels series.

Chase and Jody fell in love in high school. Chase is two years older than her, and Wyatt strongly disapproved. But being teenagers, they found ways to be together. Later those teenage decisions come back to haunt them. They truly loved each other, and it takes them a long time to find that young love once again. And it takes a lot of help from the Rebel family.

With a touch of sadness I say goodbye to Grandpa, Miss Kate and the gang.

With my heartfelt thanks,

Linda

PS: You can email me at Lw1508@aol.com, or send me a message on Facebook.com/authorlindawarren or on Twitter @texauthor, or write me at PO Box 5182, Bryan, TX 77805, or visit my website at lindawarren.net. Your mail and thoughts are deeply appreciated.

HEARTWARMING

A Texan's Christmas Baby

—

Linda Warren

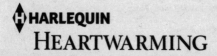

H HARLEQUIN®
HEARTWARMING™

ISBN-13: 978-1-335-42646-8

A Texan's Christmas Baby

PLEASE RECYCLE
THIS PRODUCT IS RECYCLABLE

Recycling programs for this product may not exist in your area.

Two-time RITA® Award–nominated author **Linda Warren** has written fifty books and short stories for Harlequin. A native Texan, she's a member of Romance Writers of America and the RWA West Houston chapter. Drawing upon her years of growing up on a ranch, she writes about some of her favorite things: Western-style romance, cowboys and country life. She married her high school sweetheart, and they live on a lake in central Texas. He fishes and she writes. Works perfect.

Visit the Author Profile page at Harlequin.com for more titles.

I dedicate the Texas Rebels series to my wonderful editor, Kathleen Scheibling, who has pushed me, praised me and lifted my spirits when I thought I couldn't write another word. Couldn't have done it without you. Thanks!

CHAPTER ONE

CHASE REBEL SNEAKED into Horseshoe, Texas, like a bandit, avoiding the square where a limestone courthouse stood proudly through the ages of time, and where anything that was important happened. He was avoiding family and friends, and most of all avoiding questions.

Today his heart was heavy. There'd be no Jody to greet him with hugs and kisses and promises of forever. She'd thrown her engagement ring at him and ended their fourteen-year relationship. That had happened over a year ago. They'd been happy—over-the-top happy. How could all that love just…stop?

He turned onto Mulberry Lane, a smile tugging at the corners of his mouth. Just seeing the street sign gave him a good feeling. This was home. He pushed a button on his visor and the garage door went up. He drove in and quickly put it down again. Hopefully no one had seen him and he'd have a little time to get his thoughts together. He'd had a few weeks to do that, but there were still a lot of questions to be answered. Maybe he'd made the decision too quickly. Maybe all he needed was time. Maybe...

Everything he owned was in his truck. He grabbed a carryall and made his way into the Austin stone house his dad had built for him. He dropped the carryall in the breakfast room and stared out the big windows to the barn, which he had years ago turned into his own man cave. There were a lot of good memories made there with his friends and Jody.

So many memories and he didn't know what to do with them...without her.

He hadn't been to the house since the breakup. He undid the latches on the windows and raised them, letting the cool February breeze waft through the closed-up house. Tree branches lay in the yard from a recent storm, tall weeds grew up around the fence and the yard needed mowing. When he'd gone off to college, his parents had kept up the property for a long time, but he'd decided they had enough to do without taking care of his house, too. A boy down the street mowed it for a monthly fee, but evidently he wasn't doing a great job. He would get in touch with him tomorrow and let him know that from now on Chase would do the mowing.

He glanced to the house. It had an open floor plan with a breakfast room, kitchen and a big living room and dining room all in one. His mom and dad had picked out everything, from the granite countertops to the white oak floors. It represented seventeen years of child support, his father had said. That sounded a little strange, but it was the truth.

At seventeen his life had changed forever. At the time he thought it had been the worst thing that could have happened to him, but it had turned out to be the best thing. He and his mom had lived in Dallas, where she had been the manager of an upscale restaurant. They had a good life and Chase had played football for a big Dallas school. He'd held the wide receiver position and the coaches had told him he was one of the best they'd ever seen—good enough to make it into the NFL. He just had to apply himself. He worked every day to accomplish that goal. Then his mother lost her job, Nana passed away and his mom couldn't pay the rent anymore. She decided to return to her hometown of Horseshoe. He'd had no idea where that was and hadn't wanted to go. Leaving would ruin his whole life, his plans. In Dallas, he had a chance of getting a scholarship to a good college to play football. In Horseshoe, he would lose that opportunity.

He hadn't realized at the time that he didn't have a choice. His mother had already made the decision, so they moved to the little town where she had been born and raised. They had to live with his mother's sister, Rosie, and her husband, Phoenix Rebel, whom Chase had never met before. It was all change. It was all different. And he hated it.

He flipped on the lights and made his way to the living room to sink into his dad's recliner. Memories flooded him and he took a moment to look back at all the things that had made him into the man he was today.

The McCrays and Rebels were bitter enemies and they had kept the drama going for years in Horseshoe. Chase's mother, Maribel, was a McCray. She grew up hating the Rebels, but that hadn't stopped her from falling in love with Elias Rebel. When she became pregnant, her dad demanded to know the name of the father. She refused to tell him because he would have killed Elias. Maribel's mother quickly got her out of the house and sent her to an elderly friend. The friend sent Maribel to Dallas to live with her sister until she could get her life together.

The sister was Lavinia Wainwright, better known as Miss Vennie or Nana. She had a large two-story house and took care of the two of them. Miss Vennie became a mother to Maribel and a grandmother to Chase. They stayed with her until she passed away. The bank took the house, since it was mortgaged to the hilt, and Maribel and Chase moved into an apartment. That had been a lot of changes for a seventeen-year-old kid. But it wasn't over yet.

Before he knew it, he was in Horseshoe, living with people he didn't know. And he did what every seventeen-year-old would do—acted up and tried to make his mother go back to Dallas. He talked a couple of guys he'd met into stealing beer from the convenience store and a beer joint. He thought if he got in trouble, his mother would see the town wasn't good for him. It didn't quite work out that way.

They were caught by the sheriff and

thrown in jail. That was a shock. He knew his mother would get him out, though that would take bail money and his mother didn't have any. So she did what desperate mothers do. She appealed to Chase's father. Chase had never known his identity. His mother had told him that it was a boy from high school who wasn't ready to be a father, so she'd raised Chase on her own. That was good enough for Chase. He hadn't cared to meet his father.

That changed quickly when he learned about Elias. Maribel agreed to release her out-of-control son into Elias's custody and Chase's life became pure hell from there. His biological father had a thing about manners, respect and rules. Chase thought he would die if his life got any worse. But he'd done the crime and he had to pay for it, as he was told by Elias. In court his father stood up and vouched for him; he got community service and the robbery was expunged from his record.

Restless from thinking about the past, Chase got up and walked into the kitchen, running his hand across the granite countertop, which was a tan and dark brown color that went well with the stainless steel appliances.

Elias hadn't paid child support for seventeen years because he hadn't known about his son. Being an honorable man, he wanted to make up for that. Since Maribel and Chase had no home, he bought them one. Back then it had looked like a run-down shack with the roof caving in and weeds growing into the windowsills. But Elias had said the Austin stone was as good as the day it had been laid. The other good thing was that it sat on ten acres at the end of a cul-de-sac. But Chase knew beyond any doubt that they would never be able to live there. Mice, varmints and roaches had made the house their home, and the rain-soaked carpets stank like sewage.

That was when Chase learned he was supposed to help fix it up. He had never done anything like that before in his whole life and he hadn't planned on doing it then. But his father had other ideas. And if anyone had ever met Elias, they knew he was a man of his word.

In the months that followed, Chase learned to work hard. He pulled out wet, disgusting carpet, stained linoleum and worn countertops. They basically gutted the place and started over. It took months to remodel the house and Elias seemed to know how to do everything, from plumbing to installing a new roof. Before those months ended, Chase knew how to do them, too. He even knew how to drive a lawn mower and a tractor. He learned a lot of things during that time, but most of all he learned how to love the man who had given him life.

He learned a lot of other things, too. Such as he didn't have to go to a big school to get scouted. The Horseshoe Cowboys won a state championship and Chase got noticed. He played football in college and went fifth in the first round of the NFL draft. Six years later his team won a Super Bowl and all his dreams had come true. Except for one.

The first time he met Jody was in the sheriff's office. After he finished his community service, he had to go there to apologize for his behavior. The sheriff's daughter was there and Chase was introduced to the most beautiful girl he'd ever seen. She had the most amazing green-brown eyes that sparkled with happiness. He couldn't look away from all that energy and vitality. It was such a part of her. He fell in love on the spot and so did Jody, but there was one little problem. The sheriff wouldn't let him date his daughter. Chase was too old for her. He was too wild. Sheriff Wyatt had always disapproved of Chase, but the two kids found a way to be together.

Chase was two years older than Jody and Wyatt thought when Chase went away to college Jody's fascination with him would end. It didn't. He came home as often as he could and Jody was always the first person he contacted. Then Jody left for college and Chase was in his junior year at a different college, and everyone thought the relationship was destined to end. But they loved each other. They finally got engaged two years ago and the wedding was planned for June, this year.

He ran a hand through his hair. That wasn't happening now. Everything had been canceled. Picking up his carryall, he headed for the bedroom. He could get the yard mowed before dark, but he needed groceries. He sank down on the bed. What he really needed was Jody.

His phone buzzed and he reached for it in his pocket, looking at the caller ID. He clicked on. "Hey, Zane, how you doing?"

Zane was his cousin and best friend. They'd stayed in touch through all the years. His cousin's intellect was a little higher than most people's, but he was down-to-earth and everybody loved him. He'd gone to Harvard on a scholarship and had become a doctor. He was in cancer research now and living in Houston with his wife, Erin. They were expecting their first child.

"I'm great. Erin and I are in Horseshoe. Wish you were here."

"I am."

"What do you mean?"

"I'm at my house."

"You're kidding."

"No. I'll tell you about it later. Can you get away?" Chase really needed his friend.

"Erin's gone baby shopping with her mother and I'm visiting with my parents. I'll be there in about thirty minutes."

Before Chase could put his phone in his pocket, the doorbell rang. He sighed. It probably was his parents. His mother seemed to have radar where he was concerned. He opened the door without looking through the peephole. He froze, words sticking in his throat.

Jody stood there.

He hadn't seen her in over a year and his heart stopped just from looking into her gorgeous eyes. In a green dress and heels, she looked more beautiful than ever, grown-up, sophisticated, except there were tiny worry lines around her eyes that hadn't been there before. Her long blond hair was pulled back and tied at her nape. It gave her delicate features a pinched look that he didn't like. He favored her hair long and around her face. But he didn't get much say in how she wore her hair these days.

She had a box in her hands and shoved it toward him. "These are some of the things you gave me and I don't want them in my house anymore."

He refused to take it, so she set the box on the floor by his feet. Her eyes were cold and hesitant as she waited for him to pick it up.

"How did you know I was home?" he asked, ignoring the box.

"I was coming from my house when I saw you turn down Sycamore Street."

"You have a house?"

She tensed. "Yes. Gramma left me her house, and when I came home, Mom and Dad helped me fix it up. I live there now."

The Horseshoe gossip grapevine had left

that tidbit out. He'd had no idea she'd inherited her grandmother's house. He wondered why his parents hadn't told him, but it didn't matter anymore. They were living separate lives now. It surprised him, though, that she wasn't seeking comfort from her family. "And not with your parents?"

"No." The clipped one word told Chase she was getting annoyed. "I have to go. Just wanted you to have those things back because I know they mean something to you."

"That's why I gave them to you. They're yours."

She turned to leave as if she didn't want to get into an argument. He couldn't let her go. Breathing the same air as Jody was intoxicating and he wanted to keep her here as long as possible, even if they were arguing. It had always been that way with him. He could be in the dumps about a game or something, but the moment he heard her voice, it lifted his spirits. She was the only drug he needed.

"What are you doing home anyway? Don't you have spring training or something or another?"

"I just wanted to come home."

She waved a hand as if she didn't care. "It's not my business."

"That's what I was thinking."

She gave him a narrow look that could singe the legs off a grasshopper.

"Can I ask you a question?"

She hesitated for a moment. "If it's not personal."

"Why did you come to my apartment that night a year ago? You usually call when you're coming so I can pick you up at the airport. I was just wondering what the surprise visit was about."

She stepped closer with a daredevil gleam in her eyes. "I should have made more surprise visits and then I would've found out exactly what you're doing in your off-time. But, oh, no, I trusted you. I trusted you right up till I saw it with my own eyes."

"Okay." He held up a hand as if to defend himself. "I'll tell you again what really happened. We lost in the playoffs. I told you that. The owner had a party to let the players know what a good job we had done. I told you that, too. I told you I was going, but I wouldn't stay long. I just wanted to come home for a couple of weeks.

"I left early and went to my apartment.

I was about to call you when my doorbell rang. A girl from the party had followed me home. She was the owner's niece and I felt compelled to be nice to her. It was pouring rain and she was soaking wet. She asked if I had a towel and I invited her in. She went to the bathroom to dry off and that's when you showed up. Nothing happened. How many times do I have to tell you that?"

"She was wearing the bathrobe I gave you for Christmas with your initials on it and it wasn't belted. I could see her breasts. I could see everything. She looked as if she'd just gotten out of the shower. That's what I saw and I don't care what you say. I saw it with my own eyes."

He didn't let her words derail him. He'd never touched the girl. "Why didn't you come in and confront her? Why didn't you demand to know what she was doing in your fiancé's apartment? That's the feisty Jody I know. The one who stands up for herself and never takes anything from anybody. Why didn't you confront her, Jody? Or me?"

"Because I was sick to my stomach at what I'd seen and just wanted to get away from you, away from the truth of what you were doing while playing games. I mean *really* playing games."

"I followed you to your car in the rain and you threw your engagement ring at me, delivering a tirade that I'd never heard from you before. Where was your trust, Jody? The trust that held us together for all those years apart, the trust that would cement our marriage. You judged me without knowing the truth."

"I saw the truth and, believe me, it was ugly."

"Okay." He held up his hands as if to give in. "Just tell me why you came that night."

"I hadn't seen you in a while and I just wanted to spend some time with you."

"You always call so I can make time. Why didn't you?"

"Look, Chase, I'm not going to stand here and be grilled by you. It happened and I know what I saw. You have the right to disagree. That's what life is about. So get over it, because you and I are through. I could never trust you again. I guess I was really hung up on the football hero making last-minute catches to win the game, but that phase of my life is over." She hurried to her car and drove away, leaving him wondering, still, why she'd really come that night.

JODY TURNED ON Sycamore Street and pulled over to the curb. She was trembling from seeing Chase. It had been so long since she'd laid eyes on him and she hadn't realized how hard that would be.

She hated what he had done to her. She'd loved him and he'd thrown that love back in her face by being with another woman. He denied it—why couldn't she believe him? Her heart answered immediately, but she couldn't go there. She couldn't go back to the pain.

She leaned her head against the steering wheel. She wanted to reach out and touch him, feel his strong muscles and run her hands through his hair. When she did that, they would fall into those curls that he hated, but she loved them. And she had loved Chase with all her heart. She didn't understand how everything between them could all end in a split second.

Her dad had said that some men cheat, and they always would. He'd added that it would be best if she put Chase Rebel out of her mind. Just how could she do that?

How could she get him out of her heart? She'd tried so many times, but once real love was given, it was everlasting. Even Chase's cheating hadn't changed that.

Her dad had said that she should have expected this, with him playing in other cities, traveling on the road. There were groupies hanging around the stadiums and all the players were tempted from time to time. But she'd trusted Chase.

She took a deep breath and drove on. Chase would be here for a few days. Then he would leave again and she wouldn't have to worry about running into him. Eventually she would see him again and she'd handle it much better than she had today, all nervous and jumpy like a schoolgirl.

Hurrying to the courthouse, where she worked as an ADA to Hardy Hollister, the DA, she realized it had been over an hour since she'd gone home to get her phone, which she'd left at her house at lunch.

Hardy's office was upstairs and she had a small one next to his. Alice, the receptionist, was at her desk, as usual.

"Has Hardy been looking for me?" she asked Alice.

Alice looked at her through wire-rimmed

glasses. "No. He has family in there." She nodded toward the closed door of Hardy's office.

Zane and Erin were home today for a visit and she couldn't wait to see her best friend. "Tell Erin I want to see her."

Erin was Hardy's daughter and she and Jody grew up as best friends. They told each other everything and went off to college together to make their dreams come true. Erin was living her dream while Jody was stuck in neutral, not knowing what was next for her.

When they were in high school, they had decided who they would be when they grew up. Erin would become a lawyer, following in her father's footsteps, and Jody would earn a criminal justice degree and go into law enforcement, like her dad. That was the plan, but things changed. Zane had gone to Harvard to pursue a medical degree and Erin missed him, as Jody had missed Chase. In high school it was Zane and Erin and Chase and Jody. The intervening years had put that love to the test.

Erin had transferred schools to be near Zane and was now a lawyer in Houston and happy. Her father was not thrilled with her

choices. He wanted her to one day come
back to Horseshoe and take over his job,
but Erin lived her life her way, and because
of Zane's job, she would probably never live
in Horseshoe again.

Jody soon realized being a police officer just wasn't her thing, so she entered law
school. She interned in Houston and then
worked for the Austin DA. When things
blew up with Chase, she returned to Horseshoe and Hardy offered her a job. It gave
her a sense of purpose and she liked what
she was doing in her small hometown. She
felt at home. But the peace she'd yearned
for wasn't there. She might never have that
again.

"Hey, friend." Erin waddled into Jody's
office.

Jody jumped up and hugged Erin, or at
least tried. She was eight months pregnant
and big. "Look at you! You're absolutely
glowing."

"I'm fat and this baby is sitting on my
bladder." Erin eased into a chair. They were
both blondes and people often asked them
if they were sisters. They were the same
height, the same weight and the same every-

thing, except Erin had blue eyes. "You might have to help me up."

Jody laughed and it felt good to be with her friend again. "I'm at your service."

Erin rubbed her stomach. "I never knew that carrying a baby was like having a basketball in your lap. I can't see my feet anymore and I need to pee about every thirty minutes or less. I'm ready for this baby to come."

"Be patient."

"Yeah, that's what Zane says, but he's not carrying this baby around." She rubbed her stomach again. "But I love her to death. I can't wait to meet her."

"You're going to make a great mother. How's the name game going?"

"We're still batting it back and forth. Zane wants something simple and I want something that's different…" Erin shrugged.

"I saw Chase today," Jody blurted out.

"What? Where?" Erin threw back her long blond hair and tried to sit up. It took three tries, but she made it.

"I went home for lunch and left my phone on the counter. I went back to get it and I saw his truck going down Sycamore Street. I have everything he ever gave me in a box, so

I turned around and went back home and got it. I took it to his house and gave it to him."

"Everything? Even those gold earrings he bought you with his name on one and your name on the other?"

Jody nodded. "Everything."

"Why, Jody?"

"I don't want them anymore. We're not together and all of that was a lie."

Erin stretched her back. "Really? I had a front-row seat, and from where I was sitting, it was a full-blown love affair."

"Don't say anything else," Jody warned. They'd had this conversation before. "You know what I went through and how long it took me to get over it."

"Jody, please, talk to your parents, talk to Chase. Get all the pain out. Until you do, you're going to continue to have this resentment. That's advice from a friend who knows what she's talking about."

Jody got to her feet, unable to sit any longer. "I can't. I tell myself all the time it's what I need to do, but…"

"Jody…"

"I can't relive what happened afterward. I'd just rather put it behind me."

"You can't until your parents and Chase

know what happened." Erin rubbed her stomach, eyeing Jody. "I've kept your secret all these years and I haven't even told Zane and I don't keep things from him, but you're my friend and I value our friendship. You have to make some decisions that will change your whole life and you have to be ready to face them. That's what adults do."

"I suppose," she admitted. But Erin didn't know how hard that would be. It would take her dignity, her pride and her value as a person. She'd never lied or cheated or stolen anything in her life, but she felt as if she'd stolen something valuable from Chase.

How did she make amends without destroying herself?

CHAPTER TWO

CHASE STOOD IN the doorway for a long time, wondering how their lives had gotten so mixed up. Would Jody ever forgive him if this was how she saw him? Right now he couldn't think about it anymore. It hurt too much, especially after seeing her.

He tried to close the door, but it bumped against the box. With his boot, he moved it aside. It would stay there until she took it back. There was nothing in there that he wanted; it all belonged to Jody.

Opening the shutters in the living room and dining room, he saw his dad's truck, pulling a trailer, drive up. The trailer was stacked with rolls of barbed wire and posts. His dad got out and walked toward the garage and the back gate. Tall, with muscles built from hard work, his dad was a typical cowboy/rancher in boots, jeans, a Western shirt and a battered cowboy hat pulled low on his forehead. Everyone said Chase looked just like him with his dark eyes and hair. His brothers were the same, though. They all favored their dad, though their mother had softened a few rough edges of their features.

The twins, John Abraham Rebel the Second, known as JR, and John Abraham Rebel the Third, known as Tre, would turn eleven this summer. There were twenty years between them. At first he felt kind of strange having brothers, especially ones so young. Now they were one big family. His mom, who desperately wanted a girl, had talked his dad into having another child, and little Eli happened. No girl. Just another boy. His mom was heartbroken, but it wore off quickly. Then his dad had said no more kids. His mom had her tubes tied and they knew Eli was the last of Elias Rebel's children.

His dad disappeared out of sight and Chase hurried to the breakfast room windows to see where he had gone. He was out there looking at the pasture and the grass when Chase opened the patio doors and shouted to him. With long strides, his dad made his way to Chase and grabbed him in a big bear hug. No matter how old he got, he would never tire of being hugged by his parents. It was love. It was security. It was the best thing on earth.

"What are you doing here?" his father asked.

They walked into the house. "I just got home." He did not want to get into the conversation too soon.

His dad removed his hat and plopped it onto the table. "Why didn't you call?"

"I thought I'd just wait until I got here."

Elias pointed a finger at him. "Your mom's going to be ticked off."

"I don't have to call every time I come home," he said in an unfamiliar voice. He sounded resentful.

"Of course you don't, but you know your mother. She thinks you're about the same age as Eli."

"What are you doing here?" Chase asked, changing the subject.

"I came to check on the yard. That boy you hired down the street moved away and he said he lost your number. I told him I'd take care of it. I was going to mow until I have to pick up the boys from school."

"I'll mow the yard, Dad."

"Are you going to be home that long?" Elias eased into a chair with a sigh. Most days, his dad worked from sunup to sundown. That was just the way he was, and he believed everyone in the family should work that hard, which caused a little conflict among the Rebel brothers.

"Yep."

His dad's phone pinged and he pulled it out of his pocket and laid it on the table. "I have several messages from your mother. Sometimes I just don't hear that phone when I'm working. Listen to this.

"Are you picking up the boys? Why aren't you answering your phone? Elias, you better answer your phone."

Chase pointed to the dining room windows. His mom's SUV pulled around his dad's truck into the driveway. "I think she's found you."

"Yep, she always does."

Chase got up and let his mom in through the back door.

"Chase! You're home." He towered over her, but she managed to hug him until he could barely breathe. With strawberry blond hair in a ponytail, she had a young look about her. She was one of the most level-headed women he'd ever known. Strong, too, knowing how to keep Elias in check, which some people considered a monumental task, not to mention four boys.

It had been just the two of them for so long and it was hard sometimes to realize he didn't have his mother's full attention anymore. They would always have a strong connection, though. "Why didn't you call? It doesn't matter. We'll have a big supper tonight to celebrate your homecoming."

He took a deep breath. "I need to talk to both of you."

His mom frowned. "Are you okay? The shoulder?"

He touched his right shoulder, which he'd injured in the playoffs. "It's coming along. I made a big decision and I need to tell you about it."

"Okay." His mom sat in a chair next to his dad.

He drew air into starved lungs. "I talked to the coach and my agent, and I decided to retire from the NFL."

"What!"

"What!" His mom was on her feet. "It's the shoulder, isn't it?"

"I still have a lot of therapy to go, but it's healing."

"They should have kicked that player out of the NFL," Elias snapped.

"He was ejected from the game and fined for unnecessary roughness. It's football and everyone wants to win."

"But not like that," Elias insisted. "He wanted you to miss the pass and he reached up and pushed your arm in a direction it doesn't normally go, but you held on to that ball all the way to the ground."

Chase remembered it vividly, the searing pain, the anger and the numbness as he realized what had just happened. It ended his career. White-hot pain had consumed his body, and when he tried to get to his feet, his arm dangled. At the hospital, they injected something into his left arm, and the next thing he knew, his parents were there as the nurses prepared him for surgery on his shoulder. The only person he'd wanted to see was Jody, but she wasn't there. They successfully managed to put his shoulder back together, but there would be lasting consequences, some that he wasn't ready to face and others he'd just as soon forget about.

It took weeks for him to make what he felt was the right decision for him. He'd spent almost eleven years in the NFL and it was time to call it quits.

"What's your plan?" Elias asked.

"I don't have one."

"So you're going to sit around and mope?"

That stung and he responded accordingly. "If I want to. I think I've earned that right."

"Sure you have." His mom patted his chest. "You do just what you want and your father will be very nice about it. But…but football has been your whole life since you were a little boy. I hope you've really thought this through."

"I have, Mom. I can't get my arm up high enough to bring in those uncatchable balls. Every therapy session it gets better, but I'm never going to be the way I was before. Football's appeal has worn off and I've accomplished all my goals, so I'm fine with it. And life's just not the same without Jody."

His mom's blue eyes darkened. "Don't get me started on Jody."

"I don't want to talk about Jody. Our problems are between us and don't include our parents."

Elias got to his feet. "Well, Wyatt seems to think it includes him, and if I hear him say one more derogatory word about my son,

I'm going to spend some time in jail because I'm going to deck him."

"Dad." Chase sighed. "Please, don't do anything foolish. It's been over a year now and you should be used to Wyatt saying things about me. It's okay. I can take it because I know the truth."

"I don't understand what's happened to Jody," his mom added. "I really liked her and thought she was the perfect girl for you. Now she's working at the courthouse, and when she comes into the diner for coffee or a sandwich, she says hi and that's it. I have a whole lot to say to her. I'm just biding my time."

"If you say anything, I'll be very upset and just might move away if I can't live here in peace."

"What? No! I will not listen to talk like that." It certainly had gotten his mother's attention. He hated to use blackmail, but it was all he had. "We will be very quiet, won't we, Elias?"

Elias thought about it for a minute. "I'm not promising anything. If someone hurts my kid, all bets are off."

"No one is hurting me," Chase said with as much emphasis as possible.

"Really? Take a good look in the mirror, son. You look like a horse that's been rode real hard and put up wet, if you know what I mean. Parents see things like that. So don't tell me you're fine. I know you're not. But your mother and I will support you in every way we can. That's who we are." He reached for his hat on the table. "Now I think I have boys to pick up."

His mom moved closer to his dad. "I'll pick up JR and you take Tre and Eli."

"Why?"

"I'll take him to the diner with me and spend some special time with him."

His mom owned the local diner. She'd finally paid off the note on the place and it was all hers, along with all the work. Yeah, his mom worked just as hard as his dad.

Elias shook his head. "Maribel, pampering is not the way to solve the problem."

"I don't like your way."

"My way works."

Chase thought he was in for a long session of whose way was the right way to raise children, but his mother suddenly stood on tiptoes and kissed Elias. "I'll see you at the house at suppertime." Then she looked at

Chase and said, "You're expected for supper, in case you didn't know it."

As his mother went out the back door, Chase asked, "What's up with JR?"

"His grades. Tre makes all As and JR can barely maintain a C. He's on those video games when he should be studying and that's coming to a stop. Until I see Bs, he's going to be one sad little boy."

The Rebels had always thought that Zane got his intelligence from his mother's side of the family, but Tre was just like his cousin, with his head always in a book. JR was more the outdoors type and Eli was the clown in the family. He always kept everyone laughing.

His dad headed for the back door and stopped. "Are you okay?"

"Yeah, Dad. I'm okay." It touched him that his father still worried about him. He hoped that never changed.

"You know, you might want to call your great-grandfather. If he finds out you're home and you haven't called him, he'll be hurt."

"I'll go out early and surprise him."

Elias nodded and went out the door.

Chase would never hurt his great-grandpa.

He was the first person in the Rebel family who'd accepted him for who he was and believed that Elias was his father. They had a special connection. Grandpa was in his nineties now and it made Chase sad that one day he would lose him. So the yard could wait.

Unpacking could wait, too.

Just as he was going out the door, Zane came in. He completely forgot about his cousin coming over. They hugged. They were the same height, but Zane was thin while Chase had muscles from working out.

"I didn't bring beer," Zane said. "Since Erin can't drink, I can't, either. It's a law she made." Zane sat in the chair Elias had vacated. Zane was dressed in his customary jeans, boots, Western shirt and a Stetson. They'd called him cowboy at Harvard and it stuck.

"How's she doing?"

"She's miserable and there's nothing I can do to help her." Zane removed his hat and ran a hand through his hair. "Oh, man. I'm going to be a father and I don't know the first thing about being a parent. I can now understand the mistakes my parents made when I was born. You don't fully understand something until you go through it."

Paige, Zane's mother, was a teenager when she got pregnant with Zane. She and Jude, Zane's father, had decided to give him up for adoption. But Jude couldn't live with that decision and went back to the clinic and claimed his son and raised him. His mother came back years later and found out the son she'd given up was living with his father. He was told it had been a lot of drama, but out of the drama a family had been reunited. Now Zane had two sisters.

"It's not the same thing and you'll make a great father."

Zane leaned back in his chair. "I saw your dad leaving. How did it go?"

Chase kept very little from his cousin, his best friend. They talked about everything and Zane knew he was retiring from football. He hadn't tried to talk him out of it. He was just there when Chase needed him.

"They were shocked, but they know it's my decision."

"How's the arm?" Zane got up and examined Chase's shoulder, then raised it high. Chase winced. "Still a little tender, I see."

"Tell me about it," Chase replied between gritted teeth.

"As I told you on the phone after I reviewed the X-rays you sent, the arthroscopy surgery was a success, as was the rotator cuff repair and the reattachment of the worn and damaged tendons." He moved Chase's arm back and forth. "It's stable and secure with a good range of motion. It will continue to be tender for a little while, but with therapy it'll eventually be as good as new. I know you can't get it up as high as you want, but that's a small price to pay for a healthy arm." Zane pulled Chase's shirt back to look at the scar. "Man, you heal nicely. Looks good."

"I just want the pain to go away."

Zane resumed his seat. "It will, but you have to be careful now until it's healed completely."

"I saw Jody earlier." The words just spilled out of Chase's mouth.

"Uh…here?"

"Yeah." He pointed to the box sitting at the front door. "She brought back everything I'd ever given her, said she didn't want it anymore."

"That's gotta hurt."

"I'm numb now. I can't talk to her like I used to." He looked at Zane. "Has Erin ever said anything to you about why Jody came that night?"

"No." Zane shook his head. "But then, as I'm accused of very often, I'm in my own time zone most of the time. This research I'm doing now is so interesting and it occupies my mind completely. We're close, Chase, to finding a cure for cancer. It's exciting to work with patients. I talk to them, share their pain and listen to their experiences. We have the technology now to examine each cell within a tumor, and it opens up so many opportunities for new treatments."

"You really love your work."

"Yeah. I get carried away sometimes, the same way you do about football."

Chase stretched his shoulder. "Not anymore."

"You know Erin and I went to many games with Jody to watch you play. After the game, we'd wait for you outside the locker room. Remember that time we were waiting and a bunch of college girls were there, too? One of them had her phone number written on her bra and handed it to you.

Jody jerked it out of her hand and told her that you were taken and for her to peddle her bra somewhere else. The girl called her a name and Jody got up in her face. The girl quickly backpedaled and walked off. That's the Jody I know. She doesn't run away from a problem, so I don't understand why she ran that night."

"I don't, either. I asked her about it and she got angry, so I let it drop."

"I'll ask Erin about it again, but to be honest, we both agreed when your relationship blew up that we wouldn't take sides and that we would still all be friends."

"Zane, I have to figure it out for myself. At least I'll have lots of time now." Chase got to his feet. "I'm going to see Grandpa. Do you want to come with me?"

"No, but thanks." Zane got to his feet, too. "We're having supper with Erin's parents, and my parents are upset because we're not having supper with them. And on it goes with the in-law war. I can't wait for the baby to come. She'll be like a wishbone between them."

Chase laughed and it was just what he'd needed to lift his spirits—an old friend who knew exactly what he'd been through and understood.

JODY SAT IN the dining room in her parents' home having supper. She had her own house and she should be there and not always at her parents', but she couldn't seem to make that move. Her mother always invited her over and she couldn't say no. What had happened to her backbone? She didn't really know herself anymore. She moved the food around on her plate, seeing Chase's face.

Erin had said he'd been injured in a game, but he'd looked fine to her, fit and in shape like he always was. She hated to think that he was in pain, even though she'd wanted to hurt him herself a time or two. She took a swallow of tea and wondered if he was seeing anyone. There was no shortage of girls who wanted him. She had witnessed that many times, but she'd always felt safe in his love. What a fool she'd been.

"It's so nice to have both my babies home for supper," Peyton, her mother, said.

John Wyatt Carson, otherwise known as JW, her brother, was home for the weekend from law school at Texas University. Jody was almost nine years older than her brother. He was actually her half brother, but it never felt that way. Her dad, Wyatt, had been married before, and Jody's mother had died soon after Jody was born. Afterward, her dad had decided to bring Jody home to Horseshoe to raise her in a small-town environment. Back then they'd lived with Wyatt's mother, Maezel Lillian Carson, otherwise known as Gramma.

Wyatt was soon elected sheriff and they settled into life in Horseshoe. Jody grew up as a tomboy and followed her dad around like a little puppy. She was a constant in the sheriff's office and grew up knowing everybody on the square. She thought her dad had wanted a boy, so she wanted to be a boy and dressed like one and cut her hair short. Her dad was her hero and he took her fishing and played ball with her in the backyard.

Until Peyton blew into town in a red sports car and turned the Carsons' world upside down. Jody had called her a fancy lady because she wore makeup and fingernail polish and nice clothes and had long hair. Her dad had been a widower for a long time and he noticed those things, too. Soon Jody had a stepmom, but she was never really a stepmom. Peyton became her mother and freed Wyatt and Jody from their dull lives. Because if Peyton was anything, she was exciting. And she brought all that excitement into their lives.

Jody learned about lip gloss, fingernail polish, makeup and hair products. She learned to be a girl and she wanted her hair long and beautiful like Peyton's. Peyton was her model and she loved her.

"I heard Chase Rebel is back in town," her dad said around a mouthful of food, startling Jody out of her reverie. "Did you know that?" The question was directed at Jody.

The urge to lie was strong because she knew her dad did not like Chase and it would upset him. She dredged up all her twenty-eight years of wisdom and replied, "Yes, I knew he was back."

"How?" Always the detective, her dad had to know everything.

"When I went home for lunch, I saw his truck go by."

Her dad wiped his mouth and laid his napkin on the table. "Is that going to be a problem?"

Jody kept moving the food around on her plate. "No."

Her dad pointed a finger at her. "My advice is to just stay away from him. It's over. Let it be."

Jody rolled words around in her head, trying to find the right ones to respond, but JW took it out of her hands.

"Maybe you should lock her in her room, Dad. That way you'll know where she is and what she's doing. Oh, wait a minute—she has her own house and she's like what? Forty now? She's probably old enough to make her own decisions."

Jody threw half her dinner roll at him. He ducked.

"Don't get smart, son. This is serious."

Jody pushed back her chair. She'd had enough. "I'm going home. I'll see y'all tomorrow. Thanks for supper, Mom."

Peyton followed her to the door. "Are you okay, baby?"

"I'd just rather not talk about Chase."

"You know how your father is. He just worries about you."

"I know." She kissed her mom's cheek and walked to her car.

Her house was just around the corner. She parked in the driveway and sat there. No, she couldn't keep thinking about Chase, but he was all that was on her mind.

She hated going into the house with Gramma's memories everywhere, but those memories got her through each day. How she wished she were here now so Jody could talk to her. She always had a unique way of looking at life and Jody desperately needed someone with a different perspective.

All her life, she had never wanted to disappoint her father, and she did everything to make sure she never did. Disappointing him would break her heart. How did she tell him what she eventually had to?

She wasn't that little girl riding her bicycle all over town, getting a free cookie at the bakery and a lollipop at the bank just because she was the sheriff's daughter. She wasn't that happy, smiling little girl anymore. She was all grown up and the decisions she'd made were crippling her today. Every morning her pillow was soaked with tears from those decisions, and the only way to free herself now was to share those decisions with the people whom they had affected—her parents and Chase.

CHAPTER THREE

WHEN CHASE TURNED onto Rebel Road, he got the same feeling in his chest as he had the first time he'd come here—a feeling of awe at the thousands of acres of ranchland and houses belonging to Kate Rebel and her seven sons and adopted son, Rico. Having been raised in a house in Dallas, and then a small apartment, he'd been unaccustomed to the wide-open spaces.

The house on the right belonged to Quincy and his wife, Jenny, and their three children. He raised paint horses and they galloped freely in the pasture. The two-story house on the left belonged to Falcon and his wife, Leah, and their son, John. Their daughter, Eden, had married and moved out.

The next house that came into view was a huge log home built by John Rebel for his growing family. The homeplace, another log cabin, was not far from it. Paxton and his wife, Remi, lived there with their daughter, Annie. Grandpa's old white frame house was in the distance, but he didn't live there anymore. Barns, equipment sheds, outbuildings, cattle pens and a large office dotted the landscape. Egan, Phoenix and Jude had built houses for their families miles down Rebel Road. Rico had inherited land across the highway from Rebel Ranch and he and his family lived there. It was one huge family, and at first, it was hard for Chase to remember all their names. But now they were relatives and he could roll their names off his tongue anytime anyone asked him.

He crossed the cattle guard to the big log house that now belonged to his mom and dad. His grandma Kate and great-grandpa Abe lived there, too. It had six bedrooms, so it was big enough. The house sat on Elias's inherited part of the land, but his parents hadn't moved in until after the twins were born because they needed more space. That was when his mom had signed over the house on Mulberry Street to Chase. Out of the Rebel sons, no one would have ever guessed that the hard-nosed workaholic Elias would be the one taking care of his mother and grandpa. But his grandmother was still very active with running the ranch and helping to take care of Chase's brothers.

He went in through the back door and saw his grandma was in the kitchen. She was a strong woman, surviving the death of her husband and raising seven equally strong men. It had taken Chase a while to get to know his grandmother, but as with everything, it had a learning curve. His mother was a McCray, and to his grandmother, McCrays were not welcome on Rebel Ranch. But life had a way of leveling things out. The McCray women had taken an interest in the Rebel men and today three of them had married into the Rebel family. Phoenix's wife, Rosie, was a McCray and Paxton's wife, Remi, was a McCray. Today the Rebels and McCrays lived in peace or as close to it as they would ever get.

"Chase!" His grandmother threw up her hands when she saw him. "What a surprise." She hugged him and he hugged her back. Her hair was now completely gray and her soft smile warmed his heart. "Do your parents know you're home?"

"Yeah. I came out to see Grandpa."

"He's in his chair, watching old Westerns, as always. He'll be so excited to see you."

He walked into the living room, and as usual, it took his breath away. It was huge, with a stone fireplace reaching toward the ceiling and floor-to-ceiling windows offering a view of the ranch. The whole Rebel family could fit in the room during the holidays. Grandpa was asleep in his chair, with John Wayne strutting his stuff in *Rio Bravo* on the TV. It was turned up loud. He picked up the remote control on the arm of the chair and switched it off. As he did, Grandpa woke up. His aged eyes blinked and then he sat up.

"Chase!" His arms reached for him and Chase engulfed him in a big hug. Grandpa's hair was now white and thinning, and the leathery wrinkles on his face showed a life of hard work and stubbornness, which made him a true Rebel. It was a family trait.

He loved this old man more than life itself. He'd given Chase courage when he had none. He'd given Chase confidence at times when he couldn't find his voice. He'd given Chase dignity when he didn't even know what that was. Grandpa had said, *You're a Rebel and I don't need a test to prove it. All I have to do is look into your eyes. Be proud of that.* And Chase was, from that day forward.

"What are you doing home?"

Chase squatted by his chair. "I retired from football, and the only place I wanted to go was home."

"I'm glad because this is your home, my boy." Grandpa rubbed Chase's shoulder. "Is your shoulder bothering you?"

"A little. I'm still in therapy."

"You'll do fine," Grandpa assured him. "Life will be a whole lot better with you here, and then I won't have to worry about you getting hurt anymore. Yep. Yep. I think that's a good thing."

"Me, too, Grandpa."

The back door opened and screams of joy echoed through the house. Chase's brothers were home. "Chase! Chase! Chase!"

Chase stood and caught them as they ran into the living room. Elias entered behind them and shouted, "Remember what I said."

Six-year-old Eli looked up at him. "Daddy said we can't hug real hard because your arm is still sore."

Chase sat on the couch and they piled on him, asking questions.

"Daddy said you retired from football and are gonna stay home now," JR said.

Eli crawled onto his lap. "Does your arm hurt?"

"Give him a break," Grandpa said.

That was the main reason he dreaded coming home. He was going to constantly be asked about his arm and he'd just as soon deal with it himself without all the fuss.

"JR, come with me," Elias said from the doorway.

"Aw, Daddy, Chase just got home."

"Come with me. You can talk to Chase later."

JR dutifully followed his dad out of the room.

"What did he do now?" Eli asked.

"Nothing," Chase replied. "Tell me what you guys have been up to." Chase knew JR was in trouble, but he didn't want his brother to get it from all sides.

Tre and Eli tried to outtalk each other. Chase was glad to see his mom when she came in. She looked around. "Where's JR?"

"He's with Dad."

"Oh." The worry lines on her face deepened. He was sure they went through this quite often with the boys, but he was never here to witness it. As the thought crossed his mind, he felt out of place. He should be home with his own family, his own kids. He and Jody had planned to have two, a boy and a girl, as if they could plan those things. They had been so naive in their relationship and in their love.

His dad and JR came in as they were sitting down for supper. JR was smiling, so things must've gone good. Even his mother smiled when she saw JR's face. After supper, they talked awhile. Then he went upstairs to help the boys get ready for bed. He always did that when he was home. Eli jumped around like a grasshopper, all excited, and it was hard to calm him down.

Tre and JR shared a room, and Tre fell asleep quickly, so Chase had a chance to talk to JR. "How's it going?"

JR put his hands behind his head and stared at the ceiling. "I thought Daddy was gonna tan my hide—that's what Grandpa always says. I don't really know what that means, but I don't want to get my hide tanned. Daddy just talked to me and told me my grades were unacceptable and I had to do better. I can't get on the computer or use my phone until my homework is done.

He says he wants me to do my best and he knows I'm not doing my best. It's hard, Chase, when Tre's so smart. That's what I said to Daddy. Good move, huh?"

"What did Dad say?"

"He said Tre and I are twins, but we're different. I'm an outdoor guy and I'm going to be like him and Tre is more like Mama. He likes to read and do all that weird stuff. Daddy said when school lets out I'm gonna be right with him, working. Can you believe that? I'm going to work with Daddy."

As Tre and JR grew older, they went to work with Elias a lot, so Chase didn't understand why it was so important to JR now, but it was, and that was what mattered.

He left soon after and was surprised Grandpa didn't want to go home with him. He usually stayed with Chase when he was in town. His dad must've said something. Chase didn't question it. He really needed to be alone. After seeing Jody, all he wanted was to be by himself and think about her. He'd probably be doing that for the rest of his life.

WHEN CHASE WOKE up the next morning, he realized he didn't have any coffee or groceries. He showered and changed clothes and unpacked everything from the truck and then went to the diner for breakfast. The place was busy, as usual. His mom, with an apron tied around her waist, was running back and forth, serving customers. He found an empty bar stool at the counter and slid onto it. Almost like magic, a plate filled with eggs, sausage, biscuits and hash browns appeared before him with a cup of coffee.

He didn't usually eat this heavy of a breakfast. It was typically a protein shake and fruit, but he dug in because his mother had made it for him, but he didn't get to eat in peace. He was well-known around Horseshoe and people would come up to shake his hand and ask about football and his arm. He answered politely. Some privacy would have been nice, but that was small-town life.

The last morning breakfast customer trailed out and his mother leaned on the counter, staring at Chase.

"What?"

"I just love looking at my beautiful first-born."

"Mom…"

"I just wish that sadness would leave your

eyes. When I think of what Jody has done to you, I…"

"Stop it. I'm not going to listen to any negative words about Jody. I told you that."

"I know, but when I look at your face, I… Never mind."

Anamarie, Rico's wife, came in and interrupted the conversation. She had a baby carrier on one arm and set it on the counter near Maribel. "Hey, Chase. Watch her for a minute. I have to get the pies."

"What pies?" Chase asked his mom as Anamarie disappeared out the door.

"Ana makes the pies for the diner now. I found I couldn't do everything after I had the twins. And her pies are better than mine."

"I doubt it."

"Oh, you're such a sweetie." At times, he wondered if his mom would ever see him as a grown man. She tended to treat him as if he were the same age as the twins.

He looked into the baby carrier and saw a little girl, or he assumed it was a girl, as she had a pink bow in her blond curly hair. "Where did the baby come from?"

Anamarie came back in with a large box filled with pies and carried them to the kitchen. "Lemon, pecan, two chocolate and two coconut," Ana said as she came back.

"Thank you," his mom replied. "Chase was asking about the baby."

"Oh, that's right. He hasn't seen her." Ana's blue eyes lit up as she lifted the baby out of the carrier. "Look at this little angel. She's your new cousin."

"She's tiny" was all Chase could say as he stared at the baby, waving her fists around.

"She weighed six pounds and five ounces at birth and we got her three days later from the hospital." Ana and Rico had three adopted boys and Chase had had no idea they'd adopted another child. Their oldest, Dustin, had to be about fourteen.

"She's another blessing in our lives." Ana had a dreamy look on her face as she stared at the baby. "We named her Mary Elizabeth, after Rico's mother and grandmother, but the boys have been calling her Lizzie and I guess that's what we're going to call her."

"Tell Chase her story," his mom prompted.

"Her mom was seventeen and in high school and got involved with her Spanish teacher, who was married. He decided to stay with his wife, and later she found out she was pregnant and hid it from her parents. She had the baby in the bathtub of her home and wrapped it in a towel and put it in a garbage bag. The girl thought the baby was dead— that's what she said. She carried the bag to a dumpster and set it beside it. When the trashman picked up the bag, he heard a whimper and opened it up. Fire ants had covered the bag. That's why she was crying. They were biting her. They managed to get most of them off her and called 911. See the red marks on her face and arms."

Chase looked closely and could see where the little baby had been bitten. How could a mother do that?

"Did they find the mother?" Chase asked.

"Oh, yeah. She wrapped the baby in her gym towel, which had her last name on it. She was arrested and sentenced to two years in prison. Her parents tried to get probation for her, but the judge didn't buy it. She'll probably be out in about nine months, but she's not getting this little one back." Ana kissed the baby's cheek.

"How do you know that?" Chase asked because he knew they'd had problems with Dusty's adoption.

"The judge took away her maternal rights and the father signed away his. Neither wanted the baby and the grandparents didn't want her, either. But that's okay. We love her to death."

His mom took the baby from Anamarie and cuddled her on her shoulder. "Oh, I wanted a little girl so bad. They're so lightweight and smell much better."

Ana took the baby quickly before his mom could get too attached. She placed her in the carrier. "Oh, Chase, I forgot to ask about your arm."

"Don't." He sighed. "Fifty people have asked this morning and I'm running out of answers."

"Touchy, huh?" Ana gave him a hug instead. She picked up the carrier and said, "I'll see you guys later. 'Bye."

Chase turned to his mother. "Ana and Rico have to be the nicest people I've ever met."

"They are. I've gotten to know Ana really well since she opened The Bake Shop. I can depend on her if I need anything and I don't think it's because we're family. I think it's because she's just a nice person."

"I don't understand how a mother could just throw her baby away."

"It happens, son, more than you would think. Young girls get scared and don't know what to do and wind up doing the worst thing possible."

"Were you scared when you were pregnant with me?" He had never asked his mother that question.

"Of course I was scared. My dad was yelling at me and my mom was wringing her hands, and I didn't know what was going to happen. But I got lucky, just like Mary Elizabeth. Miss Vennie saved my life."

"Did you ever think of giving me away?"

"Not for a second." She pinched his cheek. "If I had to live on the streets, I would have kept you. No one was taking my baby."

"Nana was good to us. I still miss her."

"Me, too."

"You know, she used to let me drive that big ol' Lincoln."

"I knew, Chase."

"How did you know? We were very careful so you wouldn't know and punish me."

"Miss Vennie told me. She'd start the conversation by saying *now, don't get mad*, and then tell me what she allowed you to do on a certain day. You were fifteen and I saw no harm in letting you drive around the block."

"She let me drive everywhere."

"What?"

Chase pointed to his mother's face. "You look kind of pale."

"I can't believe she let you do that."

Chase got to his feet and hugged his mom. "I have to go to the grocery store. I'll see you later."

"What else did she let you do?" she called as he went out the door. At that point, he realized there were just some things you should never tell your mother.

SATURDAY AND SUNDAY passed in a blur. On Sunday afternoon, the family came over and helped him clean up the yard. Grandpa watched and Grandma helped his mom make pizzas for supper. His mom made the best pizzas.

By six o'clock he had a brush pile to be picked up. He had city services, so he would find out tomorrow when they would get to it. His dad offered to haul it off to Rebel Ranch. Chase refused. He paid for services, so there was no need to do that. For once his dad listened.

On Monday morning, he got up and went to the diner for breakfast again, and then he walked across the courthouse lawn to the city offices, which were located across the street. Two old vacant stores had been converted for the city's use. They used to be on the first floor of the courthouse but outgrew the space. A girl he had gone to high school with was at the desk. She asked about his arm and football and went on and on until he had to stop her and ask about trash pickup. They would pick up his trash on Wednesday. He headed for the door before she could start talking again. He knew she was dying to ask about Jody and he wasn't discussing Jody with anyone.

As he neared the courthouse steps, there she was. Jody paused halfway and stared at him. She recovered quickly and continued to the bottom, where he was standing.

"I thought you would have been gone by now," she said matter-of-factly. She looked very businesslike in a dress and heels with her hair pulled back, and she clutched several files in her arms.

He thought this was as good a time as any to tell her the truth. "I retired from football."

"Oh. I didn't realize that. You could've told me the other day."

"You weren't in the mood to listen to anything. And my activities don't seem to concern you anymore."

"No, they don't," she said almost to herself. "But I do need to talk to you."

She glanced at the files she had a death grip on. "I have an appointment in Temple, so it'll have to wait." She strolled to her car, which was parked next to Hardy's. They had private parking spots at the courthouse.

As she drove away, Wyatt came out of the diner, followed by chief deputy and investigator Cole Chisholm. His dad followed them. What was his dad doing here? He should be out on the ranch by now.

He didn't have time to think about it as Wyatt reached him. "Stay away from my daughter." The words were aimed at him like a bullet meant to wound.

Chase straightened his back. "I have a right to walk across the courthouse lawn, just like everybody else."

"I saw you talking to Jody. Leave her alone. Haven't you put her through enough? If you keep harassing her, I will arrest you."

"Harassing?"

"She doesn't want to see you or have anything to do with you, and when you try to talk to her, that's harassment. I'm telling you again to leave her alone. Do you hear me?"

"The whole town can hear you."

People were stopping and staring and listening. The sheriff was losing his cool and the people of Horseshoe would certainly have something to gossip about.

"Wyatt." Cole spoke up. "This isn't the place…"

"Stay out of this, Cole."

"What's your problem, Wyatt?" Elias asked as he reached them.

Wyatt turned to Elias. "I knew your kid was trouble the moment he came to this town, and now look what has happened."

"You don't want to get in my face, Wyatt, because I don't care if you're wearing a badge. You're out of line. Even your chief deputy knows that."

"Stay out of this, Elias."

"I'm not…"

"Stop it!" Chase shouted. "Both of you, just stay out of it. This is between Jody and me." He turned his gaze to Wyatt. "You can't arrest a man for harassment when he's talking to his wife."

CHAPTER FOUR

THE URGE TO run was strong for Chase, run fast and hard down the field to outdistance the defenders to the end zone for the chance of a lifetime moment with shouts of victory in his ears. But this time there would be no shouts or cheers. He'd just thrown Jody under the bus. How could he have done that?

He gathered his courage and stood his ground. It was time for everyone to know. The sheriff's mouth fell open, his throat muscles worked, but no sounds came out. "You're lying" finally erupted from his throat.

Elias frowned. "Is this true, son?"

"Yes," Chase admitted. "We got married the fourth year I was in the NFL."

"He's lying," Wyatt charged again. "My daughter wouldn't do that. She wouldn't get married without her parents being there."

"Did you ever give her a choice? There was always an excuse for her not to marry

Chase Rebel. Think about it, Sheriff." He walked to his truck without a backward glance. His dad was on his heels.

"Son, just a minute…"

"I don't have a minute. What's done is done and it's nobody's business but mine and Jody's. How many times do I have to say that? I'll talk to you later if I feel like it, but otherwise this conversation is over."

"Chase…"

He drove away with his dad's stern voice echoing in his ears. He didn't owe anyone an explanation, but he did need to call Jody and warn her. The words had just flown out of his mouth before he knew what he was saying. All these years he'd given her time to gain the courage to tell her father. Time had just run out.

His phone pinged and he pulled it out of his pocket—his mother. He heaved a deep sigh. He wasn't in a mood to talk to anyone, even his mother. Before he could put the phone away, it pinged again. His mother wasn't going to give up, so he pulled over at a roadside park.

He was supposed to be heading for Temple for an appointment with the director of the therapy center he was visiting. Calling his mother would only be a barrage of the same questions over and over. Why? Why? Why? After all the planning his mom and Peyton had put into Jody and Chase's wedding, they were going to demand answers. The main reason had been that their parents treated them like children waiting for their approval to get married. They had gotten tired of that.

He called Jody. She didn't answer and it went straight to voice mail. He left a message for her to call him as soon as possible. She probably wouldn't since she didn't return his calls these days.

The temperature was in the forties, a nice cool day mixing with the frosty winds of February. A good day for football. The team would take a vacation before they started practicing in earnest for the next year. He had to admit he would miss the camaraderie with his teammates. The wind played with the leaves, blowing them against the cement tables. An 18-wheeler was parked to the side and the driver was taking a nap. A car honked and traffic sounds rumbled along the highway.

His mother called again and he clicked on. He then received a dressing-down as if he were sixteen years old and had stayed out too late. Enough was enough.

"Stop it. Just stop it."

"How could you go behind our backs and get married? We're your parents."

"I'm well aware of who you are and we've had this conversation many times. You and Peyton wanted a big wedding. How many times did Jody and I say we wanted a simple wedding? Simple. That never seemed to reach either one of you. And then the sheriff wanted Jody to wait until she was out of college and then when she finished her internship and then when she had a better job. On and on it went until we decided to do what we wanted. We were both adults and we got married, just the two of us, and it was one of the most beautiful moments of my life." It had been at six o'clock in the afternoon and the evening lights sparkled in Jody's eyes as they pledged their love forever. Two hours later they were on a plane to Hawaii.

"Why couldn't you tell us?"

"We tried many times, but planning a big wedding was just another stalling tactic used by the Carsons and you. Dad said he didn't care and to do whatever we wanted, and I'll always love him for that."

"Your dad didn't want to spend all that money."

"I didn't, either. Trumpets, doves and a band that cost more than my truck? Even you have to admit it got out of control."

"Then why let us keep planning the wedding?"

"Neither one of us had the courage to break our parents' hearts, and I'm sorry I hurt your feelings. There's not going to be a wedding now. I'm also sorry for the way it turned out, but Jody and I are married."

"After Jody accused you of cheating, why didn't you get a divorce?"

"She's the lawyer and I left it up to her, but she never sent me papers and I wasn't in a rush to get them. I'm still not."

"Oh, Chase, I'm so sorry this happened, but it's not your fault. It's Jody's. She just couldn't tell her parents."

Chase felt like beating his head against the steering wheel. "I'm going to Temple to get my therapy schedule set up and I won't be home early and I'd appreciate it if no one came over tonight. I need this time for myself. I have to talk to Jody and figure out what we're going to do, and that doesn't concern anyone else."

"Yes, yes, I understand."

Chase burst out laughing. "Really, Mom? Since when?"

Before he drove on, he made another attempt to call Jody, but it went to voice mail again. He left another message: *Call me back. It's important.* He made it to the clinic in time for his appointment. He had all his X-rays, MRIs, doctor's notes and therapy notes, so it didn't take long. He would go three days a week at first until the therapist working with him decided otherwise. He asked for early sessions so he'd have time to work around his house. But with everything that was happening in his life, he knew the house would be the last thing that would get any attention.

HORSESHOE WAS A small town without much crime until recently. A seventeen-year-old girl had been found in a bar ditch outside of Horseshoe. The officers on the scene thought she'd OD'd, but she was very much alive when she arrived in the Temple ER. Now the Horseshoe sheriff's office and the DA's office were coordinating things with the Temple Police Department and the Bell County DA because the crime had happened in Temple, but the girl's body had been found in Horseshoe.

Hardy sent Jody to interview the young girl, who was still in the hospital. The girl gave up the names of the two guys she had been with that night. She went to school with Victor Garcia and Tommy Clark, but she barely knew them. They forced her, she'd said. Through the entire interview she kept saying she wanted to go home, but it wasn't going to be that easy. She would have to face drug charges, and crying on her mother's shoulder wasn't going to change that. She'd made a bad mistake and she was lucky to be alive.

The rest of the afternoon Jody spent in the Bell County DA's office, and through a long discussion and a phone call to Hardy, the Bell County DA decided to take the case, which she saw as a good thing because she didn't want to be the one to put the young girl behind bars.

When she got in her car, she opened her phone and saw she had dozens of messages. She'd turned off her phone while she'd been in the hospital. There were several from her dad, her mother and Chase. Why was Chase calling her? And why were they calling her around the same time? Something had happened.

Since it was late and she was tired, she decided to go home and deal with the calls there. She had no sooner made it into the living room of her home than her doorbell rang. She opened the door, and her father walked past her with an angry scowl on his face. Her mother followed him.

"Wyatt, you promised."

Her father turned to Jody. "Were you ever going to tell us?"

"What?" Jody was totally confused, but one thing was very clear. Her father's anger was directed at Jody. "What's going on?"

"Up until about a year ago, you and your mother were planning this extravagant wedding, and no one thought to tell us that you were already married. Can you imagine my shock when Chase enlightened me? My daughter chose to get married without her parents present. I keep asking myself how could she do that. But ever since you met Chase Rebel, you haven't been the same."

They had found out that she and Chase were married. How could Chase do this to her? He'd agreed to wait until they both were comfortable with telling them, but then she found out Chase was cheating on her and nothing was the same. Nothing ever would be again.

"Just tell me it's not true," Wyatt said. "Tell me you wouldn't disrespect your parents and run off and get married."

"Run off? Chase and I loved each other and we planned that day for just the two of us, and it was the most beautiful moment of my life. And it would have been more beautiful if my parents had been a part of it. We told you a thousand times that we did not want the big wedding. No one considered our feelings, so we did it our way, and I don't regret one moment of that."

Peyton slid an arm around Jody's waist. "Where did you get married, baby?"

"In this little old chapel in Austin. It wasn't anything elaborate and it took a total of twenty-four hours to plan it."

Her mother gasped.

"The wedding was in the spring and I found a dress in this quaint wedding shop known for its gorgeous gowns. It was made of silk and Italian lace and…"

"Isn't that the dress hanging in your bedroom at the house?"

"Yes. I just told you I'd found the perfect dress and it was."

"And you were going to wear that same dress in June?" This was where Jody should have felt guilty and ashamed for hoodwinking her parents. She didn't.

Wyatt sighed. "Jody, we didn't raise you like this. Honesty and truth were always big things in our house. Remember?"

Jody stared down at the floor. "I'm sorry I've disappointed you." She shook her head as she found herself falling back into the same old pattern of apologizing for disappointing her father. "Wait a minute. I loved Chase and I married him because I wanted to."

"He forced you."

"Truth and honesty, Dad? You've always known how I felt about Chase and so has Mom. The wedding plans from hell got out of control and we decided to do our own thing. Every couple is entitled to have the wedding of their choice. Now, if you don't mind, I'd appreciate it if you would leave. I have a big day tomorrow and I haven't had supper yet."

Her mother rubbed Jody's arm. "Come home with us and we'll talk."

"No, thanks, Mom."

After her parents left, she grabbed her purse and headed for Chase's. How dare he!

She went in through the front door. It wasn't locked. He lay in a recliner, with his feet propped up, in shorts and a T-shirt.

He waved a hand. "Come right in, Mrs. Rebel."

"Shut up. You just couldn't wait for the opportunity to tell my dad, could you?"

"Most women would want their father to know their marital status. You said we'd wait a couple months and then tell them, and then it was six months, and then it was a year, and then I forgot all the times you said we'd tell them. I fell for every one of them because I thought you wanted the same thing that I did. A home and a family."

"I did, until I saw you with that woman."

"Oh, please." He got to his feet in a shaky movement and she noticed that he winced.

"Are you in pain?"

"What does it matter, Jody?"

She snapped her fingers. "That's it. That's why you're retiring from football. You've injured yourself."

He ran a hand through his hair. "Jody—" He stopped as pain echoed through his shoulder.

She threw her purse on the sofa. "How bad is it?"

He held up his hands and stepped back as she tried to touch him. "Wait. Are we gonna be all touchy-feely now?"

"I just want to see how your arm is."

"You gave up that right."

They stared at each other, weighing the odds, the moment. She slowly ran her hand along the bottom of his T-shirt and pulled it over his shoulder. A scar zigzagged across his right shoulder and she knew he had to be in a lot of pain. Her stomach clenched.

"How long ago did this happen?"

"In January." He pulled his T-shirt back in place.

"In the playoffs?"

"You would have known if you had watched."

She didn't want to get into that. "So what are you doing for it?"

"Therapy and ice."

She touched the ice pack on his chair. "This is lukewarm. I'll fix another."

"I don't need help, Jody."

She didn't listen and she made a new ice bag and put it on his shoulder over a towel.

She sat on the sofa sideways so she could see him. "What's the prognosis?"

"Good. Not as good as I wanted."

"And it has to be for you?"

"Yes."

"Football means everything to you."

"Not anymore, so let's just drop it."

"What's your plans?"

"I'm going to college online and finishing my degree in sports management."

"I think that's wonderful."

He straightened the pack on his shoulder. "What are you doing here, Jody?"

Her heart dropped suddenly. Chase was always glad to see her, but then she realized she was pushing an old relationship that had been dead for a long time. Old habits were hard to break.

She picked up her purse and stood. "I just came by to tell you that I've spoken with my parents and I don't think they'll bother you again."

"I'd appreciate that."

"The marriage idea was my fault and I fully admit that, as I told my parents. And I'll be drawing up the divorce papers soon."

"Your choice. I'd just like to know why you haven't done it before now."

"I don't know if I can explain."

"Until you do, I'm not signing anything."

"What? You can't do that."

"I will, and you know it. Before I sign those papers, we're going to have a long talk."

She stomped her foot. "You're so aggravating and you've always been. If you need a reason, there it is." She walked out the door and slammed it harder than she needed to, but it released a lot of tension.

Jody hurried out the door, feeling as if she were chased by every Carson lawman, including her grandfather who was a Texas highway patrolman and her great-grandfather who was a deputy sheriff and a great-grandfather down the line who was a Texas Ranger in the olden days.

As a lawman's daughter, she knew when to run.

CHAPTER FIVE

THE REST OF the week Chase didn't see Jody and that was just as well. Every time they spoke they ended up in an argument. Wyatt ignored him and that was just as well, too. His mom sniffled every time he was around her and he didn't understand that at all. So he gave her time in hopes that it would die down and everyone would forget the secret Chase and Jody had kept from everyone.

His dad, uncles and cousins were busy making sure all the animals and water pipes were safe from the freeze tonight. It was a constant thing in wintertime. His mother, for some reason known only to herself, dropped off Chase's brothers and Grandpa at his place on Sunday afternoon to spend the night.

He could only assume that his mother thought he was lonely and needed company. The crowd was loud as they played pool and tag football. Chase decided to make tacos with hot fudge sundaes for dessert. Then they sat around and watched an old Western of Grandpa's and he told them all about it, especially the day he met John Wayne and Clint Eastwood. Chase didn't know if it was true or not, but Grandpa made you believe. He wished he had inherited that talent.

The next morning, they crawled into his truck and headed for the diner, where Elias was supposed to pick them up. Chase's phone pinged and he stretched to get it out of his pocket. Zane started talking, nonstop. "Hey, slow down."

"Erin's having the baby and I want you here. I can't do this by myself."

"Take a deep breath. I'm on my way."

"Thanks. I'm sending directions to your phone. Just follow them and you'll be here in less than forty-five minutes. Hurry."

Elias flagged them down at the diner. Chase swerved into a spot.

"Erin's having the baby and no one can find Angie."

"She's probably with Hardy and on the way to Houston. Besides Zane, her mother is the first person she would call, right?"

"Hardy's at a DAs' luncheon in Austin,

but I'm sure by now he's on a plane to Houston."

"I've got to go. Zane is waiting for me and he's a nervous wreck."

Jody walked up in slacks and a green pull-over sweater that matched her eyes. He tried not to stare.

"Are you going to Houston?" she asked.

"Yes."

"I'm going with you."

"No, you're not." He took a hard stance because he didn't want her messing up his head again. He pointed across the street to her car. "That's your car and that's what you'll be driving to Houston."

"Come on, Chase. You know how I drive when I'm nervous."

She drove all over the place, endangering everyone's life, including hers. How could he say no? He was such a soft touch when it came to her.

"Okay, but no talking. Just be quiet and everything will go smoothly."

"Thank you."

They had no sooner turned onto Main Street than they saw Angie run out of her office with two big packages and her purse, waving them down. She opened the back door.

"Can I ride with you?" She then proceeded to dump all her stuff in the back seat and climb in. "Your mom said you were on the way and I had to leave my car at Bubba's this morning for it to be worked on. We're getting a new car. That's it. I'm not having that old junker to drive my granddaughter around."

The ladies weren't paying any attention to the traffic and yakked all the way to Houston. That suited Chase.

Angie tapped him on the shoulder. "Hurry, Chase. I want to get there before the baby's born. Of all the times for Hardy to be out of town, it had to be the day our granddaughter is being born."

"I'm driving as fast as the law allows."

Angie's phone buzzed and she answered it. It was Hardy. He was landing in Houston and would meet them at the hospital.

Chase drove into a specified spot and turned off the engine. Zane stood at the head of the parking space. Jody and Angie stared at each other.

"We're here." They grabbed their things and ran into the hospital.

"Do they know where they're going?" Zane asked.

"I don't know. They didn't ask." Chase hugged Zane. "How are you doing?"

They walked into the hospital arm in arm. "She made me promise not to give her an epidural even if she begs for it. Now she's begging for it and I don't know what to do."

"Give her the epidural. You want your baby born in peace, not trauma."

Zane slapped him on the shoulder. "I knew you'd say the right thing. I'll be right back."

They met Angie and Jody. "Where's my daughter?" Angie demanded.

"Down the hall to the right," Zane said, "but you'll have to wait."

Over the next thirty minutes, a lot of the Rebel family showed up, sitting in the hallway or standing outside.

"I want my mama" echoed along the hallways, and everything became quiet. Zane and Angie were in the room and Hardy hurried inside. Everyone milled around, worrying, but it didn't take long. Thirty minutes later Katherine Rebel, named for the grandmother who had helped raise Zane, made an appearance into the world. Chase peeked around the door. Zane gently laid the baby on Erin's chest so the grandparents could get a good look. He gave Chase the thumbs-up and Chase smiled at his friend.

Jody was waiting to hold the baby and he wondered if she had plans to get back home. The Carsons would be here soon. They wouldn't miss the birth of Erin and Zane's daughter.

He said goodbye to everyone and strolled to his truck. He stopped for a moment to talk to Uncle Jude, Zane's father, who looked a little pale.

"You okay, Uncle Jude?" He'd come straight from feeding cows, wearing worn jeans and a chambray shirt. Nothing could stop him from seeing his first grandchild being born.

"Yeah. The miracle of life is amazing. Paige said Erin and the baby are fine, and that's all that matters." He wiped his forehead with the sleeve of his shirt. "My boy has a child and I'm going to enjoy watching her grow up."

Paige opened the door. "Jude, your granddaughter wants to see you. You can't let Hardy have all the attention."

Uncle Jude was an easygoing kind of guy and wasn't all that fond of talking. When he looked at his uncle Jude, he saw strength and courage, as he saw in all his uncles, but it was different with Jude. His was wrapped in kindness and silence. He would love that little girl with all his heart. And in return she would adore him.

Jude went into the room and Chase hurried to his truck and found Jody sitting on the curb.

"Waiting for someone?" Chase unlocked his door and slid into his seat, trying very hard to ignore her.

Before he could back out, she tapped on his window and motioned for him to roll it down.

He shook his head without complying.

"Chase!" she shouted. "I need a ride home."

He didn't know why he was fighting this. He would eventually give in. He always did. And he didn't know why she wanted to ride with him. There had been no word from her in almost a year. She had refused to talk to him when he'd called. Now she was showing up every time he turned around. What was going on in her head? She wanted a divorce. Why wasn't she filing for one?

He unlocked the doors and she ran around to the passenger side and crawled in. "Thanks. I have to do some paperwork this afternoon and I have an early meeting at the Bell County Courthouse in the morning."

He held up a finger. "No talking."

That lasted until they got on the freeway. Jody pulled out her phone and started looking at photos. "Oh, she's so precious with those little curls on the top of her head."

"Curls? Katie doesn't have any curls. She's bald with a little white fuzz. What baby are you looking at?"

"Forget it." Jody closed her phone and was silent for a long time. What was going on with her?

"We didn't have lunch," she finally said. "Could we stop and get a bite?"

"I thought you had to get back?"

"An hour or so won't matter."

He was hungry, too, so he wasn't going to fight it. Maybe they could talk, actually talk. He stopped at Olive Garden and they went inside.

She ordered spaghetti with meatballs, as always, and he ordered a combo. A couple with two kids sat next to them at a table. It was clear they were arguing. The little girl sat in a high chair and smeared spaghetti sauce all over her face, unable to find her mouth.

"Can't you do something?" the man said to his wife, who was helping the little boy, who looked about three.

"Why can't you?" the wife shot back. "I've had them all morning and it looks like you could help a little."

The man glared at his wife and took the baby out of the high chair, wiped her face and held her while he fed her. The spaghetti finally went into her mouth.

Chase and Jody ate while the other couple continued to argue. Finally the woman threw her napkin on the table. "I'll walk home. I need the fresh air."

"Suit yourself."

Jody and Chase soon left the restaurant.

They rode in silence on the way to Horseshoe, each consumed with their own thoughts about the couple. Jody flipped through photos of the baby on her phone. Every now and then she would show him one. Suddenly she laid the phone on her lap and stared at the scenery.

"I was thinking about that couple at the restaurant. They must have a miserable marriage."

"Yeah."

"Our marriage wasn't like that. Even

though we were miles apart and our marriage was a secret, we were happy."

"Do you know why?"

"Why?"

"You trusted me. Even with the girls hanging around the stadium, following me, calling me, you trusted me. Why can't you trust me now?"

CHASE PULLED INTO the parking spot next to her car at the courthouse. Jody opened the door and got out without another word. Freezing cold air hit her in the face and she drew it in deeply, needing to clear her senses.

She stood on the courthouse lawn, taking several more deep breaths. But all she could hear were Chase's words. She hadn't broken their trust. He had by sleeping with someone else. And he wasn't going to make her believe otherwise.

"Jody. Jody."

She turned around to see Maribel running across the street, huddled in a big coat. It was just what she needed to finish her off for the day, a round with Chase's mother.

"Why didn't Chase come to the diner?"

"You'll have to ask him that."

"You can carry that snotty attitude around all you want, but it's not going to wash with me."

Jody stiffened. "What are you talking about?"

"Never mind." Maribel jammed her hands into the pockets of her coat. "How's the baby?"

Jody was thrown by the quick change of subject. "Uh…everyone is fine."

"Do you have a photo?"

Still puzzled, she pulled her phone out of her purse and realized her fingers were ice-cold, just like her heart. She showed Maribel pictures of the baby.

Maribel pointed to one. "Can you send that one to my phone?"

"Why?"

"I have a spot on the wall I put pictures of the newborns in the community and I'd like to put up a photo of Zane and Erin's daughter so everyone can see her."

"Oh. I remember that. I'll send it to you."

"Thanks." She made to walk across the street, but Jody stopped her.

"What did you mean earlier about my snotty attitude?"

"You go all over town boo-hooing about

my cheating son and everyone gets a real bad image of Chase. I don't like that. Chase did not cheat on you. I don't understand why you can't see that."

"Maybe because you weren't there. You didn't see the naked girl in his bathrobe with her hair all wet like she'd just gotten out of the shower. That's what I saw, Maribel, and nothing you say will ever change that."

"What was Chase wearing?"

"What?" The question had knocked her off balance.

"You said the girl was naked in the bathrobe and you could see everything, so what was Chase wearing? His underwear? Or nothing?"

"Oh—" She touched her forehead as her head began to throb. What was he wearing? "I'm trying to remember."

"Remember, Jody. It's important."

"He was still fully dressed in the clothes he'd worn to the party. His jacket was on the arm of the sofa."

"Was his hair messed up or her lipstick on his face?"

"No, I don't think so. I don't know. When I saw the woman, I just ran. I…"

Maribel put an arm around Jody. "Think

about it. It's important to you and to Chase. You and Chase promised each other a lot of things when you were teenagers with your heads in the clouds. One of those things was that you would never lie to each other. I don't believe he's ever lied to you."

A smile spread across Jody's face. "Oh, Maribel, you are so good at this. You almost had me believing, but again, you had to be there to really believe the truth."

Maribel dropped her arm from Jody's shoulders. "No. I didn't have to be there. All I have to do is know my son and trust him." She pulled her coat closer together and ran across the street to the diner, leaving Jody frozen in place.

Jody wasn't so much aware of the cold as she was of the pain in her heart. Trust Chase? Why couldn't she do that?

CHAPTER SIX

FEBRUARY TURNED INTO March and Chase was busy with classes and therapy. His arm was much better and he could sleep at night without the pain. If everything went according to plan, he would graduate by the end of August. In the back of his mind, two words taunted him: *What's next?* He had time to work it out.

Since the ranch was deep into spring roundup, he didn't see much of the family, just his mother and Eli. He made a point of avoiding Jody and she seemed to be doing the same thing, which suited them both. When he wasn't studying or exercising, he turned his thoughts to the house and the remodeling job he and Jody had planned. He still intended to remodel. Everything in the house was to his mother's taste and now he would make it his. That should keep him busy for a while.

On Friday morning, he swam in the heated

pool at therapy and it was good for his arm. Ginger, his therapist, worked with his shoulder.

"It's so much better than the first time you came here. You don't wince anymore."

He slipped a T-shirt over his head. "I'm happy how things have improved. I'm planning to put a pool in to keep up the swimming."

Ginger clapped. "That would be so good for you."

Ginger was young, very young, with auburn hair, and full of enthusiasm. He didn't miss the subtle overtures she'd made, but he ignored them. He wasn't ready to get involved with anyone, if ever.

"When you get it installed, I'll come visit. I've never been to Horseshoe."

There it was, a subtle hint to take their relationship further. He sat on the bench and slipped on his sneakers. He didn't want to tell her an outright lie, but then again, he didn't want her coming to his house.

He stood and decided to be blunt. "I'm married."

"Sure. I've just enjoyed working with you."

"Me, too. See you on Monday."

He walked out, hoping they could laugh

about it on Monday. She was a good therapist and he didn't want to lose her.

Back at his house, he crashed in his recliner, his mind full of ideas for the house.
They were really Jody's ideas, but he liked
them, especially the bigger master bedroom
with a Jacuzzi. He would have to knock out
some walls and he didn't know how his parents would feel about that. He would take
it one day at a time and slowly work up to
it. *Why?* he asked himself. It was his house
and he could do what he wanted. But then...
There was a tap at the front door. And then
another. Why weren't they ringing the doorbell? He got up and opened the door. Eli
stood there. He wasn't tall enough to ring
the doorbell.

He raised his hand. "Hi, Chase. It's me,
Eli."

He forced himself not to smile. "I know
who you are. Why are you here and how did
you get here?"

"I walked," he said, following Chase into
the house.

"Does Mom know you walked here?"

Eli shrugged.

"Eli!"

"Okay, I didn't tell her. I was bored. There's nothing to do in the diner."

"Do you know how much trouble you're in? You're never to leave the diner unless you have permission. Did you forget?"

Eli shrugged again.

Chase pulled his phone out of his pocket and called his mom. "Chase, I don't have time right now. We can't find Eli and everyone is searching. I'm so worried. I called your father and he's on his way in and…"

"Mom, Mom, slow down. Eli's here. He's okay."

There was a long pause, and then she said, "I'm going to kill him. I'm on my way."

"That's okay. I'll bring him to the diner."

"Are you sure he's okay?"

"Yes, just a little bored."

"Oh, no. I called your father and he's going to be so upset that it was for nothing."

"Just keep reminding him that Eli's okay." Chase didn't know what else to tell her because he knew his father was not going to be happy making the trip in because Eli was bored.

Eli looked up at him with big brown eyes. "Is she mad?"

Chase nodded. "You better start praying because Dad is on his way in, too."

"What did she call him for?"

Chase knelt in front of his brother. "Because they love you, and when Mom couldn't find you, she thought someone had taken you. Do you know what that means?"

Eli nodded. "Is Daddy gonna whup me?"

"I don't know." But he did know that the boys had never been spanked and Elias wasn't likely to start now, but Eli didn't need to know that. He needed to understand what he'd done was wrong.

It was lunchtime and cars were parked everywhere at the diner. Then he saw the sheriff's car and the deputy's car. Oh, heavens. His mom had called the sheriff. Chase parked behind the sheriff's car in the street and Maribel ran out of the diner and jerked open the passenger door. She grabbed Eli, stroking his hair and kissing his cheeks.

The crowd that had gathered clapped.

"Are you okay?"

Eli nodded.

Elias drove up and got out of his old work pickup. He stopped for a moment, stared at his youngest son and could see that he was okay. Obviously his mom had already called. He thumbed toward the truck.

"Get in."

"Elias." His mother couldn't leave it alone. She was going to make sure her baby was protected. "I'll take care of it. I shouldn't have called you when you're so busy. I didn't think. I was just worried."

"In the truck." The words were strong enough to crack the cement and Eli felt them.

"I'll call off the search," the sheriff said, looking at Elias.

"Don't say anything to me, Wyatt," his dad said. "I'm not in the mood for your aged wisdom."

Wyatt nodded and got in his car.

"In the truck," Elias said again to Eli.

He looked up at his mother for help. "Go," she said. Then she addressed her husband. "He's a little boy and was bored. That's all. You don't need to get all stone-faced and angry."

"He broke a big rule today, Maribel, and I'm not going to mollycoddle him like you do. Anything could have happened to him. He's going to be punished."

"Elias—"

His father strolled away to his truck. Eli sat on the passenger side, peering out the window, his eyes big as if he were begging for help.

Maribel pulled off her apron. "I'm going home."

Chase caught her arm. "Mom, let Dad handle it. Eli could have really gotten hurt today. He needs to know that he just can't walk everywhere he wants to at his age."

"I know."

"Look at me. I had a big old attitude when I came here and Elias changed it quickly and never laid a finger on me. I'm proud of the way I've changed because of Dad. Eli will be, too."

"Chase!"

Chase turned to see his old coach waving at him from the sidewalk. He walked over and his mom went back into the diner. They shook hands.

"I heard you retired."

"Yeah," he replied. "The shoulder injury. But the therapy is going well and it's much better."

Coach Pringle nodded. "Still, I hate to see you leave the game. You're the best player I've ever had the opportunity to coach."

"Thanks. I learned a lot from you. Patience doesn't come easy for me, but you drilled it into my head that I just had to wait and the ball would come my way. And, oh, did it. Many times. But the state championship and the Super Bowl will always be my favorite memories."

The coach patted his shoulder. "You earned them."

"Thanks."

"I just wanted to let you know that I'll be retiring soon and the school board is looking for another coach. I thought you might be interested in the job. It would be perfect for you since half of the team are Rebels."

Mr. Pringle had been coaching in Horseshoe for over thirty years. He knew the game inside and out, and Chase couldn't imagine him retiring. When he thought of Horseshoe football, he thought of Coach Pringle. He was an icon.

"Well, I never thought of teaching or coaching. Right now I'm trying to get my degree."

"Good. Good. Just think about it. I'm sure the job is yours if you want it." He patted Chase's shoulder again. "I'm sorry about you and Jody. Now, there was a relationship I thought would never end. Just remember what I told you about patience. Hang in there. And rumors that I hear are just that. Rumors. I know the real Chase Rebel."

"Thanks, Coach."

He turned around and saw Jody standing there. "I heard Eli was missing."

A yellow dress showed off her blond hair. Genuine concern filled her eyes.

"Yes, he's okay. Dad took him home to dole out punishment."

"Punishment? What did he do?"

"He walked to my house without permission."

"Oh. Your dad is kind of rough. He wouldn't hurt him, would he?"

That sparked his temper. "My dad loves us and he would never hurt any one of us. Now, your dad, that's a whole different story."

"My dad—"

"Is a manipulative jerk. He controls you with an iron fist, and don't start shaking your head because you know it's true. Our lives had to be put on hold because of his attitude."

"How dare—"

He turned his back on her and walked

to his truck. "I want to see the divorce papers on Monday. You seem to have forgotten about them." He got in his truck, backed up and drove away, not even taking a second to look back. He was tired of looking back. He was tired of trying to get her to listen to him. He was just tired and ready to move on.

JODY STORMED BACK into the courthouse, fuming. How dare he say that her father was manipulative. He wasn't. He was a loving, caring parent and brought her up to respect herself and others. Yes, there were goals in life he wanted her to achieve. Goals she'd rather have chosen on her own, like where to go to college and where to do her internship. Her dad had helped her make the right choices… But had they been the right ones for her?

Her dad wanted her to go to the University of Texas so she would be close to home. She wanted to go to a university closer to Chase so she could see him when she wanted to. She went to Texas to please her family, which had hurt Chase. Looking back, she couldn't believe she had done that. She was a grown woman and had let her father control her life.

She sat at her desk. Chase was right. Her father was too involved in her life. She'd made so many mistakes, but she couldn't go back and change anything. She had to go forward and salvage something of her life, something she wanted. Her main decision had to be what she could live with and what she couldn't. Once she had that clear in her mind, she could move on.

She clicked on her computer and pulled up the necessary forms that she needed: State of Texas Certificate of Divorce. Maybe if she closed the door on her brief marriage, she could go forward. She stared at the form and filled in the names. Her phone buzzed.

Erin.

"Hey, new mother, how are you doing?"

"Katie and I are lying on a quilt in the living room and I love just watching her and her actions."

"Is your mother still there?"

"No, she went home yesterday, and now we're all by ourselves and it is wonderful. I don't want to wake up from this lovely dream."

"When are y'all coming home?"

"I don't know, but hopefully soon."

"I'm filling out my divorce papers," she blurted out.

"Jody, no."

"Every time I see him, that scene in his apartment flashes through my mind, and I know I'm never going to forget it. So it's time to move on for me and him."

"You're not going to like this, but I'm going to say it anyway. Zane knows Chase really well. They're first cousins and best friends. If Chase were seeing other women, Zane would be one of the first ones to know. Chase would feel so guilty he would need to talk to someone. That's just the way he is. Even I know that."

"Why are you trying to talk me out of it?"

"Divorce won't help you move on. The only way for you to move on is to talk to Chase. Be honest. Be truthful and bear the blame without breaking down. I know you can do it. You'll never have the freedom you're searching for if you don't."

"I've already told my parents about the marriage. That's enough for them to handle right now."

"It's not about them, Jody. It's about you and the burden you've been carrying around. You need to share it and then face the consequences. I told you that before, and nothing in your life is going to change until you do. I will come to Horseshoe and be with you if you want me to."

Jody stared at the certificate of divorce on the screen and knew Erin was right. It wasn't going to change anything. The same old heartache would still be with her.

"I'll talk to you later."

"Jody—"

She tapped the off circle on her phone and then went to a special folder she kept for herself on the laptop. It needed a password to open. She gulped air into her lungs and a tear slipped from her eye.

Erin was right. She always was. She'd never had a problem standing up to her father. Maybe that was because she was ten years old when she met Hardy for the first time. Jody didn't have that strength. Her father's word was law to her, and she never had the capability to stand up to him and let him know that it was her life, not his. Now she had to find that strength. Her very life depended on it.

CHAPTER SEVEN

DURING THE AFTERNOON, Chase went over the plans for the house again and then drove into Temple to see an architect. On the way home, he decided to go by the ranch to check on Grandpa and to see how Eli was faring.

Grandma was in the kitchen working on supper. "Chase, how's your arm?"

He raised it toward the ceiling. "Much better. Therapy is really helping. Where's Grandpa?"

"In the den, watching TV. He's not feeling too good. When I mention going to the doctor, he gets all bristly, but he has an appointment on Thursday."

"Good." He walked into the living room. Grandpa was sound asleep in his chair with the TV blaring. Clint Eastwood was hanging 'em high. Grandpa was pale. His skin had a chalkiness to it that it hadn't had the last time he'd seen him. He made to sit and Grandpa woke up, coughing.

"Chase...my boy."

"Hey, Grandpa." He bent down to hug him and he was reminded once again of Grandpa's frailty. Chase wasn't ready to let him go and he held on a little tighter.

"Turn the TV off so we can talk."

Chase did as Grandpa asked. "How are you feeling?"

"Ah." He waved a hand toward the kitchen. "Kate's been talking, hasn't she? I'm just fine."

"We love you, Grandpa, and we worry about you. If you don't feel good, we need to know. I can take you to the doctor since I'm not doing much."

"Deal. If I feel bad, I'll tell you."

"Will you?" Chase lifted an eyebrow, letting his grandfather know that he didn't believe that for a minute.

"Okay. I'm not feeling like myself. When you get my age, you never know what the morning is going to bring. I'm just grateful to still be with my family."

The back door opened, and Elias and the boys came in. Eli's head rested on his dad's shoulder. All of them were dirty from their heads to their boots, hay clung to their hair and clothes, and they smelled like puppies that had been rolling in the dirt.

"Bath time," his dad said, and they made their way to the stairs.

"Eli is being punished," Grandpa murmured. "I told Elias it won't hurt him to work. Your dad worked at that age. It will calm his free spirit and he will learn to obey."

"You're tough, Grandpa."

"I had to be tough to help Kate and John raise seven boys. You can't be soft. That'll get you every time."

It wasn't long before Eli came charging downstairs in his boxers and a T-shirt and jumped into Chase's lap.

"I worked today, Chase."

"What did you do?"

"Daddy made me drive the truck so he and Uncle Paxton could throw bales of hay to the cows. I had to really stretch my legs to reach the pedals and to see over the dashboard." Eli rubbed his legs. "They hurt."

"Did you get a spanking?"

Eli shook his head. "No. Daddy gave me a lecture like he gives JR, and I was really scared. I almost peed my pants."

"Did you learn anything?" Grandpa asked.

Eli nodded. "Yeah. Never make Daddy mad."

"I hope you learned more than that," Chase said.

Eli's chin bobbed on his chest. "Yeah. I'm not going to be bad ever again."

His mom came into the living room just as his dad and the boys came downstairs. Eli jumped up and ran to his mother.

He wrapped his arms around her waist. "Daddy made me work."

His mom squatted in front of Eli. "Do you know why he did that?"

"Because I was bad. I walked to Chase's without telling you."

"Yes, and I don't want you to ever do that again. I was so scared that someone had just taken my baby, and the sheriff had people looking for you."

"I'm sorry, Mama." Eli hugged her, tears glistening in his eyes. Chase feared they were crocodile tears.

"Boo-hoo," JR mocked him.

"Stop it," Maribel said. "Get to the table. We're ready to eat supper."

They gathered around the large dining room table. Chase helped Grandpa, holding his arm as he made his way there. He trembled as he took a seat and Chase knew something was wrong with him.

Grandma said grace and everyone started to eat, the boys jabbering away about their day.

"I can almost lift a bale of hay by myself," JR boasted. "I'm getting really strong. My coach is going to like that. I'm going to play football just like Chase."

"You'll never be as good as Chase," Tre told him.

"Wanna bet?"

"Stop it," Maribel said. "No arguing at the table." She got up and went into the kitchen and brought back a chocolate cake.

Eli stood on his knees and dragged his finger through the icing. Maribel slapped his hand.

While his mother was dishing out cake, Chase said, "I saw Coach Pringle today. He said he's retiring."

"Yeah," JR said. "The high school is getting a new coach after the first of the year and then he'll be my coach, too. I hope he's good 'cause we're going to win another state championship."

"He asked if I wanted the job."

Everyone stopped eating and looked at him as if they were at a loss for words.

Finally JR said, "Like, you mean, you could be my coach."

"When you get to the high school, yeah."

"Oh, boy, I like this."

"Are you thinking of taking it?" Elias asked.

Chase shrugged. "I haven't really thought about it. It was a shock when he mentioned he was retiring. High school football is Coach Pringle to me. I thought when I came here there wouldn't be any coaches like there were in Dallas, but I found out there was an even better one in Horseshoe. I'd have to file an application and get my degree, but I like the idea. I'm thinking about it."

"It might be just what you need right now," his mother said.

"Let the boy do what he wants." Grandpa's voice rose and then he coughed. "You two—" he spluttered, pointing to Elias and Maribel "—are always trying to run his life. He's a man now and you have to respect that."

Once again there was silence at the table.

"Grandpa, we just want him to make the right decisions," Elias said.

"You make your decisions and now let him make his." Grandpa wasn't backing down. "Remember how you and your father went round and round many a time."

"Yeah." Elias leaned back in his chair. "Dad was a stickler for discipline, structure, manners, and, man, I had to learn them the hard way." He looked around at his boys. "Just like you."

"Tell us what he did, Grandpa," JR begged.

"He'll tell you one day and you'll never be able to top anything he did. There is only one Elias." Grandpa broke into a coughing spell and couldn't stop. Grandma brought him a glass of water and he was able to calm down.

"I think I'll go to bed."

The back door opened and Uncle Quincy called, "Anyone home?"

"In here," Elias hollered in return.

Uncle Quincy walked in. Tall, broad-shouldered with dark hair and eyes, just like all the brothers. "Ready to go, Grandpa?"

Grandpa looked at him with a frown. "Where?"

"You're supposed to eat supper with us tonight." Uncle Quincy and his family lived across the meadow, a good walking distance from Grandma's house.

"I forgot."

"Are you okay?" Quincy asked.

"Just catching a cold. Nothing to worry about."

Quincy placed the back of his hand on his grandpa's forehead. "You look a little pale."

"Now, don't start."

Chase could see he was having a hard time standing, so he held his grandfather's arm and helped him to his feet. "I'm a little tired, though. I'm going to bed. Sorry about supper. Tell Jenny we'll do it another night."

"She made cottage cheese pie for you. I'll bring it over in the morning. Lord knows I'm not eating it."

"You kids don't know what's good."

Quincy hugged him. "We probably don't, Grandpa. Good night." His eyes zeroed in on Eli. "I heard you got in trouble today."

"I'm being punished," Eli replied.

Quincy looked at the chocolate cake on his plate and most of it was on his face. "Chocolate cake is always a good punishment. See y'all later."

Chase helped Grandpa to his room, got his

pajamas and laid them on the bed. Grandpa sat on it with a long sigh.

"Grandpa…"

"I'm just a little tired, my boy." His hands trembled as he tried to unsnap his Western shirt. Chase did it for him and helped him out of his jeans and boots. After getting his pajamas on, Grandpa crawled beneath the sheets and pulled the comforter over him.

"It's really cold in here, Chase. See what the temperature is."

It was March and Grandpa's room was hot because he always kept the temperature at seventy-eight degrees. "It's fine in here. I'll get you another blanket." He placed a blanket over him and he went to sleep. Chase went back into the dining room and the boys were finishing up chocolate cake and milk.

"Is he okay?" Elias asked.

"I think he's coming down with a cold. I'll check on him again in a little bit."

"Okay, boys. Time for bed. We have to be up with the chickens."

Eli squirmed in his chair. "Daddy, I'm going to go with Mama tomorrow."

"Eli, son, there's one little problem with that. You don't get to make that decision. I do. Tomorrow morning you'll be up early with your brothers. Y'all will go to school and then y'all will go to work."

"I don't want to." He started to cry, tears rolling from his eyes,

Elias plucked him from the chair and held him in his lap. "We talked about this, son. You do something bad, you get punished. No deals. Not even with tears. After a week of feeding cows, you'll be glad to go back to the diner and stay there. Let's go to bed."

His mom looked after them with a woeful expression.

"He'll be fine," he told her.

"It's so hard being a parent. I know he needs to be punished... I never want to relive those minutes when I couldn't find him today. My heart was about to pound out of my chest, thinking that someone had taken my kid."

"It's over, Mom, and Dad's going to make sure it doesn't happen again."

Chase helped clean up the kitchen and then he checked on Grandpa. He was still asleep, but his breathing was labored.

When he went back into the dining room, his parents were sitting at the table, eating cake and drinking coffee.

"How is he?" Elias asked.

"He's breathing very hard. I think I'll spend the night and sleep in his room just to make sure he's okay."

Elias got up and went to check on him. "I don't like the way he's breathing, either. You take half of the night and I'll take the other."

Chase shook his head. "You have to work tomorrow. I don't. I'll be fine. I just want to make sure that Grandpa's okay."

Grandma handed him a glass of tea.

"You don't have to wait on me."

She touched his hair. "It's a pleasure. Now I'm going to bed to watch TV. I'll see you guys in the morning."

When he first met his grandmother, they weren't on the best of terms. She hadn't believed that Chase was Elias's son. It took her some time to accept it. Beyond any doubt, everyone now knew he was. She'd been riddled with guilt over rejecting one of her grandchildren and every day she tried to make up for it in any little way. He loved his grandmother and he knew she loved him, too.

"I saw an architect today," he said as a way to bring up something he wanted to talk about.

"An architect? Why?" his mother asked.

"I'm going to do some remodeling, like putting in a pool so I can swim every day. It really helps my arm."

"A pool?" His mother frowned. "Why can't you just go to Temple and swim?"

He took a deep breath, trying to control his emotions. "Okay. I'm not asking for permission. I'm telling you what I'm going to do with the house my father gave me. Everything in the house is your taste. Now I'm just going to remodel with my taste."

"Oh, Elias, he's going to make it modern."

"Whatever. It's his house, Maribel. We don't live there anymore."

"It's a perfectly good house and there's nothing wrong with it. I don't—"

Elias put a hand over his wife's mouth. She bit his finger and he howled. Then he grabbed her and carried her up the stairs.

"I'm thinking of making it a two-story," he yelled after them, smiling.

"Chase!"

"He's just goading you."

That was when he realized that whatever he wanted to do, his mother would have her own personal views. She loved the house that she and Elias had built. It was the only home she'd ever owned and he understood her displeasure at changing anything. That was what life was about, though—changes. He was adding a workout room and probably a lot more. His mom was in for the shock of her life.

Chase had a room on Rebel Ranch. His mother had insisted on it. He didn't understand why he needed a room here when he had a house. He often thought it was his mother's way of staking her claim to his grandmother's house. The dynamics of a family were sometimes overwhelming.

He took a quick shower, then slipped on a T-shirt and jogging pants. He went back downstairs, checked all the doors and turned out the lights. Grandpa's room was like an oven. Chase turned down the thermostat so he'd be able to sleep in Grandpa's recliner. Chase didn't get much sleep. Grandpa coughed most of the night and he got up three times to use the bathroom. Chase had to help him.

Grandpa woke up at five o'clock, like always. Ever since he'd known his grandfather, he woke up at 5:00 a.m. every morning. Chase could hear noises in the kitchen and knew everyone was up, getting ready to go their different ways. Grandpa put on a shirt, but Chase had to help him with his jeans. Instead of slipping into his boots, he put on his slippers and walked into the kitchen. He sat at the kitchen table and Grandma brought him a cup of coffee.

"What would you guys like for breakfast?" Grandma asked.

"Some of those biscuits like you make." That was one of his favorite things about coming to the ranch, eating Grandma's biscuits.

"A pan is in the oven."

"Add some eggs and bacon to that," Grandpa said, sipping on his coffee.

Chase had to admit his grandpa looked better this morning. He wasn't so pale and he didn't seem tired. He finished breakfast and went into the living room and flipped on the TV.

"He watches the news in the mornings," Grandma said. "If you're going to be here today, I need to run to the grocery store. I really don't want to leave Grandpa alone."

"You got it. We'll play checkers or dominoes or something."

"Thank you. I won't be long. I always like to shop early, when there isn't such a crowd."

"Take your time. I'll be here."

Chase played dominoes with Grandpa until Grandpa had to go to the bathroom. When he came back, Grandpa looked pale again and he was coughing uncontrollably.

"Are you okay, Grandpa?"

He reclined in his chair, not making any attempt to play dominoes or talk. Chase remained by his side, sitting on the sofa, watching him.

"Cha-se, I…I…can't…breathe."

Chase was immediately on his feet and brought the chair to a sitting position. "Try to breathe in." His grandfather struggled to get air into his lungs and his skin was pasty white. He coughed up blood-tinged phlegm. Chase grabbed tissues at the same time he grabbed his phone and called 911. He told the lady on the phone the situation while wiping Grandpa's face and shirt. The woman asked a ton of questions and Chase knew his grandfather needed to get to a doctor as fast as possible. "We live way out in the country. I can get him there faster in my truck."

"Does he have any injuries?"

"Not that I'm aware of. I think he might have the flu or a bad cold."

"Okay. It would probably be best if you

brought him in, but be very careful and keep me on the phone. Give me information about your truck, and the highway patrol will look for it and guide you into Temple."

He gave her the make, color and model of his truck, and the license plate. He reached for the pillow on the sofa, lifted Grandpa into his arms and headed for the truck. He got Grandpa into the truck, put the pillow behind his head and then ran around to the driver's side.

His hands shook and his heart jolted in his chest. "Grandpa, we're on our way to the hospital."

Grandpa leaned his head back and didn't say anything. Chase reached over and touched the old man's hands, which lay limply in his lap, and noticed the liver spots and wrinkles. Grandpa had lived a long life, longer than most. But they still needed him. Chase still needed him.

"Just keep him calm and quiet," the woman on the phone said.

As he turned onto Highway 77, he heard the siren and looked back to see a highway patrol car. It passed him and the patrolman gave him the go signal. With the siren wailing, they roared toward Temple.

He told the lady thanks and called his dad. "What is it, son? We're kind of busy."

"Grandpa can't breathe. I'm taking him to the ER."

"I'm on my way."

Hang on, Grandpa. Please, hang on.

CHAPTER EIGHT

WHEN THEY REACHED the hospital, two guys ran out with a gurney. They lifted Grandpa from the truck to the bed. "Cha-se." Grandpa's voice was barely a whisper, but Chase heard it.

"I'm right here." Grandpa waved a hand toward him and he caught it and held it all the way into the ER.

"You're going to have to leave," a doctor in scrubs said.

"He's kind of scared and I don't want to leave him."

"Stand back, then."

"I'm going to step back, Grandpa. The doctor and nurses need to work on you, but I'll be right here. I'm not going anywhere."

At that moment Grandpa's hand dropped to the bed. Chase looked at the doctor. "What happened?"

"He's out. We have to do a procedure called intubation to help him breathe. You can step out now, Mr. Rebel. He won't know the difference. We'll be taking him to ICU in a little bit. You can see him there."

"If he wakes up, tell him Chase is here."

The doctor glanced at him. "I will."

Chase stayed frozen to the spot, shaking from head to toe. The doctor tilted Grandpa's head and the nurse held something that looked like a ball that had a long tube and Chase knew she was going to put it down Grandpa's throat. Chase turned away and stepped into the hallway. He walked toward the waiting room, hoping someone had arrived, but there were only people there whom he didn't know. At that point, he saw his dad come through the double doors and he ran to him as if he were Eli's age.

Chase hugged him fiercely. "He's really sick, Dad."

"He's tough. We just have to hope and pray that he pulls through it."

Falcon and Quincy arrived, followed by the other grandsons. They all paced with worried looks on their faces. Chase had called Zane and didn't get a response. He had texted him earlier so he'd know what was going on. Chase expected him to be here. Chase turned to see a doctor and Zane standing in the doorway.

Zane hugged everyone. "This is Dr. Mullins. He will be treating Grandpa. I'm going to be honest with everyone. Grandpa has pneumonia and he's not good. He's breathing with the help of a ventilator and resting comfortably for now. But it's a long road ahead. We all have to be prepared."

A nurse appeared in the doorway. "Dr. Mullins, Mr. Rebel woke up and he's agitated. He's trying to say someone's name, but I can't figure it out."

Everyone looked at Chase. They all knew he and Grandpa had a special bond. He followed the nurse and donned gloves and a protective gown and then went into the ICU. There was a central unit that was connected to small rooms and each room had a private nurse. Chase paused as he saw his grandfather hooked up to several machines that were beeping. Grandpa's skin was even paler against the white sheets and it took him a moment to get his emotions in order. The moment Grandpa saw Chase, he leaned back and relaxed.

Chase stroked his grandpa's white hair.

"What are you up to? I told you I'm not leaving. I'll either be in here or outside the door."

Grandpa shook his head and looked at the ventilator. "Yes, you can't talk right now. The machine is helping you breathe."

Grandpa slapped at his chest.

"He's trying to tell you something," the nurse said. "He might want to know what's wrong."

"Is that it?" Chase asked.

Grandpa nodded.

"You have pneumonia. Did you get a pneumonia shot this year?"

Grandpa nodded.

Chase looked at the nurse. "Then why does he have pneumonia?"

"It happens sometimes. We'll check his records to see when he had his last shot."

Grandpa tried to ask something again. The nurse brought a pen and a pad to the bed for him to write what he wanted to know. She raised the bed and Grandpa scribbled on the pad. Chase leaned over to see, and scrawled on the pad were six shaky letters. *C-A-N-C-E-R*.

"No, no, Grandpa. You don't have cancer. Just pneumonia. Now rest so you can get better."

He sagged against the pillows, his eyes closed. Zane and Dr. Mullins walked in. Dr. Mullins checked all the monitors. "He's breathing much better, thanks to the machine. We just have to wait and see." Chase walked out with Zane.

"How come you didn't answer your phone?"

"I didn't have time. A doctor at the hospital was leaving to go to Dallas on his private plane and I wanted to catch a ride with him. He agreed to drop me in Temple. That took a flight change and some time, but I'm here instead of talking to you from Houston."

"Did Erin come with you?"

"No. She's driving home with the baby."

"Next time, answer your damn phone."

"Whoa. Is that anger in your voice?"

"Yes, it is. Our grandfather is about to die and you can't take the time to pick up the phone and talk to me."

"Are we having an argument?"

"I am. You're lost somewhere on another planet most of the time." He took a deep breath. The last thing he wanted to do was get into an argument with Zane. "I was scared. I'm scared of losing my grandfather and I could have used your calm voice."

"I'm sorry, man." Zane threw an arm around his shoulders. "You're right. Most of the time I am on another planet, dealing with other people's problems. I promise to do better."

"Oh, shut up. Now you're making me feel bad."

"Chase, everyone is going to die, even Grandpa, but I'm going to make sure he gets every breath he deserves on this earth."

"Now that I'm older, life seems to be sad all the time. I hate change."

"We'll get through it because we're family."

Because of Zane, the doctor allowed everyone to see Grandpa for a few seconds. All the wives had arrived and so had all the great-grandchildren, but the great-greats were too small to be at the hospital.

Grandpa's grandsons went in with their families. His mom and dad went in with the boys. Elias carried Eli. The boys were very quiet as they stared at Grandpa. "I want Grandpa to come home," Eli cried.

Grandpa nodded his head.

"Not today," Elias said. "He needs a break."

"But I want him to come home."

His mom took Eli and the boys and left the room. Elias leaned over and kissed Grandpa's forehead. "Come on, old man. You're not through giving me aggravation, are you?"

A slight smile touched Grandpa's face.

"If you need anything, Chase or I will be outside the door."

Grandpa nodded and Elias walked out. Chase was sure he glimpsed a tear in his eye. His father wasn't a man who cried easily or one to show his emotions, unless it was anger. And today his father had run the full gamut of his emotions. And it wasn't even lunchtime.

Outside the door, Elias asked Chase, "How long are you staying?"

"Until Grandpa goes home."

"Now, son, you can't keep up that pace. We'll take turns as everyone else will want to."

"No. The ranch is everyone's livelihood and the uncles need to work. I'm staying here with Grandpa until he's ready to go home. If he gets worse, I will call you, but for now I'm just waiting for him to get better."

They walked into the waiting room and

found Grandma sitting there by herself. Chase sat beside her.

"Are you okay, Grandma?"

"Yes, I guess. I'm just so worried about Abe. I knew he wasn't feeling good and I should have made him go to the doctor, but he's so stubborn. I...I..." She wiped a tear from her eye. "I just don't know what I'll do if something happens to him."

Chase put an arm around her shoulders. "Ah, Grandma, he's going to be just fine."

"That's not what the doctor said, son, and we have to be honest. Grandpa is up in years and he may not pull through this. I'm bracing myself and you have to do the same thing."

Chase got to his feet. "No, I don't. I will never give up on Grandpa."

Elias ran a hand through his disheveled hair. "Okay, suit yourself. I'll take you home, Mom."

"Thank you, son, but I'm going to stay here with Chase. Quincy said he would come back later, and I'm going to wait a little longer to make sure Abe is okay."

Quincy was the peacemaker in the family and he was always there if anyone needed anything. He'd taken care of Grandpa until he got married, and then Elias took over, or as his dad had said, he'd inherited Grandpa.

Elias threw up his hands. "I'll be back as soon as I can, and if anything happens—" he pointed a finger at Chase "—you better call me."

"Yes, sir."

"Your great-grandpa and I drink coffee all day long, just about. I switched to decaf and he hasn't noticed the difference and neither have I. It's just a habit."

"I'll get you a cup."

Chase took the elevator down to the cafeteria and got coffee and a snack. They sat in the waiting room, drinking coffee and eating a cinnamon roll.

"Abe has only been in the hospital one other time."

"What happened?"

"This was way back when John and your great-grandmother were still alive. It was roundup time and John was bringing the cows to the pens. Abe was holding the gate and this red-and-white-faced cow with long horns was leading the pack. When she saw Abe, she turned in his direction, determined not to go into the pen. Abe waved his hat and his arms, trying to scare her away, but she went right for him, hooking him with her right horn and throwing him out into the pasture like he was a rag doll. Martha screamed and the boys huddled at my feet like little chickens. I was pregnant with Jude.

"John made it to his dad and held him in his arms. I've never seen so much blood as it was that day on Abe and John. I told the boys to stay with Grandma and I ran for the truck and drove it out into the pasture. John picked up his father and got in on the passenger side and I took off for Temple. It was a long night. The cow had punctured his lung and the doctor had to operate. The days dragged on, but eventually he came home to the boys and Martha. John never left his side."

"I wish I had known him."

Grandma rubbed his arm. "Look at your dad. Elias is more John than any of my boys. They share a lot of the same qualities. John went to work at daylight and he wouldn't quit until the sun went down. Elias is the same way. A workaholic."

"I know. He taught me how to work. He taught me everything I know. Up until I met my father, I was a big mama's boy."

"I'll tell you something about your dad.

He had this uncanny strength from the day he was born. When Abe came home, he couldn't get up and down. His lung and incision were still very sore. John would go over every morning at five a.m. and get him in his chair so he could eat breakfast and watch the news. One morning a neighbor called and said one of our bulls was in his pasture. John hooked up a trailer, saddled a horse and drove over there to get the bull. He said his dad would have to wait until he got back.

"I knew Abe wasn't going to like that. I took the boys and went over and told him where John was. He said, *Come over here, boys, and help your grandpa.* I had no idea what he had in mind. Falcon was almost seven and Elias was two. I didn't think they could do much. I was pregnant and couldn't help. He told Egan and Elias to crawl on the bed and get under his back, like two little rooting pigs. Falcon and Quincy held his arms. Abe told Egan and Elias to lie on their backs and push with their feet flat against his back. They did and I was surprised at their strength. They pushed and Falcon and Quincy pulled and Abe came right up and sat on the side of the bed."

They talked on and it helped pass the day. His dad called a couple of times. His mom brought them lunch and the day wore on. As darkness claimed the daylight, the grandsons and wives trickled in. Grandpa was out and resting comfortably. After everyone left, Chase tried to get some sleep on the small sofa in the waiting area. The nurse brought him a blanket and a pillow. He was surprised that his dad hadn't come back, but he would probably be here first thing in the morning. Someone touched his shoulder and he jumped up. His dad stood there in a pair of shorts and a T-shirt.

"Go home and get some rest. I'll stay until daylight."

Chase ran his hands through his hair. "I'm not going anywhere, Dad. I told you that. I'm not leaving Grandpa until he goes home."

His dad put his hands on his hips. "I wish you weren't so much like me."

Chase could see what his grandmother was talking about, an indefinable strength that belonged only to Elias. He would work all day and still stay at the hospital all night. Family came first for him. Underneath all that rough and toughness was a man who would do anything for his family. Chase was really glad that he was a lot like his father.

JODY HAD THE divorce papers ready and waited and waited for Chase to show up, but he never did. She went over to the diner, but Maribel wasn't there, either. After work on Tuesday, she drove to Chase's house. Of course, the door was unlocked again. She hollered and hollered, but no one responded. Chase wasn't there, either.

As she went out the front door, a car drove up to the curb. A man in a suit carrying a briefcase got out. They shook hands on the sidewalk.

"I'm looking for Chase Rebel," the man said.

"I am, too, but he's not here."

The man pulled out his phone and evidently called Chase. All she could hear was his side of the conversation. "Oh, I'm so sorry to hear that. Do you mind if I look around while I'm here? Okay, thanks."

He slipped the phone back into his pocket. "Mr. Rebel said it's okay for me to look around."

"Are you buying the place?" That was the only thing that made sense and yet it made no sense. Chase would never sell this property, so what was the man doing?

"No. I'm an architect. Mr. Rebel is doing some remodeling and he's hired me to see if his plans are feasible."

"Oh." They'd had plans to remodel the house a long time ago. Now he was doing them by himself. What did she care? She was divorcing him.

She started for her car and thought about what the man had said on the phone. "Hey," she called. "When you were talking to Chase, you said you were sorry about something. Is he okay?"

"Yes, as far as I know. He said his grandfather is in ICU and in bad shape."

"Mr. Abe?"

The man shrugged.

That was where Chase was, with his grandfather at the hospital. Horseshoe was a small town and someone should have mentioned it to her by now. She drove back to the courthouse and saw that Maribel's SUV was now parked in a spot. Inside she found her dad and Cole, the deputy, having coffee. She spoke to them for a second and then went over to Maribel. "Is Chase still in Temple?"

Maribel looked up. "Yes, and he'll be there until Grandpa comes home."

"How is Mr. Abe?"

"Not good. We're all worried. He has pneumonia, and at his age, we just don't know."

She needed to be with Chase was all she could think. Moments like this he needed her, too. "Thanks, Maribel. Do you think it would be okay if I went to see him?"

"Now, sweetie, I don't think it's a place for you. Chase is upset enough."

She turned and walked out. It may not be the place for her, but she had to see how Chase was doing.

"Jody," her dad called.

With her hand on the door handle, she looked back and her dad hurried to her side. "Where are you going?"

"To the hospital to see Mr. Abe."

"Only his family can see him. I think it's best to stay away, especially with the divorce and all."

"So you knew Mr. Abe was ill and you didn't tell me?"

"I didn't see the need."

"Chase and I have been together for years and we spent a lot of time with Grandpa

Abe. I didn't just suddenly stop caring about people because Chase and I broke up."

"Jody—"

Her mother came walking across the courthouse lawn in slacks and sensible heels. "Hi." She kissed Jody's dad and then looked at Jody. "Please tell me y'all aren't arguing again."

"She found out Mr. Abe is in the hospital, and with some misguided ideas, she feels she needs to go see him."

"Well, that's…nice, but there are so many Rebels, and I'm sure they don't let many people into the ICU. Why don't you wait another day or so?"

There was that pressure that they always put on her. Not liking her decision, they always had another way for Jody to do things. Well, no more. She was doing things her way. She didn't know how much older she had to get before her backbone stiffened enough for her to say no.

"Come for supper tonight," her mom kept on. "I'm making lasagna and it's Anamarie's recipe, so you know it's good."

"No, thanks, Mom. I have things to do." She got in her car and drove away. She stopped at the corner and glanced in her rearview mirror. Her parents stood there staring after her. Two parents who didn't know how to control their grown-up daughter. Two parents who never wanted to let go. Two parents who were holding on with all their might. Jody loved them, but she had to be the one to let go.

CHAPTER NINE

JODY WENT HOME, took a shower and changed into jeans and a top. She was just about to open her laptop when there was a knock at her front door. Erin stood there holding a baby carrier.

"Erin! What are you doing here?"

"Are you going to invite me in or let me stand here holding this heavy kid? I swear she's gained ten pounds."

Jody hurriedly stepped back. "Come in. Come in. Oh, look at her." Jody took the baby out of the carrier and bounced her around. "She's growing so much. Are you home just for a visit?"

Erin sat on the sofa. "Haven't you heard? Grandpa Abe is sick. Zane came yesterday." She reached up to wipe drool from the baby's mouth. "I thought I'd just drop by to see you for a minute on my way to my mom's. I'm leaving the baby with her while I go to the hospital."

"I can keep her." Jody stroked the baby's soft cheeks with her finger.

"Yeah, and when my mom hears that you have her, you will see all her bad qualities come out. I mean, she's like a lioness."

"Well, I get to hold her for a little while." She sat on the other end of the sofa and the baby slept peacefully on her crossed legs.

"Zane said that Chase is taking this hard. He won't leave the hospital."

"He's close to his grandfather." That was why she wanted to go to the hospital to be there for him…but he may not need her anymore. She had so many emotions churning inside her and she wasn't sure what to do with any of them. Her life was a mess.

"Have you been to the hospital?"

Jody shook her head. "My parents felt it would be best if I didn't."

"Your parents, huh? What do you want, Jody?"

"I have the divorce papers finished. I just have to get Chase to sign them and then we'll be legally divorced."

Erin shook her head. "I can't believe you're doing this. It's like I don't know you anymore. And, please, if you have any feelings for Chase at all, do not give him the divorce papers at the hospital. I know you're hurt and…"

"I wouldn't do that."

"Thank heavens." Erin reached over and took the baby and put her back in the carrier. "I better go before my mom starts calling."

"How long are you staying?"

"Depends on Grandpa Abe." Erin reached out and hugged Jody. "You've been my best friend forever and I love you and hate to see you hurting like this. For once in your life, do what you want. You have a good head on your shoulders, so go with your instincts. Go with your heart and you can't go wrong."

Jody blinked away tears. "Thanks, friend."

Erin left and Jody returned to the couch, lost in thought. The TV wasn't on and the house was quiet. She could hear the kids across the street playing ball. She lay on the sofa, staring straight ahead at an old lamp of Gramma's. It was an Elvis Presley lamp with fringe around the shade and was probably more than fifty years old. Her gramma had been a big Elvis fan and Jody couldn't bear to part with some of the things she'd collected over the years.

What do you want, Jody? The words danced around in her head, demanding an answer. Most of her life she was never asked that question. Everything had been decided for her and all she had to do was agree and it made her parents happy. Chase was the first thing they'd disagreed about. They thought he wasn't good enough for her and too wild. Her dad had thought that Chase would never make it in the NFL, but he'd proved him wrong and now Chase could retire on the money he'd made.

Tonight Jody knew exactly what she wanted. She grabbed her purse and headed for her car, not taking a moment to think it might be wrong. She was going to the hospital to see if Chase was okay. He had family who would take care of him, she told herself, but it wasn't the same thing as her being there. She was still his wife.

It was after nine o'clock and she didn't think about taking him supper because she knew Maribel had that covered. Rebel ranch trucks were in the parking area and she stayed in her car for a while. Elias's truck was the last to leave.

Jody got out and hurried inside, going straight to the ICU. She knew where it was because Gramma had been there for a week.

"Wish me luck, Gramma," she murmured under her breath.

The hallways were dimly lit and quiet. The beep of a machine was the only sound piercing the silence. She walked up to the nurse's desk and it was a nurse she knew from Gramma's stay. "Hi, Jody. What can I do for you? Everything is locked up for the night."

"I'm just checking on Grandpa Abe."

"He's doing better." She pointed to the waiting room, where someone sat. "His grandson is always here." She leaned over and whispered, "He's an NFL football player. My boyfriend knows him. Well, not really knows him like drink-beer-with-him, but he knows who he is and he's going to sign a football for him. Believe me, if I didn't have a boyfriend, I'd be flirting big-time. He's got handsome all over him."

"Yeah."

"You know him?"

"Yes. I'm his wife."

She walked into the waiting area, leaving the nurse with her mouth hanging open. Chase was stretched out on the sofa, covered with a blanket and with a pillow under his head. She didn't know if he was asleep or not. There were several vacant chairs and she sat in the one closest to him to wait. The place was deserted tonight, no footsteps, no voices, no movements. It reminded her of something her gramma used to say during bad weather. *When it gets this bad, the devil's coming to town.* And then she'd add, *We don't have to worry about a thing. Your daddy is the sheriff and he'll put his handcuffs on him and throw him in jail. No, no, Jody, the devil can't get near us.* Her dad had been her whole life until Chase. Nothing bad could happen because he was always there to protect her. It hadn't exactly turned out that way.

"What are you doing here, Jody?"

She jumped at the sound of Chase's irritated voice.

"I…I heard about Grandpa Abe and came by to see how he was."

"He's not your grandfather anymore."

Chase was in one of those moods.

"I still care about him."

He sat up. His hair was disheveled and he wore a T-shirt and what looked like shorts. A wave of attraction flowed through her. She'd seen him many times like this and she never grew tired of looking at him. The nurse was right; he was handsome, covered with it right up to his indignant nose.

"They're only letting family in to see him and that's at certain hours."

"I know that. I just wanted to see how you were doing. I know how much you care for your grandfather."

Chase rubbed his hands together. "He's doing much better. It was touch and go there for a while. They're taking the breathing tube out in the morning to see if he can breathe on his own again. The whole family will probably be here."

"And you're scared?"

He looked up and she got caught in the darkness of his eyes, even though there was no light in the room. They focused totally on each other. "Yeah. All the times I was away from home playing football, I feared he would die while I was gone. When Nana died, it was the worst feeling I've ever felt in my whole life. How could this wonderful, kind woman suddenly be gone? And now it's the same with Grandpa. Mom and Dad keep telling me that he's lived a good long life and everyone has to die, even Grandpa. They don't understand how it's going to rip my heart out."

Jody slid onto the sofa, put her arms around him and just held him. That was what he needed the most, for someone to be here for him. She knew that feeling when Gramma had been so sick. "I know, Chase. No one knows that feeling unless they've lost someone they loved deeply."

His arms gripped her, but he didn't say anything.

"Life will never be the same again," he whispered against her hair.

She leaned back and looked at him. "Hey, we're talking like he's already gone. Grandpa has a lot of fighting left and I don't think he's given up yet. I think he's got a lot more living to do."

"You do?"

"Yes."

"Thank you for coming by. I'll tell Grandpa when he wakes up."

She kept waiting for him to ask her to stay, but he didn't make the offer. Where was the bitterness, the anger and that sense of betrayal? It was usually right there in her chest, fueling everything she said and did, but tonight it wasn't there anymore. Had she forgiven him? With everything in her, she just wanted to wrap her arms around

Chase and lie on the sofa with him until his grandpa woke up.

AT SEVEN THE next morning, Jody was back at the hospital and it was a lively affair. People were everywhere, talking and walking around. She made it up to the ICU unit and it was packed, as well. Rebels filled the waiting room and down the hallway. She saw Zane and Erin and went up to them.

A doctor came out of the double doors of the ICU and motioned for Zane. "This is it," Zane said. "Keep your fingers crossed and a prayer on your tongue."

Zane walked toward the doctor and Elias noticed Jody. She tensed as he came toward her. "What are you doing here? It's not a good time."

"I'm still Chase's wife and have as much right to be here as you do."

Elias held a hand to his head as if it were throbbing. "When in the hell did all these kids grow up and start telling me what to do?"

"Dad," Chase called, and his eyes caught hers.

Elias made his way to Chase and the doctor raised a hand. "Everyone, please be quiet.

I'm going to remove the ventilator from your grandfather. Dr. Rebel will be with me and I will allow one other family member. It's your choice, but I would not like to hear any squabbling."

"Chase hasn't left the hospital," Falcon said. "I think he should be there with Zane."

Everyone nodded.

Jody crossed her fingers and held them up so Chase could see.

A slight smile touched his face and he went through the double doors with Zane.

She sat next to Erin to wait and it seemed like hours, but she knew it had only been minutes when Chase came back out. "He's breathing on his own."

Everyone's shoulders sagged with relief.

"And he's mad at me because I let the doctor put the ventilator in. He's not too happy right now, but he's breathing. He's breathing without difficulty."

The brothers hugged and Jody slipped out. She had to go to work and now she could concentrate. Grandpa Abe would be okay.

CHASE STOOD AT the foot of Grandpa's bed as his uncles and their wives came in to see him. Grandpa wouldn't look at him and it made Chase mad. His grandfather had never been mad at him and he had no reason to be mad at him now. His mom and dad were the last ones to leave the room and Chase followed.

"What did you say to Jody?" he asked his dad.

"Was she here?" Maribel looked around.

"Yes, and Dad went over to talk to her. What did you say to her?"

"Elias, what did you do?"

"Nothing. I just asked what she was doing here."

Chase ran his hands through his hair. "Dad, please, stay out of my personal life. Grandpa is going to be okay and I'm not going to get angry anymore. I'm tired of being angry. But I would so appreciate it if you'd let me handle my own life."

His parents didn't say anything and he appreciated that. Zane came out of the ICU. "Man, Grandpa's on a tear and blaming you for bringing him in here. You better go in and do some of your magic. Erin and I will be leaving in a couple of hours, so this is good-bye, cousin, until the next time."

They hugged and Chase made his way back into the ICU. Grandpa was sitting up, his white hair shaggy, and he had a wild look in his eyes. Chase didn't know whether to walk back out or stay and take it. He was never one to run from a fight, so he planted both feet about a foot from the bed.

"How could you do that to your grandpa?" were the first words out of Grandpa's mouth.

"You couldn't breathe. What was I supposed to do?"

"They put that tube down my throat. You should have told them no."

"Okay, Grandpa. You want to be mad at me? Go ahead. Be mad at me. But it saved your life and I would do it all over again for that reason. Do you know what it's like, watching you gulp for air and not knowing if it's going to be your last? I had to deal with that on my own and I made the right decision and your anger is not going to change that. If you had to endure a little discomfort to save your life, then I think it was worth it. You're my grandpa and you mean the world to me. I've been here since I brought you in and I'm not leaving until you go home."

"You've been here all this time?"

"Yes. I've been sleeping on that hard sofa out there because I love my grandpa. So if you want to be mad, just stay mad. You're breathing without a problem. You're breathing. I'm going to get something to eat."

"Chase."

He stopped at the door and took a breath and looked back at a grouchy old man he loved more than anything on this earth.

"I love you, son. I just lost my mind for a minute. When you get to be my age, your mind doesn't work real well. I'm not mad at you. I can never be mad at you. I'm mad at life and what it does to a person. Then look what it gave me, a bunch of boys at my back my whole life. Then I get the greatest gift of all, a great-grandson who is just like my boy John." Tears rolled from his eyes and Chase dashed back to him.

"It's okay, Grandpa. Don't cry." He reached for tissues on the nightstand and wiped away his grandpa's tears. Then he combed his hair with his fingers. "Now, calm down. They're going to put you in a room later this afternoon. You'll like that much better and you know why?"

Grandpa shook his head.

"Because I'm going to be right there beside you on a cot until we go home. Okay?"

A smile split the cracks and crevices of his worn face. "Okay."

Later that afternoon Grandpa was moved to a room. The room was big enough for a cot and a recliner, which were already in there. Grandpa's mood was much better when he was away from the beeping of the machines. He still had an IV and was on oxygen, but he looked so much better.

The first thing he said was "Look for a Western on the TV."

Chase sighed. His job for the next few days. He found the channel and handed Grandpa the control. The doctor came in and asked if family members could keep visiting to a minimum. It was just too much for the old man. When given the news, the family wasn't too happy. But Chase solved that by gathering everyone on Zoom at nine o'clock.

About ten minutes into the meeting, Grandpa said, "Y'all keep talking. I'm going to sleep."

Chase tried very hard not to laugh as he crawled onto the cot. He'd spent most of the afternoon setting everything up and Grandpa really didn't want to talk to anyone. But at least they got to see him, and in the next day or two he'd be able to go home.

He really thought Jody would have come by tonight. He waited and waited, but she never showed. And he had to wonder if his dad had hurt her feelings, which wasn't unusual. He was known for speaking his mind.

Grandpa's heavy snores drowned out the TV. Chase reached for the control and turned it off. He flipped off the lights and sank onto the cot. Before he could get comfortable, someone pushed the door open slightly and a tiny beam of light slid its way inside the room. "Chase?"

It was her.

CHAPTER TEN

CHASE PULLED THE door a little wider while Jody juggled two Blizzards from Dairy Queen, her purse and her briefcase in her hands. "I know it's late, but I wanted to see how Grandpa was doing."

"He's doing much better. Come in. He's asleep."

"I don't want to disturb him."

Chase took the Blizzards from her, which were in a cardboard carry box. "Oreos and Snickers?"

"Yes." After class in high school they'd drop by the Dairy Queen to get Blizzards, and most of the time they would meet Erin and Zane there. They'd had no worries in the world, except her father being on her case for spending so much time with Chase. He wanted her to study all the time so she would have the best grades to enter her freshman class in college. They'd spent most of that year talking about which college to attend and it always came back to the same thing—her dad's choice was never hers. She should have stood up for herself like she had been taught by the man himself.

The room darkened as the door closed and the only lights in the room were on the machine hooked to Grandpa. As her eyes adjusted, she could see the Temple skyline from the opened blinds on the big double windows. In pajama bottoms and a T-shirt, Chase scooted onto the cot and patted a spot by him. "Are you just getting off work?"

"Yeah." She placed her purse and briefcase on the cot and sat beside him, kicking off her heels as she did. "It's been a long day interviewing people who don't want to be interviewed and who don't want to tell the truth."

He handed her a Blizzard.

"Snickers?"

"I wouldn't give you my Oreos."

"Yeah." She took a sip and smiled as the coolness and sweetness filled her mouth, reminding her of so many days at the Dairy Queen with Chase.

"We were so young back then. I was sixteen, and you were eighteen. We were just kids, as my father kept telling me. It seems strange now that I can see his worry so clearly."

Chase sat very still. She didn't want him to think that she was taking her father's side because she wasn't. They had just handled it badly. She didn't want to keep rehashing it over and over. She just wanted to feel some normalcy again.

"I filled out the divorce papers" came out blunt and honest.

There was a long silence, then, "Did you bring them?"

"No. They're at my office. They just need our signatures. Then I have to file it for it to be official."

"Seems very simple."

"Mmm."

"It's not simple," Grandpa said from the bed, and they jumped as if a ghost had appeared.

Chase got to his feet and threw his cup in the trash. "You're supposed to be asleep, Grandpa."

"How can I sleep when you two are throwing away your lives?"

"Grandpa—"

"I want to talk to Jody."

"I'm right here, Grandpa Abe." Jody stood

by Chase, holding the Blizzard cup tightly as if somehow it would give her strength.

"That young love you felt back then will last forever. Nothing will ever touch it. You might marry someone else, but that first love you'll never forget, nor can you ever replace it. Take my word for it. I fell in love with my wife, Martha, when she was seventeen and I was nineteen. Her daddy was a baptist preacher and he could stretch a sermon to hell and back. He said she was too young and had to learn about life first. I tried seeing other girls, but I only wanted Martha and luckily she wanted me, too. We got married against her daddy's wishes and moved in with my parents until I could build us our own home. The only thing Martha ever really wanted was children. Dear Lord, how that woman loved children. Miscarriage after miscarriage and then we had John. Sadly, we were only able to have our boy, and she adored the ground he walked on. I thought he would grow up to be a mama's boy, yet he was just the opposite. He followed me around like my shadow."

Grandpa took a deep breath. Jody knew Grandpa was long-winded and loved to talk about the old days. Jody had heard the stories many times, but she didn't want to be disrespectful and stop him. Usually his stories had a point and she was waiting for him to get to it.

"Grandpa, you've talked enough for tonight. Why…?"

Grandpa paid no attention to Chase. "He was our whole world and then he met this girl Kate in school and we worried. She was all he ever talked about, but they were too young, we tried to tell him. You can see those kinds of things when you're older. She was a city girl and would never fit into his way of life. That only made him angry, so we let it go. Above all else, we wanted one thing for our son—we wanted him to be happy, and that city girl seemed to do that."

"Grandpa…"

"Oh, when the babies started coming, my Martha was the happiest person on earth. We thought Falcon would never learn to walk because someone was always carrying him, but we didn't have to worry. Quincy was on the way and soon we didn't have enough arms to hold all those boys. Those were happy times."

Jody had really wanted to talk to Chase,

but she could see she wasn't going to get the opportunity. "I better go."

"I got sidetracked, didn't I?"

"Yes, you did, Grandpa," Chase replied.

"I just want you to understand that first love is a once-in-a-lifetime thing. You can't take it back. You can't get a refund. And you can't pretend it never happened." The old man turned his attention to Jody. "Do you know that a Rebel man only loves once in his lifetime?"

"Yes, I'd heard that."

He pointed to Chase. "This boy here has loved you since the first day he met you."

"I know that, too."

"Then why can't you trust him? You trusted him when he was in college with all those girls chasing after him. You trusted him all those years in the NFL. What is different this time?"

"You don't understand, Grandpa. I really have to go." She hurriedly walked to the trash can, placed the Blizzard cup in it, grabbed her purse and briefcase, and slipped into her shoes on the way out the door.

"Jody—"

She took the stairs and kept running. She didn't want to talk anymore. It only brought her more pain, indecision and confusion, and there was just no way to explain what was going on in her head that night.

Liar. Liar.

She did know how to explain it and she would have to face up to that soon. There was just no other way to live a normal life without doing so.

Grandpa had chipped away at her resolve. He was right about first love. To be free from it, she had to bare her soul to Chase and be strong enough to accept the consequences.

ONCE GRANDPA WAS HOME, he'd make a trip to the courthouse and sign the papers. Then he'd walk out of that place half of who he used to be. It was time to say goodbye to a relationship that meant the world to him. Letting go would be a test of his strength.

Over the next couple of days a therapist worked with Grandpa; he was getting stronger and now able to get around using a walker. It was time to go home to Rebel Ranch. They didn't leave the hospital until noon. Grandma had called to say she had chicken and dumplings ready for lunch. It was March and a blisteringly cold day with a windchill factor that could rip the wool right off a sheep, or that was what Grandpa said. He helped Grandpa into his long johns, an extra T-shirt, wool socks and a big jacket with a hood. He fitted the hood over his head and tied it. Grandpa complained, but Chase put it on anyway. He didn't want him to have a relapse.

All the grandsons were waiting at the house to greet Grandpa. Falcon had called to tell him to park in Grandma's spot in the garage so the old man wouldn't get too much of the cold freezing wind. Rico lifted him from the truck and carried him into the house as if Grandpa were no more than a child. Grandpa didn't protest.

Rico sat him in a chair in the kitchen. Grandpa pushed the hood from his head and looked around. "My, it feels good to be home." He looked at Kate. "Are those chicken and dumplings ready?"

"Yes, and a big banana pudding."

Grandpa stood up. "I need to get out of these clothes first. Come with me, Chase."

"Hey, Grandpa," Phoenix called. "You know, we can help, too."

"Ah." Grandpa waved a hand at him. "Y'all got wives and kids and not enough time to take care of yourselves."

"But we're always here for you."

"I know that. Y'all are good boys. John's boys. And he'd be so proud of all of you, just like I am."

Grandpa got a little misty-eyed and Chase followed him into his bedroom. He helped him out of the big jacket and extra T-shirt. "I'll leave my long johns and house shoes on." He sat on the bed. "I want to talk to you."

"We've been together for days and we've talked enough."

Grandpa pointed a finger at him. "Now it's time for you to get your life straightened out. Stop worrying about me. I'm fine. I'll be right here in this house with Kate. She watches over me real good, like John knew she would. I just want to ask you one thing."

"What?" Chase had a feeling it was going to be something he didn't like.

"To not sign those divorce papers. Trust me on this one. You'll regret it if you do. Just don't sign 'em. It will give both of you some time to adjust before you take that big step that will end it forever. That's all I got to say. Now I want some chicken and dumplings."

Chase shook his head. Grandpa didn't understand that he didn't have an option. Jody was never going to trust him again—she'd said as much. But… He didn't have to run over to the courthouse as soon as possible, either.

Laughter and loud voices came from the dining room and Chase went to join his family and forget about Jody for a brief moment. They had a good lunch, talking about the things they needed to get done before spring arrived. Grandpa joined in, talking his head off, which meant he was feeling much better.

Falcon got to his feet. "Brothers, it's time to make sure the pipes and the animals are safe during this freezing night." They trailed out, hugging Grandpa on the way. Grandpa headed straight for his chair, completely worn out from the morning's activities. Chase helped Grandma with the dishes. He thought of going to his house, but his brothers would be home soon from school and he wanted to see them. His dad came in with them at about five o'clock. They walked slowly and quietly into the house. Obviously they had orders from their dad.

Grandpa sat up when he saw them and said, "There's my boys. It's awfully quiet around here without you guys to keep me entertained."

The boys looked at Elias. "You can hug him. He's not going to break."

All three tried to hug him at the same time. "Are you better, Grandpa?" Eli asked.

"You bet I am. I'm ready to get on my horse and go for a ride."

"You can't," JR told him. "It's cold enough to freeze the nuts off a billy goat."

"JR!" Elias shouted.

"What? I didn't say nothin'."

"He's stupid, Daddy," Eli said. "Nuts don't grow on billy goats. They grow on trees. I learned that in school."

"See?" His dad raised an eyebrow at JR. "Come with me."

"Grandpa says it. Why can't I?"

Elias looked at Grandpa. "Do you need me to talk to you, too?"

"No, sir." Grandpa was trying very hard not to laugh. "I've always been known to say cold enough to freeze the horns off a billy goat."

"See, JR, that's the way to say it. You don't know nothin'."

"You both are idiots," Tre announced.

"Don't call your brothers idiots," Elias said, putting his arm around JR and leading him toward the back door. "We're going to see just how cold it is outside."

"It's good to be home with you guys. Nothing's changed."

Grandpa was right. There was always something going on at the Rebel house.

His dad came back in. JR trailed behind him with a red nose.

"How cold is it outside, JR?" Tre asked.

Everyone started laughing. Tre and Eli rolled around on the floor, playing, and JR joined them, with everyone watching them, smiling.

"Homework and baths," Elias finally ordered.

"But Mama's not even home," Tre pointed out.

"Your mother closed the diner and she's delivering food to the elderly who can't get out in this weather. She'll be home soon."

The boys were bathed and in their pajamas when their mother came home. She had a chicken fried steak for Elias and everyone else had chicken and dumplings again.

The boys had their supper and headed for bed. "Are you coming upstairs, Chase?" JR asked.

"Yeah. I'll be up in a minute to say good-night."

"Daddy, Daddy, Daddy!" JR screamed from the upstairs. "There's water every-where."

Elias threw his napkin on the table. "Dam-mit. Just what I need tonight, a broken pipe."

His mom grabbed a bunch of towels from the utility room and followed Elias upstairs.

"Do you need my help?" Chase asked.

"I'll call if I do."

Elias sent the boys back downstairs while his mom helped to figure out if there was a leak or not.

His dad came down with a scowl on his face and a handful of pennies. Chase was puzzled.

"Eli," his dad called.

Eli jumped up and stood as close as he could to Chase. "Yes, sir."

Elias held the pennies out toward Eli. "Your brothers say you've been putting pen-nies in the toilet. Why in the world would you do that?"

"Well, Daddy, you see—" Eli shifted from one foot to the other "—this boy at school told me if I wanted Grandpa to get better, I had to drop a penny in a wishing well and make a wish and say a prayer. We don't have a wishing well and I asked him what it was. He said a pool of water. The commode has a pool of water, so I thought it would work."

His mom rubbed Elias's chest to calm the storm that was brewing.

Elias let out a long breath. "You boys are going to kill me, do you know that?"

"Elias." His mom always kept his dad on an even keel. "He was doing a nice thing and he didn't know it would stop up the toilet."

"I know." He reached down and picked up Eli. "That was nice of you, praying for Grandpa, but you have to be careful what you put in a commode. It stops up." He walked with Eli in his arms to the utility room and came back with a fishbowl. He half filled it with water and brought it into the living room and set it on the coffee table. "There's your wishing well." He dropped the pennies into it. "You can make a wish and pray for anyone you want."

Eli's smile beamed across the room. "Thank you, Daddy." And then he ran and crawled into Grandpa's lap.

"You're a sweet boy. Thank you for praying for me. Where did you get all those pennies?"

"The waitresses at the diner don't like it when they get pennies for tips, and they give them to me."

His mother groaned. "Eli, sweetie, I told you… We'll sort this out tomorrow. Now we have to clean up the bathroom."

Chase, his mother and his dad spent the next thirty minutes getting the floor dry in the bathroom and fishing more pennies out of the toilet. He put the boys to bed and told them good-night. Eli was restless.

"Chase, did I do something bad again?"

"No, little brother. Praying for Grandpa was a good thing."

"But Mama was mad at me for taking the pennies."

"Only because the girls wait tables for less than minimum wage and they count on the tips."

"Then why don't they take the pennies?"

Chase ruffled his hair. "I don't know, but I tell you what. We'll show them what a difference a penny can make. When you get that bowl full of pennies, we'll take it to the bank and see how much money it is and at Christmastime donate it to the Horseshoe Children's Christmas Fund to buy gifts for the kids who otherwise don't get anything.

You might fill it up three or four times by then."

"Oh, boy." Eli smiled from ear to ear. "I can do that."

"Do you know how lucky you are?"

"Yeah. I have the best mama and daddy, JR shows me how to do things, Tre helps me with my homework, Grandpa is home and better, Grandma cooks me anything I want and I have a big brother named Chase who loves me. I have lots of good stuff."

Chase kissed his forehead. "Yes, you do."

Chase thought how idealistically beautiful it was that Eli valued the people in his life more than the material things that he had. How he wished he'd stayed that way for a lifetime. And he hoped his little brother never fell in love with a girl who would break his heart.

THE TEMPERATURE STAYED in the thirties and forties most of the week and Jody kept busy at the courthouse. She hadn't seen Chase, but she'd heard that Grandpa had gone home. The divorce papers were in a drawer, waiting for his signature. Every time the door opened, she jumped, thinking it was Chase coming to sign the papers. But so far he was a no-show. He was probably trying to catch up with his therapy and classes.

Hardy Hollister, the DA and her boss, walked into her office. Tall, broad-shouldered with striking blue eyes, the same as Erin's, he'd once been a sought-after bachelor, but when Hardy had met Angie, he became a family man.

"I was just talking to the DA in Bell County. He's shorthanded and asked if you could continue to help with the Holden case. He liked your work."

Jody turned in her chair to look at her boss. "Really?"

"Yes," he said and sat on the edge of her desk. "But don't let it go to your head."

"Why?"

"It's politics, as usual. The Bell County DA wants to get Heather's father off his back. Do you want to take him on?"

"Oh." She was startled. Up until now, she'd been assisting Hardy.

"You're giving me my own case?"

"If you want it. The way I'm looking at it is the father is going to try and get Heather's crime swept under the rug, and the two teen-agers, Garcia and Clark, are going to take the blame for more than the drugs. Of course, they're guilty of selling drugs in school and are going to spend some time in prison. But I don't believe they forced Heather Holden to take the drugs. I don't believe they forced her into the vehicle like she's claiming. And I also believe she's been on drugs for a while now. It wasn't a onetime thing."

"I agree with you," Jody said. "And, yes, I'll take the case." At first she'd thought that she didn't want to try the case because of Heather's age, but in her job she had to be prepared for every case. And it would take her mind off Chase.

Hardy nodded. "Go with your instincts and double-check the facts. Call if you need me. Now I'm taking my wife to see our granddaughter and daughter. Zane will be MIA, as usual."

"Zane is saving lives. His job is important. I thought you would come to see that. But you really don't have to see it. Only Erin does."

"I know. I just don't like that my daughter spends a lot of time alone."

"She doesn't anymore, and when she wants Zane's attention, she gets it. So please let them be happy."

Hardy didn't say anything and she let it

drop. "Get in touch with the DA and I'll talk to you tomorrow."

Jody sat there for a moment and went back to work. She had already been researching Heather's friends, and most newsworthy was a high school football player she'd been involved with, Brad Thornberry. As she was flipping through stories of players, something caught her eye and she stopped and went back. *Notable Football Injuries* was the title. Chase Rebel's name was right there at the top. She clicked on the link and watched how he got the injury that ended his career.

The camera was on the quarterback as he ran out of the pocket, looking for Chase, who was dashing toward the end zone. The quarterback lobbed a long pass and she watched with her heart in her throat. Chase went up to catch it. With one hand, he snatched the ball from the air and the guy guarding him pushed his arm back and they fell to the ground. She could see the ball was still in Chase's hand and his arm was in an unnatural position. He pushed to his feet and the arm dangled by his side. Oh, no! The pain tightened his facial features.

She touched the screen. *Sit down, Chase. Sit down, please.*

Suddenly he was surrounded by medical people from the team and they forced him to the ground. One man, the team doctor, examined his arm. Sweat broke out on Chase's forehead. The camera was focused on his face. His helmet lay on the ground. The crowd stood, silently waiting. A cart backed a stretcher onto the field. His teammates lifted him onto the stretcher and they drove out of the stadium.

She wiped away a tear and realized she'd been crying. She should have been there. *I should have been there.* It took a moment to gather her composure, and then she opened the drawer and pulled out the file with the divorce papers. Taking a deep breath, she tore it into as many pieces as she could and tossed it into the trash can.

CHAPTER ELEVEN

JODY SPENT THE rest of the morning talking to the DA in Bell County and knew Hardy was right. He wanted someone out of the area to handle Glen Holden, the father of the girl who'd been found in the ditch. It was the perfect way to get Holden off his back and still look good. A meeting with Heather, her attorney and Mr. Holden had already been set up by the DA at the Holden home this afternoon. That was allowing privilege and Jody didn't like it.

She had an interview with Garcia and Clark, who were still in jail. They told a completely different story than Heather's. She then had a couple of phone calls to make and a visit to see all the evidence that had been collected. The more information she had, the better the interview with Heather and her attorney would go.

She met with the high school principal and Heather's best friend, Haley. Neither told her anything she didn't already know. She headed for the gym to locate Brad Thornberry. Since football season was over, he was now on the basketball team, and they were practicing. The place oozed with testosterone and sweat. An assistant coach asked her what she wanted and she told him. He whistled for Thornberry to come over. They sat in the bleachers to talk as the basketball team kept pounding the ball against the floor and shooting her and Brad curious glances.

Brad had a towel around his neck and he wiped his face. He was handsome, with dark eyes and hair that reminded her a lot of Chase. But he didn't have the charisma Chase was known for.

"I know why you're here. Haley's already called. I don't know anything, either."

She pulled a pad and pencil out of her briefcase and placed it on her knees. "She's called you, huh? Why is everyone so nervous? Just tell me the truth. That's all I'm asking."

"I'm not nervous," he said. "I just wish you'd leave Heather and Haley alone."

"Miss Holden almost lost her life because

of a drug overdose, and we in law enforcement take that seriously."

"They wouldn't leave her alone."

"Who?"

He closed up fast when he realized what he'd said.

"If you're withholding any other information concerning this case, I can prosecute you for withholding that evidence and it will go on your record."

"What!" His eyes grew large. "I'm depending on a football scholarship so I can play in the NFL. I can't get involved in this. I'll lose everything."

"Then tell me the truth."

"I can't do that, either." He ran his hands through his hair. "Oh, man. What do you want to know?"

"Was Heather kidnapped as she's claiming?"

He took a long breath. "No. She needed something to get her through exams before the holidays."

"And she knew who to call?"

"Yeah. She's been using for about two years."

And just like that, Brad Thornberry threw Heather under the bus to save his NFL career. She remembered another young man whose dream was the NFL, but Chase would never betray her. Wait. What did she just tell herself?

She got to her feet. "If you have anything else to say, just call my number." She handed him a business card. At his hangdog expression, she added, "If she's addicted to something, nothing good will come of it. Would you rather see her dead or alive? Like a poker player would say, look at your aces, Mr. Thornberry. You aren't holding any."

"Yeah," he muttered under his breath, staring at the card in his hand.

"Your name is Rebel. Do you know Chase Rebel, the football player?"

"Yes. He's my husband."

After years of using her maiden name, it was easy to say her married one. She even had business cards made with Rebel on them. Now, why would a sane person do that if she were planning to get divorced?

Brad jumped to his feet, his worries forgotten. "Are you kidding me? I've watched all his games and that was a bummer when he got hurt. I heard he retired. I can't believe that. I'd love to talk to him."

She tapped the card in his hand. "Call me and I'll give my husband your regards."

As she walked out of the gym, a couple of brash teenagers whistled at her, and she ignored them as she made her way to her car. She took a deep breath and looked out at the nice sunshiny day. Sitting in the bleachers made her feel as if she were back in high school, waiting on Chase. She'd spent most of her time waiting on him because she didn't want to be away from him. She thought back to that night once again and the girl in his apartment. Seeing the almost-naked girl had forced her faith in Chase to take a nosedive and she couldn't see anything beyond that. She had to make the right decision, just as Brad had to.

She backed out of the parking lot and headed for her appointment with Heather and her father. It wasn't going to be an easy one. Mr. Holden owned a large construction company and was used to handling people. She hoped she could at least keep pace.

The family lived in a plush neighborhood in a redbrick two-story house with several detached garages. It sat on more than an acre of land and mature trees shaded it. Mr. Holden had built it himself and it was very impressive. She parked in the circular drive and walked to the front door with a briefcase in her hand. A maid in black slacks and a white blouse answered the door.

"I'm here to see Miss Holden and Mr. Holden."

"Miss Heather is in the living room." The maid pointed directly ahead and disappeared.

Someone was beating on a piano and Jody followed the sound. It wasn't any music Jody recognized and she learned why when she saw Heather using her fists and pounding on the piano. The baby grand didn't stand a chance.

"Heather," she shouted, and Heather's head jerked up.

She brushed the blond hair from her face and took a breath. "Sorry, I got carried away." The piano was situated in a corner, the perfect spot to play for people in the large living area. Heather got up and walked farther into the room with two facing sofas, a huge stone fireplace and enough greenery to fill a forest.

"Do you play when you're not angry?"

In jogging pants and a matching top trimmed in yellow, she fell onto the sofa with a scowl on her face. "I can barely get through 'Chopsticks,' but my dad tells everyone I'm an accomplished pianist—" she waved toward the corner "—hence the expensive piano."

Heather's phone buzzed and she pulled it out of her pocket. "Yes, Haley, I know. I have to go." She placed the phone in her lap, staring at it.

"Have you been back to school?"

"No. How can I? Media has made me the number one story in this town, and now my dad has hired a tutor so I don't have to face everyone. Why are they doing this to me?"

Jody sat on the other sofa with the briefcase at her feet. She had a feeling that all of Heather's problems were, according to her, somebody else's problems. Everything had always been taken care of by her parents. Jody could probably sing that tune; she'd lived it. Her parents were just as controlling as Heather's, but Jody didn't have the attitude. Her life had actually been happy until her father took a dislike to Chase.

Jody cleared her throat. She couldn't get distracted. "Heather, I'm going to be honest and tell you what I've uncovered in this investigation. At the time of the incident, your blood work showed you had ingested wine, liquor, methamphetamines and cocaine."

The blood drained from her face, but she didn't say anything.

"I've spoken with your friends—"

Heather sat up straight with fire in her eyes. "They don't know anything about me."

"They know a lot about you and so do I, so don't give me another cock-and-bull story about the boys kidnapping you. You know them. Quite well."

Heather chewed on a nail and frowned at it. "I have to get my nails done before we go to London."

That startled Jody. "You're going to London?"

"Yes. My mom is taking me to get me away from everything."

Before Jody could tell her she wasn't going anywhere, Glen Holden and his lawyer, James Archer, walked into the room, followed by Mr. Holden's wife, Karen. Heather jumped up and ran to her father. "Daddy, she's saying awful things to me. Make her stop."

Jody got to her feet and the men glared at her. Her heart jumped into her throat, but she held her ground.

"You have no right to come in here and disturb my daughter."

"I'll handle it, Glen," the lawyer interrupted him.

"You asked for the meeting in your home so Heather would be more comfortable. The DA agreed and that gives me a right. The paper is in my briefcase where you agreed to the meeting. Would you like to see it?"

"I agreed to meeting here but not to you bullying her. I will be speaking to the DA."

"You have that right, but first I'm going to have my say. It comes down to Heather's word against two boys who she says she doesn't know, and she has never been out with them."

"That's correct."

Before Jody came to the Holden house, she had gone through Heather Holden's OD file, every little note and everything that had been collected by the Horseshoe Sheriff's Department and the Temple police. She found something that gave her some leverage. She was hoping that it worked. "If that's true, then their names wouldn't be on her phone and she wouldn't have their numbers."

"No, and I assure you they are not."

"Do you mind if I look?"

A flicker of doubt crossed his face and he

LINDA WARREN   185

glanced at the attorney. The attorney nodded to go ahead. Holden picked up the phone
from the sofa and looked through all the
contacts. "I don't see their names on here."
He handed it to Jody. "See for yourself."

For once Jody had the upper hand. When
she'd interviewed the boys, they told her
they didn't have phones in their names. They
had phones in their grandmother's name and
that was how Heather got in touch with them
when she needed something.

Jody scrolled through the contacts. "Do
you know a Maria Rios?"

"No," Mr. Holden answered for his daughter and then looked at Heather. "Who is
that?"

"Just some girl in school."

"Heather, you should know before you dig
this hole any deeper that your phone was
in police custody for several hours while
they were trying to ID you. They copied
everything and it was still in the file when
I got this case. The cops didn't see the boys'
names on your phone and stored the information away. I interviewed the boys and dug
a little deeper. Maria Rios is their grandmother and their phones are in her name.

She will testify to that. And Tommy Clark is the one you've been calling."

Mr. Holden swung toward his daughter. "Is that true, Heather? Do you know those boys?"

Heather didn't respond.

"Tell me the damn truth."

The lawyer jumped in quickly. "Don't worry about it, Glen. I can get the phone thrown out. Anybody could have had access to the phone while the police had it."

"It's been in police custody and not just anyone can see the file or the evidence. You have to show identification and sign for it and it's all on record who's had access to it."

"Make her go away, Daddy."

Heather started to cry and her mother took her in her arms. "Don't worry, baby. Daddy will take care of it."

"No," Mr. Holden shouted, to everyone's surprise. "Daddy will not take care of it. You lied to me." He pointed a finger at his daughter. "You lied to law enforcement. Do you know how that looks on my reputation?"

"Not now, Glen," his wife told him.

"Yes, now," he said into his wife's face. "We have to deal with this now. Our daughter is a drug addict and it's time we faced it."

"She'll go to jail. I can't stand it if she goes to jail."

"Well, you better tighten up your bra, Karen, because that's where she's going." He turned to Jody. "How much time is she looking at?"

"Probably two years."

"No, no, Glen!"

"I can take care of this," Mr. Archer interrupted. "There's no need to jump off the deep end."

"Look at my daughter, James. Can't you see the signs? Her skin is pale and blotchy and her eyes are sunken in her head. She's so skinny and nervous I hardly recognize her. I've been seeing this for a long time, but I've been ignoring it because I thought my daughter wouldn't get involved with drugs. That's what I kept telling myself. Now I have to ask myself if I want my daughter to live or die. If she keeps using, she will be dead before much longer because usually she gets what she wants. Today I'm putting a stop to it."

Heather continued to sob on her mother's shoulder, letting her parents decide her future. It wasn't exactly what Jody's life was like, but similar in so many ways that she could feel Heather's pain. She knew what the girl was going through.

"Heather." Jody took steps toward her. "Don't you have anything to say for yourself? This is your life we're talking about."

"I…I…" She looked up at her mother. "I need something, Mom. I'm shaking. Please."

"Are you buying her drugs?" Mr. Holden pounced on his wife.

"Somebody has to help her!" she screamed at her husband.

"I can't believe you."

"Everybody, calm down," Jody said. "I'm going to make this short and sweet. For you to get help, Heather, you have to admit what happened that night, and it has to be the truth."

"I…I need something first."

"No, it doesn't work that way. You tell me what happened and your part in it. Then I'll call an ambulance and it will take you to the hospital and they'll give you something to calm down. After that, you will go into a lockdown rehab until you're clean. I'm almost positive I can get that by the DA. Rehab instead of jail, but the kidnapping charges on the boys will be dropped and they'll get a better deal."

Jody looked at Mr. Holden. "Are you in agreement?"

"Take it," the lawyer advised. "At this point, it's the best you're going to get."

"What kind of rehab? Do we get to choose the place?"

"You have to talk it over with the DA, but it has to be locked down or she'll try to escape." Jody glanced at Mrs. Holden. "And certain members of your family would help with that. We want to be absolutely sure she gets the help she needs."

"Yeah, I'm beginning to see her mother is most of Heather's problem."

"I resent that."

"It is illegal to buy drugs, Karen. Assistant District Attorney Rebel might like to know where you're getting these drugs."

The woman paled. "It's our daughter, Glen."

"I'm not interested in Mrs. Holden, but I suggest you lose the connection, for your daughter's sake."

Jody called the Bell County DA and set everything in motion. An officer came out with an ambulance. He arrested Heather, and Karen insisted on riding in the ambulance with her daughter to the hospital. It was very clear that Heather would be going it alone from there.

On the drive home Jody's mind pounded with thoughts of the past and her insecurities. Her life was similar to Heather's in many ways, yet different, too. Jody did everything to please her father. She wanted to be perfect so he would be proud of her. Why couldn't she see that he had already been proud of her? A little bit of confidence would have saved her a lot of heartache.

Grandpa Abe had said that all he and his wife wanted for their son was for him to be happy. Looking back through that damn rearview mirror, she could see that was all her parents had ever wanted for her.

EVERY MORNING BETWEEN 5:00 and 5:30 a.m. Grandpa would call Chase to let him know that he was doing fine. Then Chase would turn over and go back to sleep. Getting up early wasn't on his agenda anymore. He hadn't seen Jody and she hadn't brought the divorce papers by his house. Maybe she wasn't as eager to get divorced as she'd seemed.

He was back on schedule with his therapy and his online classes. He'd reinjured his shoulder when he picked up Grandpa and put him in the truck. Ginger had worked it into feeling normal again. He wasn't in too much pain and he was grateful for that.

The architect had been out a few times and they had gone over ways to redo the house. There was a big oak tree in the backyard and it would have to come down to make room for the pool. He wasn't too fond of that idea. The tree shaded a lot of the yard. He'd make that decision later. He'd never realized that it would be such a headache to remodel the house.

His phone pinged and he pulled it out of his pocket. It was Grandpa. Evidently Grandpa missed him. He might go out and pick him up so he could come and stay with Chase for a couple of days.

"Hey, Grandpa."

Eli started laughing. "It's not Grandpa. It's me." Eli had been begging for a phone for a long time. He was the only one in the family who didn't have one. When he had someone to call, he always used Grandpa's. In August he would turn seven and Chase knew his parents were getting him his first phone so they could keep up with him.

"You fooled me."

"Yeah, you have to come home. I want to show you something."

"Can't you just tell me?"

"No. It's a surprise and Grandma said you have to have supper with us."

"Okay. I'm on my way." There was no need to fight family when he had nothing else to do.

Eli met him at the back door, hopping around like a grasshopper. "You're not gonna believe it." He grabbed Chase's hand and pulled him into the living room.

"Hey, Grandma," Chase called as they breezed past her in the kitchen.

"Look." Eli pointed to the fishbowl, which was almost full of pennies. "We have to take it to the bank to see how much money is in there."

Chase squatted in front of the fishbowl. "You've been saving a lot of pennies." He tapped the quarters that were in the fishbowl. "How did those get in there?"

"Angels."

"What?"

"That's what Grandpa said when I saw them for the first time. He said angels were helping me."

Chase glanced at Grandpa, who was smiling. "And Grandpa wouldn't lie."

"No. He rode with John Wayne and he was a good guy."

Chase laughed. He couldn't help himself. "Well, yeah. If you rode with John Wayne, you would never tell a lie."

"Now, let's get this straight." Grandpa fidgeted in his chair. "I met John Wayne and he said I could ride with him anytime I wanted. Gotta get your facts straight."

"When can we take the money to the bank?"

"You're out of school on Saturday, so I'll take you then, and we might open an account so we can keep it all together and see just how much money you can donate to the Christmas Fund."

His dad came in with the other two boys and soon his mom arrived. They sat around the table, talking, and Chase realized, not for the first time, just how lucky he was. This togetherness was everything to him. He just wanted his own family, his own home and his own kids who would drive him crazy, but he wasn't sure if that was ever going to happen.

CHAPTER TWELVE

ON SATURDAY CHASE drove out to the ranch and picked up Eli and they went to the bank, which was two doors down from the diner. Chase carried the fishbowl in, without the water, since he felt it was too heavy for Eli.

The Horseshoe Bank & Trust was an institution and had been there for over a hundred years. The Stedman family sold it about ten years ago and the townspeople were afraid it would lose that small-town feel, but it was there to accommodate the people of Horseshoe and it was still going strong.

Chase set the fishbowl on the granite counter. Eli wasn't tall enough to see over it, so he stood at Chase's feet. The place had changed since the last time he was here. Everything had been updated, from the hardwood floors to the granite countertops to new oak desks and leather chairs. The large shiny, clear windows gave it a professional feel.

"We'd like to deposit this money," he told the woman who came to the window. He knew just about everybody in Horseshoe, but he'd never met this woman before. She was probably in her forties, had two and a half kids and was a hometown girl. She had that look of being healthy, happy and predictable.

"We?"

"Eli. He's down here, but you can't see him."

"It's me, Ms. Newman," Eli called.

She leaned over the counter. "All I see is a big hat." She glanced at Chase again. "You want to deposit these pennies?"

"Yes, ma'am, and open an account for Eli."

"Okay. We'll have to do that at my desk. I'll open the gate." By gate she meant the half wall that separated the employees from the customers. He followed her to a desk and Chase carted the pennies along since she didn't seem inclined to take them.

"You're Chase Rebel, Maribel's oldest son, the football player?"

"Yes, ma'am."

"I'm Ms. Newman. It's nice to finally

meet you." She turned her attention to Eli. "I hardly recognize you in that big ol' hat."

As if remembering something Grandpa had told him about how a cowboy always removes his hat indoors, Eli quickly pulled off his hat. "See, I'm Eli, and I'm a cowboy like my daddy."

"You certainly are. What can I do for you today?"

"I want to know how much money I have in my fishbowl." And then he went on to tell her why he was saving pennies.

"Elaine," she called to another woman in the bank. "Take these pennies to the back and have them counted."

"Where is she taking my money?" Eli was instantly on alert.

"To count it like you wanted," Chase told him.

"But…but she'll bring it back, right?"

"No. That's why we're here. To deposit the money in an account so you can fill up another fishbowl. Do you understand?"

Eli frowned. "I don't like it."

"It's so sweet what you're doing, Eli. It will help all of the little kids who won't otherwise get gifts. I'll even add ten dollars to the fund," Ms. Newman said.

"Wow! Did you hear that, Chase?"

"Yep, I did, buddy. Now let's fill out these papers and set up a bona fide banking account for Eli Rebel."

"Since this is for charity, I'm assuming you want a tax-free, plain-vanilla account."

"Yes, ma'am."

"There has to be at least one adult account holder and I'm assuming that's you, Mr. Rebel."

He thought about his parents and knew they wouldn't mind. They had enough to do and this was his and Eli's project. "Yes, that's fine."

The other lady came back with a receipt and handed it to Ms. Newman. She also handed Eli the fishbowl.

"It's empty."

Ms. Newman handed Eli the receipt. "That's how much money you have in the bank, and with my ten dollars it comes to $61.92. Keep it somewhere safe and don't lose it."

"But…"

Chase pointed to the amount. "Look at that. I'm so proud of you."

Eli was stone-faced. Chase poked his

cheek. "If you don't smile soon, I'm going to cry."

Eli jumped into Chase's lap. "Let's go tell Mama."

"Mmm?"

"Can I come see my money?"

Ms. Newman groaned.

"Eli, money is not like people. You don't visit money," Chase reminded him.

"But how will I know they still have it?"

"Trust me on this." He tipped his hat to Ms. Newman. "Have a good day."

They went down to the diner and spent thirty minutes telling Maribel about the pennies. Eli followed her around, wanting to make sure she heard everything that had happened. It was eleven o'clock and people were hustling in for an early lunch.

"Take him to Elias so he can work off some of that energy."

"Did you tell him what to wear this morning?"

"No." Maribel wiped the counter as she talked. "I was surprised to see he wore his good clothes."

"Me, too. I guess he figured if he's going to a bank, he needed to dress up."

"When he gets home, you make sure he

takes those clothes off or they'll be filthy by the end of the day."

"Eli, let's go." Eli was sitting at a table with an elderly gentleman, talking his head off. The man probably didn't understand half of what he was saying.

"Why we gotta go?"

"Your dad is expecting you."

"Ah, jeez. I'm still being punished?" He glanced at his mother.

"You'll have to ask your dad. Why did you wear your good clothes this morning? Those are your church clothes."

"You have to wear your good clothes when you go to the bank—that's what Grandpa said—so they'll look kindly upon you if you need money."

"He listens to everything Grandpa says and most of the time it doesn't make a lot of sense."

"But could you think of a better role model for him?"

"Honestly, no."

"I gotta show Daddy my receipt." Eli searched his pockets and couldn't find it. "Chase, what did I do with the receipt? I can't find it. Oh, no!"

Chase reached down into Eli's jeans and

pulled the receipt out of his pocket. "Calm down. There it is. Why not let Mom keep it?"

"No. It's mine and I want to keep it. I promise to be very careful." He frowned at his mother. "Don't wash it if it's in my jeans."

"Now, listen, young man, I'm not keeping up with your receipt. When you get home, put it in a drawer or something."

"I got it." Eli pulled his wallet out of his back pocket. The wallet had nothing in it and Chase wasn't sure why he carried it. He carefully tucked the receipt inside. "I keep all my important papers in my wallet, just like Daddy."

Maribel laughed. "Your dad does not keep—"

Chase could almost see her mind working and she thought it best just to leave it alone. With Eli, you never knew.

Chase kissed his mom's cheek. "We'll see you later, and I just wanted to warn you that Eli will probably be asking to visit his money."

"What?"

"He's under the impression that he needs

to see it to make sure it's still there in case it's been stolen or misplaced."

"Chase, they're not going to let him in and out of the bank to visit his money."

"Good luck explaining that." He flashed a grin and headed for Rebel Ranch.

IT WAS SATURDAY morning and Jody planned to sleep in and then drink coffee at her leisure. Her phone jingled before she could even get out of bed.

Hardy. What did he want?

Brushing hair out of her eyes, she picked up her phone. "It's my day off and nothing can be so important that I would have to work today."

"You haven't had any coffee yet, have you?"

"No."

"I hate to wake you up, but I got a call from the Bell County DA. Heather Holden is asking for you."

Jody sat up in bed. "What? Why would she want to see me?"

"I don't know, but he also said that Mrs. Holden is there, too, and she's causing a scene. He asked if you could come since the girl asked for you."

"Why doesn't he go?"

"You know a DA is not going to do that. It's showing favoritism."

"And sending an ADA is not?"

Jody lost the battle and thirty minutes later she was on the road to the rehab center. On the way she called Mr. Holden to make sure he knew what was going on. She had no authority to release his daughter—that would have to come from the DA himself. Mr. Holden didn't answer, so she left a voice mail.

The rehabilitation center was in Temple and seemed to be in the middle of nowhere. A couple of big live oaks shaded the plain rectangle building made of Austin stone, but there were no flowers or anything to make the place look inviting. She couldn't imagine Mr. Holden agreeing to this place that looked more like a prison. The windows were high and narrow but at least there were no bars that she could see. The center sat on several acres and it was peaceful and quiet, just what an individual needed to get off drugs. A water fountain near the door seemed out of place. A statue of an angel stood in the center, holding a water pitcher in her hands. Water poured from it.

It gurgled behind Jody as she went into the building.

A lady sat at a desk in a large nondescript foyer. She wore a gray dress with the rehab center's name on her left pocket. Her hair was also gray and curled into a bun at the back of her head. She looked at Jody through wire-rimmed glasses. "Can I help you?"

"I'm Jody Rebel. Heather Holden is asking for me."

"Sister Carter, the supervisor, will speak to you shortly. Just take a seat."

"Ms. Rebel, Ms. Rebel." Karen Holden ran up to her and grabbed her arm. Obviously Mrs. Holden was waiting to see Heather. "You need to do something. I can't get anyone to listen to me. Heather is not made for this kind of life and I know you can get her out of here."

She removed her arm from the woman's grasp. "We went through all this over a week ago. Your daughter committed a crime, and instead of going to jail, she's spending time here until she's clean. There's no way around it."

"Don't tell me that. If you'll just get her out, you'll never see us again."

"Are you trying to bribe me?"

"Ms. Rebel." Someone called Jody's name and she swung around to see a woman about six feet tall in the same gray dress the receptionist wore. Sister Carter. Rosary beads and keys were attached at her waist and it became clear to Jody this was a religious place. Her height, stern features and a face that Jody was sure never smiled gave her an imposing presence.

"Yes."

"Come with me, please."

She followed the woman through the double doors and through more locked doors. The clanging steel made her nerves jump. There were no pictures hanging on the cream-colored walls, just long bare hallways and common areas. What amazed her was the sound—just an echoey silence as if the place was empty.

Sister Carter stopped at one of the steel doors. "Miss Holden has been upset since she arrived. She spent the first night crying and the next night yelling and screaming for help. She's not adjusting well, but then, they rarely do. I have to give her credit for trying. Last night she learned that her mother was here and she asked to see you. When she didn't get her way, she started the yelling and screaming again, but most of these walls are soundproofed. There was something about her that changed during the night and I thought this one might be saved. I don't want to miss that chance. Every kid saved is a prayer bead on a rosary."

"That's very nice of you to give her a chance." Jody's view of rehabs and jails for teenagers changed, in light of Sister Carter's words. There had to be someone there to support them, to help them get to the other side, where they could see the light to make the right decisions. Sister Carter was definitely a gem.

"No offense, but is this a religious rehab?"

"It's run by the sisters of the Good Samaritan. We offer the kids hope and faith. We don't shove religion down their throats. It has to be a choice. Some of these kids have never been to church and they're looking for someone to save them."

"I hope you're right. Can you tell me what changed about Heather?"

"Her attitude. She started listening to me."

Sister Carter reached for the keys attached to her belt and unlocked the door. "You have fifteen minutes."

Jody stepped into the room and paused. It

was small and simple, almost monastic. No pictures on the walls. Not any kind of decoration to give the room a warm, comfy feeling. This was it. Bottom of the barrel. There were no fairy tales lurking in these walls. You either dug your way out with sheer determination or rotted here in your own misery. It was a sad fate for a beautiful young woman who'd had the world at her fingertips. Now all she had was her own strength. Would she have enough to save herself?

"Ms. Rebel." Heather rose from the bed and Jody barely recognized her. Her hair was in tangles, as if she'd run her fingers through it many times. Her pale skin stretched over sharp bones that stuck out and the white gown was too big for her thin frame. It fell off one shoulder. The blotches on her face told their own story.

"Thank you for coming."

That startled Jody. The young woman she'd met hadn't been too high on manners.

"You're welcome. I just don't understand why you want to see me. There's really no way I can help you."

"It's not about that." Heather sat on the bed and Jody took a seat in the only chair in the room. "My mom is trying to break me out of here. I mean, she's hiring people to break me out, and then we'll leave the country."

"Is that what you want?"

She bent her head, staring at her shaking fingers. "I did the first day I came here and my head was all messed up. Then my brain started to clear. I heard the birds singing outside my window the other morning. I haven't heard them in two years. I did my own laundry for the first time. We have to cook in the kitchen and I helped to make the food that I ate. No one is pressuring me to do anything. If I don't help with the food, I don't eat. If I don't wash my clothes, they stay dirty. It's a revelation."

She scooted back on the bed. "I don't want to go to a strange country. I want to get better with my life here. There's a small chapel and the church bell rings every morning at six. You can go to services or not. It's up to you. I've been twice and I can't explain it, but I feel good when I'm there. I've never felt good about myself. Please talk to my mother so she'll stay away."

This was the total opposite of what Jody had expected, and for a moment she was speechless, wondering if this were some kind of trick to get her out.

"The first two days were terrible and I don't think I would've made it without Sister Carter. The first night I was shaking and my teeth were chattering. Sister Carter had me put on shorts and a T-shirt and she took me to the heated pool and let me swim around in the warm water until I felt better. It helped tremendously. I did that the second night, too. The pool is available for everyone and I really needed it at the time. I want to live a life without drugs. I want to play that piano in my dad's living room one day, too."

"I'm so proud of you, Heather, and, yes, I can help you with this. Keep leaning on Sister Carter to help you until you're strong enough to handle it on your own."

"I intend to."

Jody looked around the sparse room. "You're really okay here?"

"Yes. It's not the luxury of my room with all the clothes, shoes and purses. But I really don't need them anymore. I need inner strength and faith in myself for a change."

Jody hugged her and wished her the best. Then she spent the rest of the day talking to and trying to deal with Heather's mother.

The officer who had arrested her came out to the center and they had a meeting. Glen Holden showed up and that solved the problem. The doctor had diagnosed Karen with a mental breakdown when Heather was arrested, but she'd ignored the doctor and refused to go to the hospital. Mr. Holden didn't give her any choices. He had her hospitalized until she could get better. She didn't go willingly. She fought the officers and had to be given an injection to calm her down. Even though it was rough treatment, Jody felt it was better for Heather's mother to get control of her own emotions before Heather even thought about going home. They both had to get well.

It was after four o'clock when she drove into a parking spot at the courthouse. She had no idea why she'd come here. Her workday was over. The day had been a stressful one but a good one, too. With the help of her father, Heather Holden was going to make it. If Heather had the courage to change her life and overcome the obstacles, so could Jody.

CHASE WAITED EVERY day for Jody to show up with the divorce papers, but she still hadn't. His goal now was to finalize the plans for the remodel. He'd gone over them several times with the architect. He just had to make a decision about the tree.

March slid into April and everyone enjoyed the mild temperatures, the bright sunshine and the beautiful flowers popping up everywhere. The crepe myrtles at the courthouse were blooming. But the summer temperatures were peeping around the door, waiting to deliver a blast of ungodly heat.

His dad and his uncles finished spring roundup and were getting ready for hay season, which would last through the summer. During this time his dad was almost unapproachable. His total focus was hay season. He worked nonstop and he and his mom fought about it a lot. But she loved him, so she learned to deal with it by taking him lunch every day and making sure the boys always had time with their father. Since the boys were getting older, this hay season they would probably be his shadow. Chase chose to sit out hay season this year so he wouldn't chance injuring his shoulder.

The two sets of plans for his house were spread across his breakfast room table. He glanced from one to the other, trying to make a choice on what would suit him years down the road. His doorbell rang, startling him.

It was probably his dad dropping off the boys to spend the night, although he usually called first. He swung open the door without looking and froze as he saw Jody. The first thing he noticed was that she didn't have any papers in her hands.

"Come in." He stepped aside to let her into the house and then they just stared at each other. She didn't say anything. Her blond hair fell down her back, the way he liked, but she seemed nervous, pushing it back behind her ears.

"Would you like something to drink?"

"Water would be nice."

They walked into the kitchen and he grabbed bottled water from the fridge. "Did you come by for a reason?"

She took the bottle and sat on a bar stool. "Yes… I tore up the divorce papers."

He gripped the bottle in his hand until the coolness calmed his senses. "Why?"

"I decided I don't want a divorce."

He stared at the lovely lines of her face, the beautiful green eyes that he loved. "Why?"

She kept staring at the bottle of water.

"Does this mean you've changed your mind?"

"Yes." She raised her eyes to his.

"What changed it?"

"I was talking to your mom…"

"You've been talking to my mom?"

"Some. She's not so antagonistic anymore."

"What did she say?" Chase could hardly contain the excitement bubbling inside him. Could she really believe him? Trust him again?

"It's not so much what she said, but what she asked. When we got back from Katie's birth, she jumped on me about spreading rumors that you were a no-good cheater and she wanted me to know that you weren't like that. Then she asked me what you were wearing that night. It startled me for a moment because I was so focused on the girl, but I suddenly remembered that you still had your clothes on and your jacket was laid across the arm of the sofa."

"Yes. I had just gotten home, like I told you."

"Then it was some of the things that Grandpa said about young love and how important and strong it is. Our love was like that." She raised her eyes to his and he saw all the love, their love, in her eyes.

"Jody—"

"I told you about the case I'm dealing with, the young girl on drugs."

"Yeah."

"I had to interview her football-playing boyfriend. His dream is to go to the NFL, like someone else I know, and nothing is going to stop him, not even the young girl whose life is in tatters. I knew then that you would never do that to me. I could always trust you to have my back."

"Trust? You trust me?" He inched his way around the counter until he was standing six feet from her.

"Yes. I still trust you. I still love you. Through all the heartache, that has never changed."

"I just couldn't understand why—"

"Please, Chase, I don't want to go back. I want to go forward with our lives. You and me." She set the water bottle on the bar and looked at him from beneath her eyelashes. "Did you by any chance look for my engagement ring that night?"

"The one you threw at me?"

"Yeah."

"Why?"

"I want it back. I love you and I can't stand being away from—"

He grabbed her then and swung her around until she was bubbling with laughter. "Chase—"

"Say it again."

"I love you and I want my ring back. Please tell me you looked for it."

He reached into his pocket and pulled out the ring that he'd kept there for over a year. "Is this it?"

"Oh. Yes, yes!" She held her shaking hands to her lips. "Please put it on again."

He reached for her hand. "Jody Carson, would you do me the honor of becoming my wife…again?"

"Yes, yes!"

He slipped the ring onto her finger.

Tears filled her eyes. "I thought I would never see this again."

"I was out there in the cold, rainy weather on my hands and knees, crawling around, looking for it. Cars whizzed by, splashing water all over me, but I finally found it before a car could crush it."

"Thank you." Tears kept streaming down

her cheeks and he wiped them away with his thumb.

He held her face and kissed her for the first time in forever. All the old emotions exploded inside him in a way he needed, like air to breathe. He needed her.

"I love you more than you'll ever know."

"Me, too. But we need to talk."

He shook his head. "Jody, we've talked so much and I don't want to talk anymore. I just want to be with you again. Everything else we can sort out later."

"But, Chase—"

He took her hand and led her to the bedroom. His heart pounded in his chest and he held on to Jody as if she might slip away into a surreal dream. It wasn't. This was real. Their love had survived and nothing would ever shake it again.

Not ever.

CHAPTER THIRTEEN

JODY WOKE UP in the most beautiful dream. She and Chase were back together. He'd even had her engagement ring and put it back on her finger. She moved her ring finger and felt it. Oh… Oh… It wasn't a dream. It was real. She turned her head to the dark-haired man lying beside her sound asleep. His hair fell across his forehead and his lips curved into a smile as if he were sharing her dream.

Darkness still claimed the night, but she knew daylight wasn't far away. The daylight would bring regrets that she hadn't done what she'd set out to do. She should have told him, but she had taken the coward's way out.

Chase's phone rang and he stirred, reaching for it on the nightstand. "Hey, Grandpa." She could only hear his side of the conversation, but she knew it wasn't anything serious. "Yeah. That's good. I'll talk to you later."

He turned and reached for her, pulling her

close. "That was Grandpa. He calls every morning this time to let me know he's okay."

"That's sweet."

"At five o'clock in the morning?" He kissed her forehead, her nose…

"Chase, we need to talk."

"Now?"

"Well…that's what I…" He kissed the corner of her mouth and all thought left her.

A long time later sunlight streamed through the windows, lighting up their day. Chase crawled out of bed. "I'll make coffee."

Jody sat up and brushed hair behind her ears. "And then we'll talk."

He pulled a fresh pair of underwear out of the dresser drawer and slipped into them. Propped up on pillows, she watched as he moved around with the agility of an athlete, all muscle and bone that moved effortlessly. His male body was flawless except for the scar on his right shoulder. She'd always regret not being there when he'd needed her.

He leaned over and kissed her. "You know, Jody, there's nothing you can tell me that will make me stop loving you. Nothing. We talked it out and I don't want anything else to stop us from being together."

You don't know everything, she thought

as he went into the kitchen. She slipped on one of his big T-shirts. And *nothing* didn't cover the secret she'd been hiding and she wondered now if she had the strength to say the words.

He came back with the coffee and sat down with one leg curled under him and the other hanging off the tousled bed. "Now, what's so important that you have to tell me?"

She squirmed, but tried not to let her nervousness show. Today, sitting on this bed, her whole life had led up to this moment. And, like Heather, she had to have the courage to face it. Strange that she could draw strength from someone she barely knew.

She gripped the cup. "You asked me several times why I came to see you that night in your apartment."

"Jody." He shook his head. "It really doesn't matter anymore."

"Yes, it does. I have to tell you for my own peace of mind."

"Okay, why did you come?"

"Like I told you, I hadn't seen you in a while and I wanted to see my husband. I had something important to tell him."

"Like what?"

She cleared her throat. "To tell you that I was pregnant."

Up until now, his face was soft, full of joy and happiness. All of a sudden it all disappeared and his face went cold.

"What?"

"I was pregnant and didn't want to tell you over the phone. Then I saw her and my whole world turned upside down. All I could do was run to get away from the scene."

He slowly stood. "You were pregnant?"

"Yes."

"Where is our baby?"

Jody swallowed and tried to say the words, but they were stuck like glue to the roof of her mouth.

"Where is our baby?" he shouted.

"She was…stillborn."

It took him a moment to digest the news. "She's dead? She died? She—"

"Yes. She was a kicker. She kicked all the time. I could barely get any sleep. Two months before she was due, I noticed she wasn't kicking, so I went to the doctor and… he said…the baby had died inside me. They induced labor and I gave birth. She weighed four pounds and two ounces, and I named her Ivy."

He sank onto the bed. "This can't be true. Your parents don't know about this, do they?"

"No."

"How did you manage to hide this from everyone? And why would you want to?"

"I didn't intend to. When I got back to my apartment that night, I didn't know what to do."

"You should have answered the damn phone!" he shouted again. "I called you about a million times. Why couldn't you pick up the phone and talk to me? Why couldn't you tell me?"

"I don't know. I kept seeing that girl in your bathrobe and I couldn't get past that."

"So you wanted to punish me?"

"No. That was never my intent. After that first week I tried to pull myself together and then I went to see a doctor and started eating healthy. I kept telling myself, I'll do it tomorrow. I'll tell my parents tomorrow. I'll call Chase tomorrow. But tomorrow was never the right day... And then... I didn't have another day. She was gone." Jody reached over and put the cup on the nightstand. That was better than staring into Chase's cold dark eyes.

She had started this and now she had to finish. "They let me hold her for a long time. She was perfect. Ten fingers. Ten toes. She had these little dark curls on her head."

"I wouldn't know. I never had the chance to see her." Chase's voice was clipped and angry.

Jody got up to get her purse in the kitchen. She pulled out her phone and went to that secret place she kept only for herself. She handed it to Chase.

"You have pictures?"

She sat again on the bed, her legs shaky. "Yes. They let me take as many as I wanted."

He walked around looking at the photos over and over and then started again. "She's so tiny, so beautiful. Her face is perfect. She looks just like you. Send these pictures to my phone." When she seemed to hesitate, he said louder, "Now."

Jody wanted to stop. She'd told him all she'd needed to, but again, that was the coward's way out. She had to tell him everything. For them to have a future, he had to know everything.

"As I held her, I couldn't stop crying, and the nurse suggested I call a family member to be with me. I knew I was having a nervous breakdown and I called Erin."

His head shot up from the phone. "Erin! You should have called me!"

"I tried… I tried…"

"Does Zane know this?"

"No. Erin swore to never tell him or anyone."

"Why? Why did you have to keep my baby a secret?"

"I wish I could understand it myself." She brushed away more tears.

"Your father." He pointed a finger at her. "You didn't want your father to know. You couldn't tell him that you were carrying Chase Rebel's child. It would be an embarrassment. My God, I can't believe you would do something like this."

"No, Chase, it wasn't like that."

"How was it, then? Because I'm out here in left field, trying to understand how you could do this to a man you claim to love."

She jumped from the bed and ran into the living room, unable to handle any more. She pulled the T-shirt over her knees and buried her face in her hands, wanting to disappear into herself. Not wanting to hear that accusatory voice one more second.

Chase sat on the coffee table, facing her. He'd slipped on his jeans. "What happened next?"

His voice wasn't so angry and she lifted her head. "The doctor advised me what I needed to do and Erin helped me. I didn't want to bury her without any clothes, so I sent Erin to buy her something white. It was a beautiful frilly dress with a bonnet that had a big bill on it. All you could see was her beautiful face. The nurse brought me white socks and a diaper, though she didn't need one, but I kept hearing a line from an old George Jones song, 'all dressed up to go away,' and I wanted her fully dressed. As I dressed her, I thought it would be my first and my last time. I burst into uncontrollable tears.

"They gave me something. I woke up the next morning and Erin was there. She said it was time to go and we went to the cemetery to bury Ivy. I don't remember much because I was crying. I had picked out a white infant casket trimmed in gold and I remember them lowering it into the ground."

She gulped a breath and brushed tears from her face. "I cried all the way to my apartment and Erin begged me to come home, but I didn't have the strength. And you're right. I couldn't tell my parents. I wasn't strong enough to listen to 'I told you so.' And I wasn't strong enough to tell you, knowing you were sleeping with someone else. I told myself it would take time and I would eventually tell you about our daughter."

"I don't understand this. You cut me out of my child's life."

"I know you don't. Sometimes I don't, either. I'd just lost Gramma and the pregnancy caused my hormones to go haywire. When I saw that woman, I was so hurt, deeply hurt. I couldn't think straight. I wanted to get as far away from you and that woman as possible."

Chase got to his feet. "There was no woman. I never slept with her. I don't even know her name. How could you believe it?"

"I guess I wasn't as secure in our love as I thought. It came crashing down with more pain than I could ever imagine."

Chase went into the kitchen for another cup of coffee and she followed, sliding onto a bar stool.

He glanced toward the big windows in the breakfast room. "Do you remember the first time we made love?"

She followed his gaze. "The man cave."

"Your dad was so worried we were going to have sex and my dad promised to watch us. Of course, my dad tended to fall asleep a lot."

"We were too young, Chase."

"I thought I knew what I wanted and that was you and nothing else. I considered myself grown and knew all the answers. Looking back, I knew nothing. I was just like every teenage boy everywhere, dreaming grown-up dreams without a clue."

"Where do we go from here?" she asked with her heart in her throat.

"I don't know. I honestly don't know if I can ever forgive you for this."

She bit her lip to keep from crying out.

"But I do know one thing—the secrets and the lies have to stop. Our parents have to know they had a grandchild. And the sooner we tell them, the sooner we can get on with our lives."

Jody bent her head. That seemed so final and for a moment she had trouble breathing. "Wouldn't it be better if we each told our parents on our own?"

"No. I deserve to hear what your father

has to say about me and you don't need to take it alone."

This was reckoning day and Jody knew that as well as she knew her own name. This was the day she'd been avoiding for over a year. She had to stand up and take the blame for everything that had happened. Chase didn't know if he could ever forgive her and she didn't know if she could go another day without his love, without knowing that at least there was a chance. And her father... She knew how that was going to go and she had to be strong enough to do what she should've done over a year ago. Stand up and take control of her life.

"Okay. I'll go get dressed."

"You call your parents and I'll call mine. We'll meet at the Carson house."

"Okay."

Twenty minutes later they parked in the Carsons' driveway. Maribel pulled in behind them, as did Elias.

"Do you want me to do the talking or do you want to?"

Jody took a long breath. "I caused all of this, so it's all on my shoulders. I'll do the talking."

"What's up, son? I have a butt load of work to do today."

"Just be patient, Dad."

Peyton opened the door in her silky bathrobe. "Come in. I wasn't expecting company, but my daughter says you're coming over, so good morning."

Pleasantries were exchanged and her dad took his seat in his favorite chair, a cup of coffee beside him, a newspaper in his lap. It was his routine for as long as Jody could remember. Peyton hated that chair. She'd wanted to leave it in Gramma's house when they remodeled and moved into the antebellum house two blocks away, but her dad wouldn't hear of it. He was comfy in his old stuff and not happy with change or surprises. He folded the paper in his lap.

"What's going on, Jody?" He used the same tone as when she was seventeen years old and got a B on a test. *Do you want to explain this?* he'd asked and she just wanted to say no. All kinds of blubbering stories came out of her mouth in her defense, but it all came down to her apologizing and promising to do better.

It wasn't going to be like that today.

"I did something bad and I need to tell everyone how it happened."

"Bad!" Peyton put her arms around Jody. "How could you do something bad? I won't believe it for a minute."

"Just let me talk. I really need to tell you something."

Peyton squeezed her around the waist. "Okay, baby, calm down and tell us what you need to."

All eyes were on her and she dredged up the last ounce of courage and started to speak. "This is going to be hard to understand, but it happened and I'm sorry for all the pain that it has caused Chase. I went to see Chase that night for a reason—to tell him I was pregnant."

"What!" echoed around the room, and the wide-open eyes stung her like a slap against her skin.

"Please let me finish." She went on to tell them the same things she had told Chase.

Peyton tightened her arms around Jody. "Oh, baby, how could you do such a thing? I am so sorry you didn't feel you could come home. That's on us, your parents, not you. But to go through all that alone just breaks my heart." Then she whirled around, pointing a finger at Wyatt. "This is all your fault. How many times did I tell you to just let her be a girl? She wanted to go out and have fun like other girls. She didn't have to be perfect and make all As and do everything you wanted. How many times did I tell you, Wyatt? Give her some freedom and now look what's happened. She couldn't come home when she needed us the most."

Wyatt got up and left the room. Peyton was immediately on his heels.

Silence dropped into the room like a bomb, shattering whatever peace Jody had. Her stomach churned with nausea. She'd never expected her father to react that way and she wasn't sure what to do or what to say. In a great big old world she stood alone with everyone pointing a finger at her.

"Let me get this straight." Elias found his voice. "You kept my son's child a secret from him, from everyone?"

Jody swallowed and held her head up. "Yes."

"How dare you do something like that to him. He deserves better and I…"

"Shut up, Elias," Maribel said with grit in her voice.

"What?" Elias was staggered at his wife's words.

"Don't you dare come down on Jody."

"You're taking her side?"

"I'm taking every teenage pregnant girl's side, like myself, who was all alone with nowhere to go. My father wanted to kill me and you, and luckily my mother got me out of town to an old friend, which saved my life, and Chase's. I was scared to death and didn't know what I was going to do, but I knew one thing. I was keeping my baby." Maribel was on a roll and she didn't show any signs of stopping. "Every time my mom would call, she would say that you were with somebody else. Every time, Elias. You were chasing girls all over the county and not once did you think of me. Not once did you think that there might have been consequences to our one night together. That's what hurts."

"This isn't about us, Maribel."

"It's the same situation. Jody thought Chase was with that other woman and she was determined to keep her child. Things didn't go well. I'm not blaming her for that. I don't approve of what she did, but I know she did all that she could. I have to believe it." She looked at Chase. "I'm sorry, son."

She hugged her son. "It's okay, Mom. I still haven't processed everything."

Jody kept waiting for her parents to come out, but they didn't and she could hear voices from their bedroom. Everyone was arguing. She had imploded both families and she wasn't sure what to do, so she did the only thing she could. "We better go."

Chase glanced toward the doorway. "Yeah."

They walked out of the house and Maribel hugged Chase once again. "I'll talk to you later."

Chase reached into his pocket for his phone. "Wait. I want to show you something." He showed her Ivy. "That's my daughter. Her name is Ivy."

"Oh, my goodness." Maribel's hands shook as she took the phone. "She's so tiny, so beautiful. Elias, look at your granddaughter."

His dad swallowed hard, his glance landing on Jody. "I'm not saying anything because I'll say the wrong thing, but I'm trying to understand."

"Thank you, Elias." That was all Jody could ask of him.

They went back to Chase's house in silence. Chase had been working in the yard, cutting low limbs off the trees. He put on his gloves and started carrying the limbs to the front yard for pickup. She helped until the pile was stacked high. At two o'clock they stopped and went into the house and made sandwiches for lunch. Still they didn't speak. It seemed that everything that could've been said had been said. There were no more words.

They cleaned up the kitchen together and Jody didn't see any reason to hang around. They both needed space now to adjust to the past. She picked up her purse. "I think I'll go home for a while."

"Okay," he said in a low voice.

Ask me to stay. Ask me to stay. She almost made it to the door when he called, "Jody."

"Yes." She swung around with eagerness in her voice.

"I think it's best if you draw up the divorce papers again. There's no way I can ever forgive you for this and there's no use pretending that I will." He turned and went through the patio doors to the backyard.

No! She stood frozen in place, unable to breathe, unable to accept they had no future. Tears rolled down her cheeks and she didn't bother to wipe them away. The crying was over. Everything was over and now she really was alone with her many sins to keep her company.

CHAPTER FOURTEEN

CHASE FOUND HE couldn't stay in the house or in Horseshoe. He had to get away from his thoughts, away from Jody. He didn't want to see her or talk to her, and he couldn't escape her in the small town. There was nothing so final as a last goodbye to a teenage love that had ripped his heart out and left him struggling to breathe like a fish on a bank. He would survive. If he knew anything, he knew that he would do exactly that because he was a Rebel and Grandpa had told him Rebels were strong; he would remember that in the days ahead.

In his truck he picked up the phone and sent a text to his mom and dad. It was simple.

I have to get away for a few days. Don't worry about me and don't contact me. Tell Grandpa and Grandma and the boys I love them. I'll be home soon.

He just started driving, weaving in and out of cars on the highway. He didn't know where he was going or what he wanted to do. He just wanted to go. He zipped through Killeen, and as he drove into Lampasas, dusk settled in like a chicken on a nest, warm and comfy. A small hotel was up ahead and he swerved into the parking lot, checked in and suddenly noticed he was hungry. He ate at a small diner across the road, similar to the one in Horseshoe, but it wasn't his mom's. It didn't feel like home. The whole place was much like Horseshoe with a white stone courthouse sitting on the square. Farmers and ranchers inhabited the place, men wearing baseball caps, Stetsons and talking about the weather, cattle and the price of oil. But it wasn't Horseshoe. It wasn't home.

He swam until midnight in the hotel pool, and the next morning, he ate breakfast at the same diner and then bought two bottles of wine at a small vineyard nearby. He was on the road by eleven o'clock. Small towns whipped by him, but he didn't spare them a second glance. The drive was monotonous, with fields upon fields of corn, cotton, wheat and maize, but it was peaceful in a way he needed. When he reached

Burnet, he stopped for lunch and then drove on to Buchanan Dam.

The dam was built on the Colorado River for generating hydroelectric power and for flood control. Needing to stretch his legs, he got out and walked toward the water, gazing out at the massive amount of area the water covered. He sat in the grass and just stared, absorbed in the scenery. People farther down were in a camper and he could hear their voices, but otherwise this stretch wasn't populated too heavily.

He pulled up his knees and wrapped his arms around them. He hadn't called Zane because he didn't want to do anything that would shake his marriage and Chase's anger surely would. As if by telepathy, his phone rang.

Zane.

Chase didn't answer. He couldn't talk to his friend and involve him in this. His phone rang again and again. When they were younger, they had this signal that they would ring three times to let the other one know that it was important. Reluctantly he clicked on.

"Zane, I don't really need to talk to anyone."

"I'm sorry, Chase, and for Erin's involvement in this."

"Do not apologize for me." He could hear Erin in the background. "I did what I had to for my friend, so stop pointing your stupid finger at me."

"Could you please be quiet while I talk to Chase?"

"No, because all you're going to do is blame Jody. But if I remember correctly, there was a young woman in his room. What was she doing there? Someone had to have let her in for her to change clothes and dry her hair. And that would be the married man Chase."

Chase started to put the phone down, but he kept holding it, listening.

"There was a reason for that."

"Zane, even you must admit how bad it looked and Jody was pregnant and not thinking like she normally would. What was she to believe?"

He wanted Jody to believe him.

A baby wailed in the background.

"Now you've woken the baby. I'm going to go put her down, and when I come back, if you don't change your attitude, I'm going home for a while."

"Sorry, Chase, I have to go. You know how Erin is when she gets upset."

"This isn't your battle, Zane. Let it go and concentrate on your own marriage."

"Love you, cousin."

Chase lay in the green grass and the April sunshine warmed his skin, lulling him to sleep. Shouts of laughter woke him. More people had arrived with boats and campers and he decided to move on. After more time on the road, he saw he was in Georgetown, Texas, a much bigger city. The historic Williamson County Courthouse was there, as were many historical museums and sights to see. But Chase didn't feel like sightseeing. He checked into a hotel with a pool and swam until it was time for supper. As he sat alone in the dining room, it occurred to him that Austin wasn't far away. Ivy was buried there, but he didn't know where. He'd have to call Jody to get the information and he wasn't ready to do that.

So he gritted his teeth and called Erin.

"Chase?"

"Yes," he managed. "I'd like to know where my daughter, Ivy, is buried."

"Why aren't you asking Jody?"

"I'm asking you. She said you were there."

"Would you listen to me for a moment?"

"I'll try." But the urge not to listen was strong.

"I didn't know about the baby until after the birth. That's when she called. Her voice... I can't explain her voice. The moment she said my name I knew something was terribly wrong. I got there just as soon as I could and she was a mess. I've never seen her like that, switching between uncontrollable tears and long bouts of silence. She was still holding Ivy and the nurses couldn't get the baby away from her. She said she had to go with Ivy and I told her that Ivy was in Heaven and she had to come home with me. That's when she started screaming no and that Ivy deserved a better mother than her. They called the doctor and he gave her an injection. That's when they took the baby."

Chase rested his head against the steering wheel, eyes closed, as Erin's words ran through his head with a sick refrain. *That's when they took the baby.* He'd never thought once how hard it must've been for Jody. He'd only been thinking of himself.

"She wanted something white for the baby to wear. I hurried out to buy the clothes and they brought the baby back so Jody could dress her. They were hesitant about doing that, but I told them it would help her to heal. Her hands shook so bad I had to help her. I thought she would cause a scene when the funeral home came for the baby, but she didn't. She just sat there looking stoically ahead, her face marred with an expression that I can't explain and I hope I never see again. I mentioned that we should call you and let you know about the baby. She calmly replied you were probably with that girl and she couldn't stand to talk to you if she was there. I told her it didn't matter if she was there or not. You needed to know. And she told me that she would do it later. She collapsed again at the cemetery and a man there helped me get her to my car, and I took her to her apartment. She cried and cried, and I decided I had to let her grieve in her own way. One night, as I was making her soup, she said she'd told Ivy about her father."

He swallowed the dryness in his throat. "What did she tell her?"

"How you met and how much she loved you. She told her how much you loved football and she even ordered one from Amazon. It was in the baby bed in her room. She wanted Ivy to have a connection to her father. I was there with her, Chase, and I know it made her physically ill to think about telling you while you were with that girl."

"I wasn't with that girl. It happened just like I said."

"I know now. Jody does, too, but it doesn't make losing Ivy any easier and it doesn't make telling you any easier. It was a tragedy and it is something we all will feel for the rest of our lives."

"Where is Ivy buried?"

Erin gave him the address.

"Thanks, Erin."

"Call Jody."

"I'm not there yet, but I'm better than I was this morning. Please don't make this an issue for you and Zane."

"I won't."

Chase drove through Georgetown and merged onto I-35 going into Austin, the capital of Texas. The traffic was congested, cars whizzing here and there, but he had his eyes searching for a street number and within minutes he found it. The first thing he noticed were trees, lots of oak trees, and of course tombstones. He hoped Ivy's grave was under a tree. He couldn't explain why, but he wanted it to be as nice as possible. Taking a long breath, he went into the office and spoke to a woman. She called an elderly gentleman who said that he would show Chase the grave.

He shook hands with the man. "My name is Joshua Foley and I've been taking care of these graves going on fifty years now. I know exactly where Miss Ivy's grave is. Her mother comes here all the time." He pointed to a bench that was beside the grave. "She had that bench put in so she'd have a place to sit and talk to her baby. See, it has Ivy's Bench written on it."

Ivy was buried beneath a large oak tree. A small flat granite stone was at the front. On it was written *Loving infant daughter of Chase and Jody Rebel*. Her date of birth was beneath that.

His knees gave way and he sank onto the bench and just stared.

He had a daughter.

"Hey, I know you," the old man said. "You play football." He looked at the tombstone. "Yeah, Rebel. You catch balls."

"I used to. I'm retired now. I hurt my arm and had to have surgery."

The man sat beside him on the bench.

"Sorry to hear that. You're a damn good player and I'll miss seeing you."

"Thanks."

"So you're Ivy's dad?"

"Yes, I am." Involuntarily his chest puffed out. "I found out the other day."

"When Miss Jody first started visiting the grave, she seemed so lonely and had no one to talk to, so I started talking to her. We sat on this very bench." He patted it with his hand. "She told me about the breakup and the other woman, and she was a sad, broken-hearted woman."

"It was all a big misunderstanding. I wasn't cheating. As a football player, I get hit on by many women, but I've been faithful to my wife."

"Does she know that now?"

"Yes. And then she told me about Ivy and I have a knot in my chest that I believe is never going to go away."

"You blame her?"

"Damn right. She should have told me."

The old man shook his head. "Carrying all that anger around is going to do nothing but cause a big old hole in your stomach."

"She should have told me."

"She thought you were with another

woman, and no matter how many times you discuss this, it will always come down to what she saw and what she believed."

"I know." For the first time he let himself see how bad it had looked for Jody.

"There's always going to be a right way and a wrong way. You have to decide how you want to live your life...with Jody or without her. I don't even know you, but I pray you kids can get your lives together." The old man looked at him with tired brown eyes full of wisdom, brimming with lessons learned and offering compassion and kindness. "Until you admit you're to blame as much as she is, that big old knot in your chest is never going to go away."

"Listening to my friends and you, I've already come to that conclusion." Chase got to his feet and stared down at the grave. "I wish she were closer so I could visit her every day."

"Where are you from?"

"Horseshoe, Texas."

"Miss Jody lives there, as well. It's hard for her to visit, too. Why don't you just have the coffin moved to Horseshoe?"

"You can do that?"

"Sure. People change their minds all the time."

Did Chase want to move her? Did he want to bring his daughter home? He thought about it, glancing around at the well-kept cemetery miles away from her parents. Peace and quiet, except for the rumbling of cars on the highway, an occasional dog barking, a door slamming and voices floating on the afternoon breeze. Ivy didn't belong here in the city.

He was taking Ivy home.

JODY WALKED AROUND in a fog, her thoughts driving her insane. Chase had been gone for two days and no one had heard from him. She knew he needed this time to grieve on his own, but it wasn't just the grieving. It was the totally shutting her out of his life. She hadn't even started the divorce papers and she didn't plan to. They would be married but living apart until Chase came to grips with what had happened.

Everyone in town had heard about the baby and she couldn't go anywhere without people staring at her. People who usually went out of their way to shake her hand or hug her were now shunning her. She didn't curl into a ball on her sofa or avoid the townspeople. She went to work every day and faced those judgmental stares.

The day had been a long one and Jody was tired. She planned to eat supper, lie on the sofa and watch a movie. There was nothing in her refrigerator but yogurt, bottled water and a ham that smelled rank. She grabbed a yogurt and cheese crackers out of the cabinet and sat on the sofa to eat her supper. Loneliness seeped under her skin. She hadn't heard from her father since he'd walked out of the room. Her mother called her at least twice a day. She supposed her dad was still upset with her for disappointing him, but she'd rather hear it from him face-to-face than be ignored.

She was half asleep on the sofa when she heard a knock at the door. *Chase.* She leaped over the coffee table to open the door. Her father stood on her doorstep with his hat in his hand.

"Dad!"

"Can I come in?"

"Yes. Sure." She'd never dreamed her dad would be the one to bend. She'd just figured that in a few days she'd apologize and everything would be back to normal, but somewhere in her mind she knew she was never going to apologize again. She'd done what she had to in extraordinary circumstances and she would fight anyone who told her differently.

She sat on the sofa and her dad took the comfy chair she'd purchased before she moved in. She gripped her hands until she could feel her nails digging into her palms. Her nerves were on red alert. She waited for him to speak.

"I came to apologize for the other day. I just couldn't believe what you went through to avoid coming home. I wanted this to be a place you'd run to, not away from. Your mother was right. It's all my fault. I pressured you too much. I did everything too much. Remember when you were little? I'd come home and we'd play baseball in the backyard and on weekends we'd go fishing. You would be sitting on the front porch with your rod and reel and your dog, Dolittle. Sometimes you'd get tired of waiting and walk down to my office. You were my little girl. Then this upstart football player from Dallas shows up and I knew from the start he was going to be trouble. The moment you looked at him, you became someone else. You weren't my little girl anymore. You didn't want to play baseball or go fishing. You just wanted to be with him. I felt as if he stole you from me." A tear squeezed from his eyes and he had to stop.

"Oh, Daddy." She slipped from the sofa onto his lap as she'd done so many times as a child. She wrapped her arms around his neck. "You didn't lose me. I grew up."

"Too fast. I wasn't ready."

"Oh, Daddy."

"I keep thinking that if I hadn't been so strict on you and if I hadn't objected to the relationship so strongly, you wouldn't have been forced to marry in secret and have a child in secret. And maybe Ivy would've had a better chance at life."

"Nothing could have been done to save Ivy. Her heart just stopped beating."

"Why didn't you come home, baby? Why didn't you come home?"

"I couldn't listen to you telling me 'I told you so.' It was just one more time that I had disappointed you and I couldn't apologize for my daughter because you disapproved of her father."

He held her a little tighter. "You thought I would disapprove of the baby?"

"I don't know, Dad. You were very upset when I told you about Chase. You even confronted Elias, which I asked you not to do."

"That's because he was cheating on you."

"He wasn't. It was all in my head. I should've trusted him."

He rested his chin on her forehead. "How did we get so mixed up, Jody? I never wanted us to have that kind of relationship. I just wanted to love and support you in everything that you did."

This was where the rubber met the road, so to speak. She had to be completely honest with her father. "But you didn't."

"What?" He leaned back to look at her face; his was a mask of astonishment.

"You never supported me, Dad. You wouldn't let me go to the college of my choice. I had no say in my future. It was all what you wanted because you wanted to keep me away from Chase. It was too late for that. I loved him."

"I'm so sorry, baby girl." He kissed her forehead. "I just thought I was doing the right thing."

"How would you have felt if I had taken an intense dislike to Peyton? As a matter of fact, I didn't like her all that much at first.

Because of that, I could have dug my heels in and made your life very miserable, but Gramma said that I had to learn to accept change. I couldn't stay a little girl forever. I was going to grow up, fall in love, and then I would be happy that you had some-one. And I am. I love Peyton. But you didn't really give Chase a chance."

He hugged her tight. "No, I guess I didn't. But you know what? I'm going to change, like Gramma said. I will apologize the next time I see Chase and ask for his forgive-ness."

She hugged him back. "Thanks, Daddy. I don't know when he'll be back in town again. He's having a hard time dealing with Ivy. He says he can't forgive me for what I did. How do I live without him?" Before she knew it, tears rolled down her cheeks, and she quickly wiped them away.

"Shh, shh." Her dad stroked her hair. "Whatever you have to go through, I'll be here to support you this time."

"Thanks, Dad."

He looked toward the coffee table and saw the yogurt and crackers. "Is that all you're having for supper?"

"Yeah. I haven't felt like going to the grocery store and I'm not hungry."

"I'll take you out for supper. Anyplace you want to go."

"Thanks, Dad, but I'm not in the mood. We'll do it another time."

He stood and twirled his hat in his hand. "Do you think we can visit Ivy's grave one day?"

She was startled for a moment as she realized how many people she'd hurt by keeping Ivy a secret. She wished she could go back and change the way she'd handled the situation. Going back was an eternal gift and no one had earned that while on this earth. But with each passing day, God gave us maturity to handle the road ahead with a better perspective than the past.

"Sure. We can go over the weekend, if you'd like."

"Okay. I'll have to talk to your mom first. She's not talking to me right now, but I think I can get through to her."

"Oh, Dad." She turned around and hugged him. "Make up with Mom. You need each other. I love you, Daddy."

"Love you, baby girl, and we're not going through this again because we're going to communicate and support each other. I'll talk to Chase as soon as I see him and welcome him into the family."

"Right now Chase wants a divorce, so please take it slow and give him time to grieve."

After her dad left, she lay on the sofa, listening to some old records of Gramma's. "Are You Lonesome Tonight?" was playing on the record player, which was as old as the records. Jody couldn't bear to throw them out. It made her feel close to her grandmother.

A knock sounded at the door. She didn't want to see anyone, but she opened it anyway.

Chase.

CHAPTER FIFTEEN

CHASE HAD COME to tell Jody about Ivy and that he was moving the body to Horseshoe, but the sight of her blotchy face and sad eyes made him forget his die-hard attitude. He thought about everything she'd been through on her own without her family's help and he didn't know how she'd done that. But he'd always known she had immense strength.

"I just came to tell you that I'm bringing Ivy home."

She shook her head. "What?"

"She's buried among strangers and I've arranged to bring her to the Horseshoe Cemetery, where she will be buried with her family."

"Without talking it over with me?"

"No," he said without pausing. "I get to make this decision and I'm telling you only as a courtesy. I know what it feels like when important things are kept a secret. I'll let you know when Mr. Foley gets it set up."

"You talked to Mr. Foley?"

"Yes, and he thought it would be best for both of us if the baby was here."

"I guess it would," she mumbled.

He walked away to his truck.

"Chase…"

"I have nothing else to say, Jody." He drove home and fell across his bed, boots and all, not even bothering to lock his doors. But he couldn't sleep. He tossed and turned, and sad dreams invaded his restless slumber. Jody sat on the bench crying and he tried to reach her, to tell her everything would be okay, but he couldn't touch her. He couldn't get her attention. As much as he called and shouted, she kept sitting there crying.

He woke up with a start, his body drenched in sweat. Taking a long breath, he calmed down and then headed for the shower. He couldn't get bogged down in the sadness anymore. It was almost 6:00 a.m. and he decided to get coffee and breakfast at the diner. The place was already getting busy. He had to weave his way through the people to get to the counter.

He slid onto a bar stool. "Hey, Mom."

She swung around and almost dropped the

coffeepot she was holding. "Chase! You're back."

"Yeah. I got back last night."

She poured him a cup of coffee. "You could have called. You know how worried we are."

"I told you not to worry, but it never sinks in. Do you know who takes care of the Horseshoe Cemetery?" He shifted gears quickly to avoid an argument.

She shook her head. "Why?"

"I'm bringing Ivy home and I need to talk to someone who takes care of the cemetery to buy a plot and make arrangements."

Her eyes widened as he talked. "Wh-what?" But being his ever-resilient mother, she regained her balance quickly. "Oh, Chase, I don't believe you should do that. Have you talked to Jody?"

"Yes." He hadn't thought that it would be easy, but with his mother, it never was. "Do you know who takes care of it or not?"

She sighed. "His name is Ernest Faust. His wife died about three years ago and he comes in here every morning for breakfast. His life is that cemetery and he can tell you everything about it."

"Thanks, Mom. Let me know when he comes in."

She eyed him closely. "Son, are you okay?"

His first instinct was to lie, but his mother knew him inside and out. "I'm getting there, but if I could get breakfast, I'd be a little better."

She winked at him. "Sure thing."

He had breakfast, waited and had another cup of coffee, and his mother still hadn't pointed to anyone.

A girl took over the cash register and he followed his mom to the end of the counter. "Mr. Faust is sitting at the second table from the door, wearing a Dallas Cowboys cap."

"Why didn't you tell me?" He was trying very hard not to get angry, but anger seemed so easy for him these days.

She took his arm and pulled him to the side. "The man deserves to eat his breakfast in peace. Bringing the baby home isn't going to make your pain go away. You have to deal with it as everyone does who loses someone they love. That's what grief is. Son, please take a moment and think about what you're doing."

Maturity kicked in for the first time in a

long time. Maybe his whole life. "Do you ever visit your father's grave?" Ira McCray died about two years ago, and even though his mother and her father had differences because of the Rebel/McCray feud, she was there for the funeral.

She blinked. "What?"

"Do you?"

"Of course Rosie and I go."

"That's what people do when someone they love dies. Nana taught me that. You visit the grave because it gives the person going some sort of peace about the death. That's what I need for Ivy. I need her here so I can visit when I want to and feel that peace."

"Oh, son." She wrapped her arms around him and squeezed. "Sometimes you're more grown-up than I realize." She pushed back and wiped away a tear. "Go and introduce yourself to Mr. Faust. You're old enough to do that."

HE TALKED TO Mr. Faust and agreed to meet him at the cemetery in thirty minutes. On the way he decided to text Jody and let her know what was going on. She deserved that.

I'm meeting Mr. Faust in a few minutes at the cemetery to pick out a plot for Ivy. Just wanted you to know.

He followed an old Chevy truck into the horseshoe of the cemetery—of course, what else? Mr. Faust, about five feet eight inches tall and in his late seventies, got out of the truck. They shook hands again. Before a word could be spoken, Jody drove up behind them.

She got out in jeans, a T-shirt and slippers. Her long hair hung down her back.

"You still have your slippers on," Chase pointed out.

"I was getting dressed for work when you texted me."

"Well then, let's get it done. Mr. Faust, we're looking for a plot to bury our daughter. She was buried in Austin and I would like to bring her home."

"Oh, sure. No problem." He pulled off his baseball cap and scratched his balding head. "The thing that I don't understand is, why do you want to buy a plot?"

"Excuse me? Isn't that the way it's done?"

Mr. Faust pointed to a wrought iron fence.

"See that? Take a look at the name on the gate."

Chase stepped back so he could see. "It says Rebel."

"Yes, it does. Mr. John made sure his sons had enough burial plots for their needs. Every Rebel who was ever born in Horseshoe is buried here, all the way back to Ance Rebel, who came here in the 1830s. Your relatives are buried here and—" he waved his hand across the horseshoe "—the Mc-Crays are buried over there."

"But that's my dad's burial plot, not mine."

"When Mr. John's mother died, he bought twenty plots for each son and put up the fence. I guess Mr. John thought his sons were going to have as many children as he had."

The more Chase thought about it, the more he liked the thought of Ivy being buried in the Rebel plot. That was who she was.

"I'll talk about it with my dad," he said.

"Or we could bury her in the Carson plot," Jody put in. "It's right next to the Rebels and we could put her near Gramma. She would watch over Ivy."

Chase glanced to the Rebel plot with all the history and family roots, and he wanted

Ivy to be a part of that. She was a part of that. She was a Rebel.

"I'll let you know, Mr. Faust."

"Good deal. Just give me a call." He shook Chase's hand and then Jody's. "I'm real sorry for your loss."

"Chase, please," Jody appealed as Mr. Faust drove out of sight. "Why can't we bury Ivy by Gramma?"

"Because when I die, I want to be buried by my daughter, and she will be right there in the Rebel plot."

That threw Jody for a moment and then she swung around and shouted over her shoulder, "You're just doing this to hurt me!"

Was he? He could be. But he didn't like to think of himself as that heartless.

He glanced again to the wrought iron fence and the tombstones and thought about all the history that was enclosed there. History he was a part of, and Ivy, too. She would be among her ancestors and that was how he wanted it. That was how it was going to be.

JODY WENT BACK to her house to finish dressing and made it to the courthouse by nine o'clock. She tried not to let Chase's stubbornness get to her, but by noon she felt sick to her stomach and had to go home. Her very eagle-eyed mother noticed her car wasn't at the courthouse and came over. She had a key, and when Jody didn't answer the door, she let herself in.

Jody lay on the couch, feeling ill.

"Oh, Jody, what's wrong?"

She sat up. "I just feel sick, like I'm going to throw up."

"Oh, dear. You probably caught a bug. I'll get a washcloth."

"I don't think it's that," Jody called after her.

Her mother came back with a wet washcloth and wiped Jody's face. "Does that feel better?" She put a hand over Jody's forehead. "You don't have any fever."

"It's not that, Mom. I've just been upset."

"Other than the obvious, has something else happened?"

She told her mother about Chase's plans to move Ivy.

"Oh, baby, I'm sorry."

"He's just so stubborn."

Peyton sat by her daughter and gently wiped her face. "Calm down. You're making yourself sick over this."

"I just wanted her by Gramma."

She tightened her arm around Jody. "Now I'm going to talk to you like a mother instead of a stepmother."

"Is there a difference?"

"Yes. As a stepmother, I never wanted to hurt your feelings, but a mother wouldn't care. So here it goes. It hasn't bothered you before that Ivy is buried in Austin and not by Gramma. Why is it bothering you now?"

"Why do you have to be so logical?"

"Because I love you and you're missing the obvious. Chase is grieving and wants to be close to his daughter. Let him grieve. We will all be the better for it." She stroked Jody's hair. "Now, I'm going to fix you some lunch."

"Mom…"

"How about chicken noodle soup?"

"Okay."

Her mom brought soup, crackers and a Sprite to the coffee table. Jody grabbed the drink. She was thirsty.

"That might settle your stomach."

"It already has."

"I'm going home to make your dad something for lunch, even though I'm still upset with him."

"Oh, Mom, please don't be. I told you we

talked and we're okay. He's hurt that I didn't trust him, but we worked it out, so please don't be mad at Dad."

"We'll see," Peyton said as she opened the door and then turned back to Jody. "You do know that I'm not your stepmother anymore?"

"I know."

"I love you the same way I love JW. You're my kid."

"I know, Mom."

As soon as Peyton closed the door, Jody wondered why she'd felt as if she couldn't depend on her mother. She would have supported her 100 percent and would have dared her father to say one negative word to Jody. She would have protected her like mothers do and Jody could have leaned on her while she went through the pregnancy. How easy that was to see now.

CHASE WAS RESTLESS and needed to do something physical. He'd missed his therapy appointment, so he called to see if he could get in. They said yes and he headed toward Temple and spent an hour swimming and exercising. He stopped at about one o'clock and got lunch, then went home to catch up on his online classes. It was about six o'clock when he finished up and decided to go to the ranch to talk to his dad about the burial plot.

When he drove up, his mom's SUV was there and so was Grandma's truck. He didn't see Grandpa's truck. Even though they didn't let him drive anymore, he still kept it. Then he noticed the truck over at Grandpa's house, which was about a hundred yards away. Sometimes he liked to go to his house and just sit there and think of the old days and his wife. Usually JR drove him. The first time Grandpa told JR to drive him home, his mom had a *McCray fit*, as his dad called it. What if he ran over somebody? What if he hurt himself or Grandpa? On and on it went until his dad told JR to get in the truck and take Grandpa to his house.

He'd been teaching JR to drive out in the pasture, so he had no fears that he couldn't do it. And JR drove without a problem. His Mom cooled down and they were back to normal, or as close to normal as the Elias Rebel family would ever get.

In the kitchen his mom and grandma were busy fixing supper. His grandma hugged him. "I'm sorry, Chase."

He knew he was going to get a lot of that,

and strangely it didn't hurt like he'd thought it would. "Thank you, Grandma."

"Now, listen, son," Maribel said, wearing her mother's cap. He didn't think she ever took it off. "Eli doesn't understand about the baby, so he has lots of questions. Just try and be as honest as you can."

"Why did you have to tell them?"

His mom paused in placing silverware on the table. "We're not keeping secrets in this family. That's what's causing all the pain. Even though your brothers may not understand everything, they need to know. And you, of all people, should understand that."

"Yes, I do. It's just an open wound right now."

The back door opened and they could hear voices. Grandpa came in first with JR holding on to his left arm and then Tre and Eli.

"Hey, Chase," JR said. "I have to get Grandpa to his chair."

"I can get myself to my chair," Grandpa shot back.

JR didn't let go and Chase followed them into the living room. Grandpa suddenly turned and hugged him. "I'm sorry, son. I'm so sorry."

Chase hugged him back. "I'll get through it, Grandpa. Thanks."

He sat on the sofa with JR and Tre on either side of him. Eli stood in the middle of the room, staring at them and twisting his hands as if he didn't know what to do.

"What's wrong, Eli?"

"Nothing. When are we gonna take the pennies to the bank?" he asked suddenly, as if he'd just thought of it.

Chase glanced at the fishbowl on the end table. "When you get it full. It's about three-fourths right now."

"Okay." He ran and crawled onto Chase's lap.

"Can't you sit somewhere else?" Tre grumbled.

"No. I want to talk to Chase," Eli replied.

"What is it?" Chase asked.

"I don't understand how you had a baby and didn't know about it."

"Oh, jeez." Tre sighed. "I'm going to tell you one more time and listen. Jody and Chase got secretly married and Jody got pregnant. She went to tell Chase, but that woman was in his room, and Jody thought they were together. She ran away and wouldn't see Chase because she thought he was with that woman."

"But he wasn't?" Eli asked.

"No," JR and Tre said in unison.

Tre continued, "Jody had the baby alone and it was stillborn, and before you ask, that means she was born dead. And Chase never knew until a few days ago. Now do you understand?"

"It makes me sad," Eli replied.

Chase tightened his arms around his younger brother. "It makes me sad, too." This was what he needed—to be around family, to talk about it, to soak up their comfort, and somewhere through all that, the healing would begin.

Elias entered the room. "What's everyone looking so gloomy about?"

Eli jumped up and ran to his dad. "Tre was telling me about Ivy and how she was born. That's her name, right?"

"Yes, that's her name," Chase said.

Elias glanced at Chase. "I'm going upstairs to take a shower, and then we can talk."

It didn't take his dad long, and before he knew it, they were sitting at the dining table, eating supper. No one spoke much. His dad was tired and he thought of asking him later, but he couldn't stop now.

"Did you drive your Grandpa's truck today?" Elias directed the question to JR.

JR swallowed a mouthful of food. "Yes, sir. Grandpa wanted to go talk to Great-Grandma." JR frowned. "How did you know we were there?"

"I told you I know everything you do, but this time you made it easy for me. You left the lights on."

JR snapped his fingers. "Dang it."

"That was probably me," Grandpa said. "Don't go jumping on JR. He does a good job taking care of me. The railing on the front step you put up thirty years ago is getting loose and I asked JR to hold on to me so I wouldn't fall. I guess that's how we left the lights on."

JR pushed back his chair. "I'll go turn them off."

"Nah. Your great-grandmother will turn them off. She never liked it when the lights were left on," Grandpa said.

After his words, silence dominated the room. Everyone looked at each other, but no one said a word. Grandpa glanced around at everybody. "What? You don't believe me?

Go look. She's probably turned them off by now."

JR and Tre shot for the back door. Eli got out of his seat and edged toward his mother. The boys ran back in, out of breath.

"Well?" Elias asked.

"The lights are off," JR gulped out.

Eli crawled onto his mother's lap.

"What are you up to, Grandpa?" Elias took a drink of his tea.

"Teaching these boys I'm not as old and senile as they think I am." Grandpa pushed to his feet. "I got 'em good. Got the rest of you pretty good, too, didn't I?"

"You got us," Chase said. "Now tell us how you did it."

JR handed Grandpa his cane and the old man ambled toward his chair. "I don't like giving away all my secrets, but as you get older, you realize just how much smarter you are than everyone else."

Elias laughed. "And when did you come to that conclusion?"

Grandpa waved a hand as if to dismiss it. "Uh…that was a long time ago. You just have to be alert and pay attention to what's going on around you."

Elias got up from the table and sat on

the sofa with his iced tea glass in his hand. "Well, Grandpa, you're about the most un-alert person I've ever known."

Grandpa shook a finger at him. "Watch your manners or I'll dump you in the pond like I did when you were a kid and misbe-having."

"You never dumped me in the pond."

"Yeah, yeah, you're right." Grandpa had a thoughtful expression. "That had to have been John. Yep, it was."

"I don't believe that for a minute," Elias said. "I have no memory of Dad dumping me in the pond."

"He didn't really dump you. He threw you like a big ol' football."

"You make up all those stories, Grandpa."

"But he didn't make up that one," Grandma said as she carried plates to the kitchen.

"Mom…"

"It's true," Grandma said, coming back into the living room. "Your dad told Falcon and Quincy to go with Grandpa, and you and Egan would go to work with him. You got mad because you wanted to go with Grandpa, and your dad told you if you didn't straighten up, he was going to dump you in the pond to straighten out your attitude. Remember that?"

Elias leaned forward, his forearms resting on his knees with the glass clutched in his hands. "Yeah, I remember now."

"What did you do, Daddy?" Eli asked. "Did you drown?"

JR and Tre started laughing. "He didn't drown, you idiot," JR said. "He's right here."

Eli squeezed in beside Elias and JR. "Did you get a spanking?"

"No, I didn't get a spanking."

"What did you do if you didn't get drowned?"

"He started playing around, swimming," Grandpa said. "That was until the fish swam up the leg of his britches and then he was running and screaming for help."

"Did you go to work with Grandpa, then?" JR asked.

"No, I went with Dad like I was supposed to."

"Okay, boys." Maribel clapped her hands. "Upstairs to take a bath and then come back to say good-night to Chase. Right now Chase wants to talk to his dad, so give him some time."

"Oh, Mom, you're always the party pooper," JR said.

"What did you say?"

JR held up his hands. "Nothing. I don't want to get dumped in a pond."

The boys ran upstairs laughing.

Chase told his father what he had in mind about Ivy.

"Son, you can put that baby anywhere you want on my plots. Just get in touch with Mr. Faust and…"

"I already have and he said as long as it was okay with you."

"You got it."

"Thanks, Dad."

The boys came charging downstairs like a herd of buffalo. "Grandpa," JR called. "You didn't tell us how you made the lights turn off."

"When you get as sharp as I am, you'll figure it out."

Eli looked up at Chase. "What did you and Daddy talk about?"

"You don't need to know everything, Eli," his mother told him.

"Is it a secret?"

"No." His mother looked from Elias to Chase. "You see, Ivy is buried in Austin and Chase wants to bring her home to Horseshoe and bury her here."

Eli scratched his head. "I don't understand. I don't think I like Jody anymore."

His mom sat on the sofa and gathered Eli onto her lap. "You know what I told you about judging people."

"Yeah, you can't judge people until you walked a mile in their shoes. Jody wears heels and I'm not walking in her shoes."

"That's not what I meant. You have to live through what Jody has lived through to experience her experiences before you can criticize."

Eli was shaking his head before his mother even finished.

"Let me explain it another way." She placed her hand on her chest. "I know what Jody's going through because I went through the same thing."

"You did."

"Yes. I got pregnant with Chase when I was in high school and I was all alone. My dad kicked me out of the house and I had nowhere to go. I didn't know what I was going to do or what was going to happen to me. I was just a scared young girl."

Eli wrapped his arms around his mother. "I'm sorry, Mama. Where was Daddy?"

"Good question."

"Okay, boys, I want you to listen to me." Elias stepped in with a growl in his voice. "Here's the real story. When we were in high school, your mom and I had sex in my old pickup."

Eli put his hands over his ears. "No, no, no. I don't want to hear."

"He's being a baby," JR said.

"I said listen."

"Yes, sir."

"Your mother's truck was older than mine and she had a flat tire. It was cold and raining and I stopped to help her. One thing led to another and Chase was created."

Chase had the insane urge to also put his hands over his ears. He didn't want to hear this, either.

"I looked for your mother in school the next day, but she wouldn't talk to me. Suddenly she wasn't in school anymore. I asked friends of hers and no one knew where she was. I asked Mrs. Peabody, a friend of Maribel's mother's, and she told me to forget about Maribel. I didn't like that answer, so I approached Malachi, Maribel's brother. He told me to stay away from his sister or they would hurt me. This was when the Rebel/McCray feud was going strong, but that didn't bother me. I kept pestering Malachi and he finally told me that your grandfather and your mother had a big argument and Maribel left." Elias looked at Maribel. "So don't tell my son that I wasn't there because you never gave me the chance. I looked every day until you returned with my son in tow and that was the biggest shock of my life. And the biggest blessing."

"Oh, Elias." Maribel crawled over her sons to get to him. "I believe that's the nicest thing you've ever said to me. I thought you just forgot about me." Then she wrapped her arms around his neck and just held on.

"No, Maribel." He stroked her hair and for a minute Chase thought they didn't even realize anyone else was in the room.

"Can we forget about the past now?" Elias asked. "Let's leave it in the past, where it belongs, and enjoy raising these boys."

Chase got to his feet. "I better go. It's getting late."

Grandma came into the room, wiping her hands on a dish towel. "I think the boys need to know my part in all of this, too."

"No, Miss Kate." Maribel was instantly on her feet.

But there was no stopping his grandma.

"Maribel came here and told me that Elias was the father of the child she was carrying, but I didn't believe her. I thought her father had put her up to it as one more way to torture the Rebels. It's all my fault. Chase should have been born here... I..."

Chase was closest to her and he grabbed her, helping her backward to her chair. Then Elias and Maribel were there reassuring her.

"You're not to blame for anything," Chase told her. "I had a very good life. I'm learning that that's just life and you never know what's going to happen or if you're doing the right thing."

She touched his face. "I love you."

"I know, Grandma."

"It's ironic, isn't it?" Tre said.

"What is?" JR asked.

"That Mom and all of us live here now with Grandma."

"No, what does *ironic* mean?"

"Shut up."

"No, you shut up."

"Upstairs," Elias shouted, and they bumped into each other trying to get there.

"Good night," they called from the landing.

Elias glanced at his grandfather. "Mr. Alert is out for the night."

"I won't wake him," Chase said, hugging his grandmother. "Stop making yourself ill over what happened."

"I'll do my best."

He hugged his parents and held on a little tighter to his mother. "Are you sure you don't want to spend the night?"

"No, thanks, Mom," he said. "I have a lot to do tomorrow."

"If your dad and I can get through all our problems, so can you and Jody. You can work this out."

"I don't know. I think all I'm going to feel for Jody now is anger."

"Don't you say that. I've raised you not to hate or judge people."

"She hurt me."

"I know, son. Just remember one of your grandpa's sayings. Time changes everything, so do your grieving and let time handle the rest."

As he drove away he wondered if there would ever come a time when he could open his heart and forgive Jody.

CHAPTER SIXTEEN

THAT NIGHT PEYTON brought over soup that she had made for Jody. Her brother, JW, came home from college and was there to eat, too. It was just the four of them, like it used to be. They were a family until Jody fell in love. Then everything fell apart and they barely talked to each other.

They cleaned up the kitchen together and her father noticed JW on his phone. "Get off the phone, JW. This is family time."

"Sorry." He slipped the phone into his pocket. "I can't stay very long in the morning, Mom. I have to get back to make up a test."

Her dad paused in putting up dishes. "And why do you need to make up a test?"

Jody could see her brother was gauging his words carefully. "I went to a party and overslept the next morning and missed the test, but the professor agreed to let me take it in the morning."

Wyatt leaned against the counter. "Okay. Fine."

JW glanced at Jody and she shrugged. Their dad was in a good mood.

JW took advantage of it. "Uh… Dad, I'd like to talk about something."

"What?"

"I'm thinking of changing my major."

This had her dad's full attention. "To what?"

JW twisted the napkin in his hand. "Uh… criminal justice."

"You want to become a lawman?"

"Yes. Gramma talked about Grandpa and his years as a highway patrolman. After I get my degree, I'd like to become a highway patrolman and then try to get into the Texas Rangers."

"Sounds as if you have it figured out."

"I do, Dad."

"You're getting your degree first."

"Yes, sir." JW threw himself at his dad. "Thanks."

"I'm the easy one. Now you have to deal with your mother."

Peyton placed her hands on her hips. "That's it? That doesn't work for me, Wyatt." She ran her hand over JW's hair. "I think my son is delusional. The answer to changing majors is a big fat no."

"Mom, it's what I want to do."

"Do you know how long I was in labor with you?"

"Forty-two hours and twelve minutes. You ask that every time you're mad at me."

"Peyton, you have to let him live his own life. We learned this the hard way. Remember?"

Peyton thought about it for a minute and then she shook her finger in JW's face. "Don't you ever get shot. Ever."

"Thanks, Mom." JW hugged both his parents.

How easy. She wished she'd had the courage to do that when she was eighteen.

"Sit down and have some cake," Wyatt said. "Your mother made it."

"That's not much of an endorsement," JW quipped, sliding into a chair. Peyton was not known for her culinary skills.

Peyton slapped at his shoulder and they sat and had coffee and cake.

The doorbell rang, interrupting the pleasant silence. Jody hurried to answer it.

"Chase!"

His sad eyes and haggard expression had her taking a step backward. "Come in."

"It's late, but I just wanted to let you know I heard from Mr. Foley and the burial won't be until next Friday, about four in the afternoon."

"Thanks. I'll be there."

Her dad stepped around her and offered Chase his hand. "I should've done this years ago, but welcome to the family."

Chase looked at his hand for a second before he shook it. "Yes, it would have been nice years ago, but today it means nothing."

"Hey, Chase," JW called as he came into the room.

Chase nodded. "JW."

"You don't mean that," her dad continued. "You and Jody will eventually get back together."

"I seriously doubt it." He turned and walked out the door. Her dad made to go after him, but Jody caught his arm.

"Let it go, Dad. Can't you see how he's hurting? He needs to be alone." And she needed that for him. Even though her heart was breaking, there was no other way.

THE DAYS SEEMED to drag for Chase. He put off the remodel and worked around his house, even washing the windows. Doing that and keeping up with his therapy and online classes kept the pain at bay.

He talked to Mr. Pringle one day at the diner and he asked Chase about the coaching job again. Chase was honest and told him that he had too many family problems right now to consider it. He wasn't interested. Mr. Pringle said that he would give him some time and talk to him later. The way Chase's life was now, he couldn't see himself taking the job. Not only was he unsure about his future plans, he didn't know where he'd be by next year.

One week turned into two as it was taking time to get all the paperwork done on moving Ivy. On Thursday Mr. Foley called and said everything had been finalized and they would be there on Friday about four o'clock. Chase got there early and walked around, looking at the graves. Mr. Faust was there, too, to make sure everything went smoothly.

Chase looked around and noticed Ance Rebel's wife's name was Byaa. "That's an unusual name," he said to Mr. Faust.

"She was a Comanche living with the white people when Mr. Rebel came here. I guess he took a shine to her because he married her and she gave him twelve kids. Seven boys and five girls. Only six lived to adulthood and they're all buried right here. Ol' Abe can give you chapter and verse on the Rebels. You need to talk to him."

"Yeah, I will."

Jody drove up and parked behind his truck. Dressed in a slim-fitting black dress with her hair up, she walked toward him, carrying a bouquet of white roses. Her features were set in place, like glass, and at any moment her composure was going to shatter into a million pieces.

The Carsons and his parents followed. The boys jumped out. Chase wished his mother hadn't brought them, but what better way to learn about life and its many heartaches. Grandma and Grandpa were with them. JR got out with a folding chair for Grandpa, and Chase hurried to help. Mr. Faust had asked if he needed chairs and he had said no. He hadn't expected anyone to come besides him and Jody. He had forgotten one very important thing: he was a part of a big family and a large community.

Grandma had reminded him that he might want a minister to say a few words. She took care of that for him, which was good because

Chase felt like he was in a fog. Quincy's daughters, Martha Kate and Bailey Rose, asked if they could sing along with Paxton's daughter, Annie.

His uncles arrived and parked to the side so the black hearse could get through. Chase didn't recognize some of the cars. They had to be people from Horseshoe. Stuart, Wyatt's other deputy, and Cole were directing traffic. He'd never dreamed this many people would show up to support two kids who had suffered a tragedy. And that was what it was. A tragedy. Today no one was pointing fingers. They were all here because they cared about Chase and Jody.

The hearse stopped at the gate to the Rebel burial plots. Mr. Foley got out on the passenger side. Chase shook his hand. "Ready?" Mr. Foley asked.

"Yes, sir."

Jody came over and gave Mr. Foley a hug, and then they walked to the grave site where the fresh grave had been dug. Chase and Jody stood together with their parents beside them. Mr. Foley opened the back door of the hearse and a young man brought the casket to the grave. It was white trimmed in gold and Chase hadn't expected it to be so small. His stomach clenched and he fought to breathe.

With Mr. Foley's help, the young man lowered the casket into the hole and a minister said a few words. Martha Kate picked up her guitar, strummed a few strings and broke into "Amazing Grace." Annie and Bailey Rose joined in. Their voices blended beautifully. The age-old words filled the cemetery and everyone's hearts. Jody trembled beside him. That was when her knees gave way and she almost crumbled to the ground, but Chase caught her.

"Wyatt!" Peyton screamed. "Jody."

"I'll take her home," Wyatt said to Chase.

"I'm okay," she insisted, leaning on Chase.

"She needs a place to sit," Mr. Foley said. "Bring the bench."

Within seconds Mr. Foley and the young guy had it set up at the foot of the grave. Jody slowly picked up the flowers that had fallen to the ground and sat on the bench with tears running down her cheeks. She made no effort to stop them. She looked at Martha Kate. "Please keep singing."

As the men shoveled dirt onto the coffin, Martha Kate's, Annie's and Bailey Rose's voices rang out. Chase sat by Jody and took her hand. He didn't know why. He just knew he had to touch her. As Martha Kate's voice ebbed away, Jody got up and placed the roses on the grave.

"Let's go home," Peyton said as she took Jody's arm.

"I'm fine, Mom. I really am."

"You're not fine."

Jody raised her head. "Mom, please."

Wyatt took Peyton by the shoulders. "Let's give our daughter some space. She knows she can call us for anything."

"Thanks, Dad."

Mr. Foley walked up to Chase. "Since we have the headstone, we'll place it at the top of the grave for now. When the grave settles, in about six months, we'll come back and set it properly."

"That's fine, Mr. Foley. Thanks."

Mr. Foley said goodbye and the hearse drove away. Chase shook hands with everyone and thanked them for coming. And then there was just the two of them.

JODY STARED AT the fresh dirt that covered their daughter and then glanced up at the live oak tree. "I think she'll like it here. She'll have lots of shade."

"Yeah," Chase said, sitting by her. "I was surprised at all the people."

"They've known us most of our lives."

"Mmm. I'm sorry it had to end like this."

"Me, too." She drew a deep breath and let the reality of that statement sink in. Was it really over? Could a love so strong be over? She got to her feet, trying not to make a fool of herself again. She reached down and plucked a petal from the roses. "Goodbye, my angel. Mommy will come to visit you often, and if you see a crazy lady sitting on your bench at night, it will be me. I love you from the depth of my heart."

She walked away and didn't look back.

Jody went straight home and fell onto her sofa, crying until she couldn't cry anymore. There was no way to stop the tears and she didn't even try. She had to get it all out so she could heal. Her mother came in and just held her.

Peyton stroked Jody's hair. "You'll be okay, baby. Mama's here."

"When Martha Kate started singing, I couldn't take it."

"I know, baby. Just rest. Tomorrow you and I will do something, even if it's just sitting around, watching an old movie."

There was a knock at the door and Erin came in. She fell down beside Jody and they held on to each other. "I'm so sorry. I should have never encouraged you to tell Chase. It's all a big mess and so many people are hurt."

"No, it was the right thing. That's why we're hurting, but we'll get better. I have to believe that."

Peyton got to her feet. "While you girls are talking, I'll fix supper."

"No, you don't have to," Erin told her. "I have food in the car from people in Horseshoe."

"What?"

"Some people started calling my mom, asking where to take the food, and being chief volunteer of everything, she set it up at the community center."

Peyton and Erin brought the food inside and it covered the breakfast room table. There was no way she could eat it all. Peyton called Wyatt and Cole and Stuart from his office to come over to make plates.

"We should take some of this to Chase," Jody said.

"Don't worry about that," Erin replied. "Rachel took twice that much out to the ranch. Since she's married to Egan and aware it's hay season, she thought it best to take the food to them. Chase is out there with Zane and the family."

How sad it was that two people who'd professed to love each other were apart on the saddest day of their lives.

Later she and Erin sat on the sofa, one on each end, like they used to do when they were kids.

"Are you okay?" Erin asked. "And I don't want your typical response of *fine*. I really want to know how you're doing."

"Terrible. That's the truth. Chase says it's over. He can't trust me anymore."

"I'm sorry, girlfriend. I just wish you could find some measure of peace."

"I don't think there's any in my future."

"Don't say that." Erin took a big bite out of a chocolate chip cookie. "Yummy. Have you tasted these?"

"I don't have much of an appetite and most of the time I feel sick to my stomach."

"Oh, Jody, you have to pull yourself out of this—" Erin stopped herself and held up her hands. "I'm not giving any more advice. But you know what we need? A couple of beers. A glass of wine. That would lighten the mood for sure."

Jody laughed, yet didn't feel any lighter. "Remember that time when we were about fifteen when I spent the night at your house and you suggested we drink a couple beers of your dad's? We crept downstairs to get them. We got light-headed and we were afraid your dad could smell it. We poured it down the toilet. We were such idiots."

"We were just kids trying to be grown-ups."

"Yeah." Jody nodded. "As if growing up could solve all our problems. In reality it only makes them worse."

Erin gave Jody a tight hug. "I better go find my kid. One grandmother has her, but I'm not sure which. I'll try to come by again before we leave for Houston. And today, let's start a new chapter in Jody Rebel's life."

"The happy chapter? I thought I already did that one."

"Sometimes you have to do it twice to get it right."

Jody stood and hugged her friend. "A new beginning."

A new beginning.

CHASE SAT IN his grandmother's backyard on the steps of the wooden deck. People were everywhere, sitting and eating good food the town of Horseshoe had provided. No one spoke. They just enjoyed the company and the food.

"How you doing?" Zane asked, sitting beside him on the steps.

"I just wanted to bring Ivy home. I didn't want to make a party out of it."

Zane slapped him on the back. "When you're raised country, that's what it means. You help out your neighbor. So get that look off your face and appreciate what your neighbors have done for you."

"Sorry, man. I'm kind of wound up."

"Everyone understands that."

"Probably."

"Don't you think Jody should have been here?"

Chase didn't respond. He had no words. They were all tangled up inside and he grew angry that Zane had mentioned it.

"I've supported you through all of this and I took your side when it looked bad because I believed you. I trusted you. I still do. You need to return the favor toward Jody. In her condition she did the best she could at the time. Now it's time to move on."

"That's easy to say when it wasn't your

daughter we buried today." He jumped to his feet and headed for the back gate.

"Chase!"

The wind caught his name and threw it into the trees, leaving a hollow echo. When he realized Zane was following him, he started to run. He couldn't take one more person telling him how he needed to feel. He passed the work barn and the other two. They'd built a new barn with a corral a few months ago. He stopped there. The back of the building faced the trees and several heifers were in the corral. When they saw him, they got up and milled around, hoping for more food.

Two benches were built into the barn, one on each side of the big door. They were rock-solid so no one could move them. Chase sank onto the one nearest him and stared into the dark night. It was a half-moon tonight and visibility was good, but his focus was on the darkness and the billion sparkling stars shining like diamonds on a tiara. God's tiara. He liked to think that each star represented someone's loved one and the brightest was Ivy. He knew from all the science classes what stars were, but he liked his version better.

He heard a noise in the barn and turned to see if it was someone. Eli peeked around the corner.

"What are you doing out here?"

Eli hopped onto the bench and got as close to Chase as possible. "I came to be sad with you. It's not fun to be sad all by yourself."

Chase pulled him onto his lap. "No, it isn't. Thank you for being sad with me."

"I'm sad, too."

"About what?"

"About Ivy...and... Will I ever grow, Chase? I want to be tall like you and Daddy, but JR calls me a shrimp because I'm so skinny and short and I don't have a butt big enough to hold up my jeans. Will I ever grow?"

Chase squeezed him around the middle. "You're going to grow as tall as Dad, as tall as me. You just have to be patient. And don't pay too much attention to JR. He's always kidding you, but he helps you when you need it." He tightened his arms around his brother. "Let's pick out a star for Ivy. See—" he pointed to the sky "—look at all of them. That really bright one is Ivy." She would shine bright in his heart forever.

He heard them before he saw them. JR

and Tre settled on the bench, one on either side of him. "What are you doing?" JR asked.

"I'm being sad with Chase," Eli replied. "You have to be quiet and not act up, JR, or it will make Chase sadder."

"We're sorry you're sad," JR said. Whenever JR or Tre talked, they always included the other one. They were one. Chase hoped they always stayed close.

"How come Jody's not here?" Tre asked. "Wouldn't it be better to be sad together?"

Before he could answer the heart-stopping question, Grandpa's truck drove up to his house. His dad and Grandpa got out and started working on the loose railing Grandpa had talked about.

"Doesn't Dad know it's dark?" JR asked as the lights in Grandpa's house and on his porch went on. His dad just needed to do something and Chase supposed he thought fixing the railing was as good a thing as any. He was sure his mom was packing up food for the freezer.

Elias drove some nails into the wood to secure it. Grandpa went up it a couple of times to make sure. Afterward, his dad put his tools back in the truck and drove back to

the house. Although he turned off the porch
light, he'd left the light on in the house.

JR laughed. "Now we can get Dad."

About that time the light went out and the
boys scooted closer to him.

"Did you see, Chase?" Eli asked.

"Yes, I did. And there's who's turning
off the lights." He pointed toward Paxton's
house, which was in front of Grandpa's.
Paxton went through his back door. "Paxton turns off the lights when they leave them
on because he knows Grandpa is forgetful."

JR and Tre jumped up. "Oh, boy, now we
can get Dad and Grandpa, too."

At that moment someone turned on the
outdoor lights and the front of Rebel Ranch
was flooded with light. "Uh... Eli... Did
you tell Mom where you were going?"

He slapped his face with both hands. "Oh,
no. I forgot. Daddy's gonna kill me this time
for sure."

Chase picked him up. "Come on. We have
to let them know everyone is okay." As soon
as they stepped away from the barn, they
could be seen because the lights were bright
and on.

His mom came charging toward them.

His dad was a little slower. Grandma and Grandpa just waited at the house.

Maribel took Eli from Chase. "I forgot, Mama. I just didn't want Chase to be sad all by himself. And JR and Tre found us."

She patted his chest. "We have to have another talk, but since it's such a sad day, your dad and I understand and we're going to let this pass." She pointed a finger in his face. "Next. Time. Think. Eli. Before. You. Leave. The. House. Got it?"

"I got it, Mama."

Elias threw an arm around Chase's shoulders. "You okay?"

"Yeah. I'm better, but I won't deny it was a rough day."

A shooting star flashed across the sky. "Look," Eli shouted. "That's Ivy. We named a star after her."

"Aw, that's so sweet," Maribel said. "Our boys are sweet."

Chase hugged his grandma and grandpa. "I'm going home now to just crash for a while. Don't worry about me."

"Hey, Grandpa." JR and Tre edged a little closer. "We saw Great-Grandma at your house." They darted into the house.

"What did he say?" Grandpa asked.

"Where? I didn't see her." Eli was giving it away.

"What are those boys up to?" His dad hugged him and then went into the house. His mom put two bags of food in his truck.

"Mom, really?"

"You won't feel like cooking and you'll have something to eat all week."

"Thanks. I'll see you in a couple of days."

Maribel laughed. "You know me well enough to know you'll see me sooner."

"I just need some peace."

"You're not going to find it being alone and brooding. You did a beautiful thing for your daughter. Now embrace it and get on with life. You were dealt a hard blow, but I know you can come back even stronger."

A lot of laughter and screams came from the house. "I better go see what's going on."

"The boys think they have one up on Grandpa. They just don't know that's not going to happen. Grandpa will outsmart them every time."

"I better go before Grandpa has all three of them crying. Come for breakfast in the morning," she shouted, running into the house.

He glanced toward the sky and said,

"Sleep in peace, sweet Ivy." He got in his truck and drove away. As he traveled down Rebel Road, only one thing occupied his mind.

Jody should have been here.

CHAPTER SEVENTEEN

BEFORE JODY KNEW IT, May had arrived. She kept telling herself that the next day would get better, but each day was the same. She woke up feeling bad and went to bed feeling bad. She hadn't seen Chase and she didn't know where he was. She visited the grave site more than she wanted to admit. That didn't help, either. Ivy's death weighed heavily upon her. But life went on.

She got a call from Sister Carter at the rehab place, who wanted Jody to know that the Holdens were trying to get Heather out of the facility and Heather didn't want out. The sister felt Heather needed someone in her corner and wondered if Jody could do something to make sure Heather had a full course of treatment before being released.

The sister was right. Mrs. Holden was out of the hospital and wanted Heather home, too. The Holdens had hired an expensive attorney from Dallas to get the job done.

She may be just a small-town ADA, but she could fight with the best of them. First she visited with the Bell County DA and reminded him of how hard she'd worked on the case so Heather could go to rehab instead of jail.

He told her his hands were tied. He picked up a document from his desk. "They're saying the interview, which they had requested be done at home, should have been conducted in my office under a controlled environment. The at-home interview allowed ADA Rebel to bully Miss Holden into a confession. In compensation, the lawyer stated that the family would be satisfied with Heather's release and would not take it to trial, but if the DA failed to make that happen, he would be happy to go to court."

"That's bull," Jody told the DA.

"I know, but how are you going to fight the big boys? I'm taking the deal to release Heather. In exchange, they will not file any charges against my office or you."

"I don't believe you. You're caving."

"Ms. Rebel, sometimes you have to know when your back's against the wall."

"Yeah. Within a month Heather Holden will be back on drugs and her life will be over. Isn't it worth being backed against the wall to save a life?"

The DA got to his feet in an angry gesture. "I know you're young and eager, but the real world doesn't work that way."

"I know. The real world is unjust and cruel." She walked out before she said anything she would regret. This wasn't her fight. She had to keep reminding herself of that. Yet Jody suddenly found herself at the rehab center.

The sister was happy she had come for a visit and led Jody out to the big garden where Heather was working. She was on her knees pulling weeds in a large vegetable garden.

"She loves it out here," the sister said. "I'll leave you to visit. Heather," the sister called.

Heather looked up and a smile spread across her face. She got up and brushed the dirt from her jeans and ran to Jody. "It's so good to see you." Her eyes were clear and bright and her skin was flawless. The drugs were out of her system. They sat in the cooling room, as Heather called it. If you got tired or hot in the garden, you could go to the cooling room and cool off and get something to drink. It was nice and open and airy with a vending machine and ice.

"You look great," Jody said.

Heather fidgeted in her chair. "I feel great."

Jody decided to get right to it. "I heard a Dallas lawyer is going to get you out."

She looked down at her nails and studied the dirt beneath them. "Yeah. My mom is out now, too, and my dad thinks I need to be at home."

"Is that where you want to be?"

She paused and looked off to the garden at the beautiful tomatoes growing there. "I hate to leave my garden." She pointed to the back wall. "We have all kinds of flowers growing there. The gorgeous roses are just blooming. I like to work in the dirt. It's amazing what you can grow." She glanced at her hands. "Gardening has done a number on my hands, though. I used to get a manicure and a pedicure about once a week. You know, I don't even miss it."

"Sounds as if you like it here."

"My dad says I'm using this place as a shield. I need to get back into the real world."

"And what do you want, Heather? Think about it. What do you want?"

"I want to stay here until all the vegetables and flowers are gone."

"This is May, so you're talking about September?"

"Yeah. I'd like that, but my father is so adamant. He won't listen to me. Oh, I got my high school diploma online and got accepted into Baylor. My mom is upset that I didn't get to walk across the stage or go to the prom. My boyfriend, who I thought was my boyfriend, went with someone else." She looked down at her hands again. "I guess he was never really my boyfriend. He was never there when I needed him and he hasn't even made an attempt to see me."

"I'm sorry, Heather."

She threw her long blond hair back and tucked it behind her ears. Her hands were still a little shaky. "I think I'm growing up. There's a line in a song I remember that says everything that glitters is not gold."

"Isn't that the truth?"

They both chuckled. "You're eighteen now, right?"

"Yeah." She smiled shyly.

Jody scooted her chair closer to Heather. "I can fight this, but you have to be with me all the way. You can't change your mind tomorrow or next week. Before I put my neck on the line, you have to know what you want."

"I want to stay here. I feel safe and secure."

"Are you sure you're not clinging to this place?"

"No. I went to lunch with my mom the other day and she ordered a drink. I wanted one so bad I could taste it. You see, I was mixing alcohol with the drugs… I had to get out of there or I would have ordered one and my mom would have let me."

Jody picked up her briefcase and went to work. Heather was not ready to leave the facility on her own or with her parents. When she informed the DA of this, he blew his top. "How dare you go behind my back."

She pointed to the file she'd laid on his desk. "My name is on that file and it reflects on me. Heather Holden is not ready to leave the facility and I'll stake my reputation on that. Until a judge or a certified counselor can talk with her, she stays where she is." She took a breath. "Or we can go to trial."

"You might get your wish."

Over the next few days Jody thought about it, and it looked as if that was where they were headed until fate took it out of her hands. Heather's mother was arrested for a DUI in McLennan County. She was two times over the legal limit. The expensive attorney was busy trying to get it erased from her record, but the state of Texas was coming down hard on repeat offenders. And it seemed this was her third offense.

Jody quickly drew up a motion, asking a judge to dismiss the Dallas lawyer's complaint due to Heather's mother's drinking. It was the root of all of Heather's problems. The judge granted her motion.

Heather stayed where she was until her next hearing, which would be in the middle of September. A judge would decide her fate. Her mother would most likely go to jail. Sometimes money couldn't buy everything.

CHASE CLEANED HIS house until everything sparkled. He even took the ventilation grille off the bottom of the refrigerator and cleaned it. He went to a nursery and bought a truckload of flowers to plant. It spruced up the yard and everything looked nice, but inside he was still hurting.

His dad and his uncles were deep into hay season and he didn't see much of them. His brothers were also helping. His mom hinted that his dad could use an extra hand with driving and he thought that was just what he needed, to get out and do something away from his house. So he found himself in the hayfields with the Rebel clan. Square bales of hay dotted the horizon as far as he could see. The goal was by nightfall to have them all in the barns or someone else's barn. So they went to work.

Three trucks with long flatbed trailers spread across the field. Egan and Jude had the first trailer with Egan's boys, Justin and Jordan, helping. Jude's daughters, Olivia and Emily, were the designated drivers. Quincy and Phoenix had the second truck and trailer with Jake, Phoenix's son, and John, Falcon's son, helping. Caleb, Quincy's son, and Martha Kate, Quincy's daughter, stacked. Bailey Rose, Quincy's other daughter, and Gracie, Phoenix's daughter, were the drivers. Everyone was involved. It was a family tradition.

His dad and Rico had the last trailer with Rico's three boys, Dustin, Ben, Logan Mac, and Elias's three boys. His dad's trailer was larger, so he had more help, and the boys were all younger. But his dad and Rico were twice as strong as the others, which made up for a lot. During hay season they got off one day a week and today was Paxton's. Since school was out, his daughter, Annie, was probably with him.

His dad and Rico threw the eighty-pound bales onto the trailer as if they weighed no more than a loaf of bread. JR, Ben and Dustin stacked on the long trailer and Tre and Logan Mac stacked on the bed of the truck. Every now and then Jericho would help Ben and Logan Mac, but they never slowed down. Chase drove with Eli in the front seat.

Their day started as the sun peeked through the cobwebs in the trees and they went full throttle. They stopped when someone shouted for water. Eli was the water boy. He'd hand water bottles to everyone, then wait for the empty bottles and throw them in a bag.

"This is hard work, Chase," Eli said as he got back in the truck.

"Wait until you get bigger." Chase glanced to the trailer. "Your butt will be back there."

"Yeah, I'll be one of the big boys."

"Did y'all get the best of Grandpa the other night?" Chase asked before Eli could start rambling. He'd noticed that about his little brother. He liked to talk.

"It was kind of hard to tell."

"What do you mean?"

"JR started hopping around, saying he saw Great-Grandma and she was big, about six feet tall with broad shoulders, and used to ride bulls. Grandpa got tears in his eyes and everyone could see. It was just like that—" he shoved a fist into the palm of his hand "—bam. Everything got quiet. Then Grandpa said *don't talk about your grandma like that.*

"Then Daddy said, in his deep voice that makes me jump three feet, *apologize.* JR apologized, as did Tre. Grandpa got up and went to bed. Daddy told us to go to bed and we raced for the stairs. When I looked back, I saw Grandpa turn and wink at Daddy. What did that mean?"

"It means JR did not get Grandpa, nor did he make him cry or hurt his feelings. Grandpa is stronger than that. Grandpa was teaching him a lesson and Daddy knew it."

"It must have worked. The next morning, JR apologized again and helped Grandpa get his cane and put on his socks and told him that he would never ever hurt his feelings again. And he loved him."

He glanced down at Eli. "Are you crying?"

Eli brushed away a tear. "It makes me sad that we hurt Grandpa's feelings. I love Grandpa. He's the smartest man I know. He rode with Sam Houston."

"I don't think he rode with Sam Houston."

"Jesse James?"

Before he could reply, someone shouted for water. Chase stopped the truck and they all paused for a moment. They sat by the shade of the truck and took a break. "This load needs to go over to Mr. Beasley's place," his dad said, looking directly at Chase. "Do you think you can do it?"

"Sure."

"You just back it up to his barn and his hired hands will take it from there. Go after lunch—it's time to have something to eat."

"Thanks, Dad," he said with a smile. He hadn't backed up a trailer in a long time, but he felt sure he could still do it just like his dad had taught him. There were some things you just never forgot, like riding a bicycle. Like loving Jody. His mind paused on that fact. He had been slowly realizing there was just no way for him to forget her. She owned his heart.

They headed for the house and lunch. He parked near the big oaks by the barn that had a large picnic table. They sat at the table under the trees, waiting for Anamarie to bring lunch. She and his mom switched days. As he made to get back in the truck to go to Mr. Beasley's, Zane showed up.

"Hey," Zane called. "I thought I'd do something un-doctorly today and help Dad."

Chase hugged him. "It's good to see you."

Zane drew back. "How are you?"

"Better, and manual labor kind of takes the rough edge off."

"I was only trying to help, but you were right. I don't know how you're feeling and had no right to tell you otherwise. You're my friend, my very best friend, and I stepped over the line."

"Please," Chase groaned. "You're killing me."

"Brothers again?"

"You bet." And that made the world a little more livable for Chase. He never wanted to lose his friendship with Zane. He'd already lost too much.

JODY WOKE UP feeling sick. She ran to the bathroom and threw up. What was wrong with her? The only other time she felt this bad was when… Oh…boy. Could she be pregnant? Maybe. She grabbed her terry-cloth summer robe and wrapped it around her. With her purse in her hand, she headed for her car. She drove to Temple and found a convenience store and bought two pregnancy tests. From there she went to Chase's. It wasn't even six o'clock, so he should be home.

She ran up the sidewalk and marched through the living room to the kitchen. He was at the counter making coffee in his shorts. His hair was tousled and he needed a shave. Every time she saw him she marveled at his rugged handsomeness.

He stared at her. "What are you doing here? Is something wrong? You're still in your pajamas."

She slapped the pregnancy tests onto the bar. "I've been sick a lot. Nausea and vomiting. It's possible I'm pregnant."

"Whoa. There's no way you could be pregnant."

"We'll see." She picked up a test and went

into his bathroom. "This way we both will find out at the same time."

"Jody—"

She slammed the door on his words. She took the test and went back into the kitchen and laid it on a paper towel. "Now we wait."

"What are we waiting for?"

"For a plus or minus to pop up. Plus means I'm pregnant. Minus means I'm not."

He looked down. "It's a plus."

"Oh, yes! I knew I was pregnant, but I'm not getting excited until I take the next test." She slid onto a bar stool. "I have to wait a few minutes."

He kept staring at her. "It's too soon, Jody. I'm still grieving Ivy. It's just too soon. I'm not ready for this."

"A child is a gift from God. And I'm ready for a child even if you're not." She grabbed the test and went into the bathroom. She brought it back and laid it beside the other one.

Chase looked at it and turned away. She glanced over. "Another plus." She raised both arms above her head. "Yes! I can hardly believe it, but I'm accepting it with both hands and with my heart wide open. I've had so much guilt over Ivy, and this is God's way of forgiving me. I'm accepting this gift with joy and gratitude, and now I'm going home to get dressed and see if I can get in to see a doctor to verify the pregnancy." She turned toward the door and stopped. "I know you're not ready, but it looks as if we're going to be parents again. When you're ready to be a father, you just let me know."

On the way out, she stopped and picked up the box that was still sitting there. "I believe this belongs to me."

Chase stood there as if he were paralyzed. His knees felt weak and his heart thumped against his chest in loud rhythms. *A baby. A gift from God.* The words kept running through his head. Could they be pregnant? He wasn't ready. How could he *not* be ready?

He hurried to the bathroom to shave and dress. He went to Jody's house, but she wasn't there. He went to her parents', but she wasn't there, either. She said she was going to see a doctor. But who? There was only one professional she'd go to without an appointment and that was Zane's mother, Paige, the obstetrician and gynecologist.

It didn't take him long to reach Temple and he knew where Paige's office was. He took the stairs instead of the elevator, needing to burn off some energy. Of course, the receptionist said he needed an appointment. Then he asked her to tell Dr. Rebel that he'd like to speak to her. He was shown into her office. Jody was there staring at a piece of paper.

Paige was sitting at her desk, writing something in a chart. She got to her feet. "Come on in, Chase. And congratulations!"

"Jody's pregnant?" His voice came out hoarse and jittery.

"Yes," Paige replied.

"There's our little bump." Jody showed him the piece of paper she'd been staring at.

It didn't look like much of anything except swirling lines in Jody's stomach. It certainly didn't look like a baby.

"It's right there." Jody pointed. "In a couple more weeks we'll be able to see much more."

"Since Jody had problems with the first pregnancy, I'm being very careful and plan to monitor the pregnancy closely. I did an ultrasound, which I don't normally do this early, but like I said, I'm being very careful. I've ordered Jody's records from the Austin hospital and I should know more once I read them. Any questions?"

"When is it due?" Chase found his voice.

"By the end of January you should be parents again."

January. It was the end of May. January was months away. His heart rate accelerated as he tried to visualize their lives with a child in it when they were so far apart. How could they do this?

"Jody is to be very careful. No horseback riding, no strenuous exercise, no lifting heavy objects. Just use common sense and be careful so we can take this baby to term."

"I will be very, very careful," Jody said.

"I know I'm not your mother, Chase, and, Jody, I'm not yours, either, but I'm going to offer you some motherly advice. You've been blessed with a child and that in itself is a gift. I suggest you two get your act together and raise this child together. He or she deserves that much. I know what I'm talking about. I made the biggest mistake any woman could ever make and Jude forgave me because he loved me. And I still loved him. I'm grateful every day for that, and God gave me two more beautiful children. I'll never get over losing part of Zane's life, but I can't go back and change anything. I know you two have loved each other since you were teenagers, so I suggest a little forgiveness goes a long way in healing old wounds and making love new again."

They went down in the elevator together and neither spoke. In the lobby Jody sat in a chair. Chase sat beside her.

"Something wrong?"

"No. It's something wonderful. We're pregnant. But I'm worried this pregnancy might be just like Ivy's."

"Please don't say that. We just have to be careful."

"We?"

He leaned back in the chair, stretched his long legs out in front of him. "Yes. We're in this together and I think we should move in together so I can be there if something happens."

"You mean like husband and wife?"

"Why not?"

"Because you're so angry."

He leaned forward, trying to get a grip on his emotions. "I want to be a part of this baby's life every day."

"I never thought that you wouldn't. It's about me. How do you feel about me?"

He looked into her green eyes and saw his

whole world, but the anger was still holding on to him. "Give me time."

Jody got to her feet. "I'm going to go tell my parents and be as excited as I can be."

"Jody, you know what the doctor said. I'm going with you."

"You have your truck."

"I'll meet you there."

He prayed that time was all he needed, because if he could never forgive, that would be the biggest stress and heartache of all.

WHEN THEY REACHED the Carson house, everything was locked up and there were no lights on. It was after eleven o'clock. Where were her parents? Her dad should've been home for lunch. She knocked, but no one answered. Fishing in her purse, she found the key, opened the door and went in.

"Mom, Dad, it's Jody. Where are you?"

"Maybe they went out with someone," Chase suggested.

Peyton came from the hallway in a long silky negligee, her hair tousled in every direction. "Jody, Chase, we didn't know you were going to stop by." Her voice was nervous, as were the hands that pushed the blond hair away from her face. Her dad followed in his bathrobe, his hair just as tou-sled as her mother's. Oh… She knew what had been going on. Her parents were hav-ing makeup sex.

"We just wanted to tell you some good news for a change." She looked at Chase and said, "We're pregnant!"

"I need coffee—" Peyton swung toward the coffee maker and then swung back. "What did you say?"

"We're pregnant," she shouted. "I know it's a bit of a shocker. It was for us, too, but it's true. You're going to be grandparents at the end of January."

"I thought you weren't seeing each other?"

"Things changed."

"I'll say. A baby, Wyatt. Did you hear?" Peyton engulfed her in a sea of silk.

"Yes, I heard." He joined the hug. "Con-gratulations, baby, and you, too, Chase." He shook Chase's hand.

"Now, we have to go and tell more people, and you can continue what you were doing."

Peyton had the good grace to blush.

"I'll meet you at the diner," Jody said to Chase because she knew telling the Rebels was next. There were so many of them that it would take all day, but Jody was so happy that she didn't mind. She could sing from the rooftops all day long. They were having a baby and she couldn't help but be reminded of when she'd found out about Ivy. This was the way it should have been.

THE LUNCH CROWD was slowly filling the diner. Chase straddled a bar stool and smiled at his mother.

"Well, this is a difference," she said, wiping down the counter. "It's like flipping a switch from dark and gloomy to bright and sunny. What happened? Or are you just grateful not to be in the hayfield?"

She was right. That weight on his chest wasn't there anymore. Could a little baby work that much magic? "Where's Dad?"

"Who knows? He's working on the baler or something. It's his day off and he should be spending time with me and the kids, but you know your father."

At the mention of his name, Elias strolled through the front door. Grease smears were on his jeans and shirt, which wasn't going to sit well with his mother.

"Hey, son." Elias patted Chase on the back. "Are you getting rested up? We have a full day tomorrow."

"That's what I—"

"Look at your mom. She's got that mad look on 'cause I'm working. Tell you what, Maribel. I'm going to Temple to get a part and then I'm going to put it on the hay baler. After that, you and I are going out."

"What!"

"Put your dancing shoes on and something low-cut so it'll keep my blood pressure up and my eyes open."

She ran around the counter and hugged him. "That's so sweet. But what about the boys?"

"They're staying with Mom and Grandpa. JR and Tre feel so bad about making Grandpa cry that they're doing anything he wants. Right now they're polishing his boots. Grandpa has them going. He's good at fake tears. I remember that from my childhood. Oh, by the way, when you get home, you'll find pennies all over the living room. Eli decided to count them to make sure the bank's not cheating him. He lost track and started over."

"Elias, why did you let him do that?"

"When I get back to the house, I'll make him put them back into the fishbowl."

Jody came in and Chase walked over

to her. His parents kept talking as if they weren't there. Chase clapped his hands. Startled, his parents' attention swung to them, as did everyone's in the diner.

"We have something to tell you."

Maribel clapped her hands. "You're back together. I knew it." A big smile spread across her face.

"Well, what we really wanted to tell you was that we're pregnant. You're going to be grandparents at the end of January."

His mom's mouth fell open and his dad seemed stunned. His mother recovered first, jumping up and down and screaming. "Oh, oh, oh, this is the best news." Then she started to cry, wrapping her arms around Jody and him. "We have to do something, Elias! Y'all come out to the ranch tonight and Miss Kate and I will fix a big supper to celebrate. I'm so happy for you guys."

"Mom, give us time to adjust. Because of what happened to Ivy, Paige wants to monitor Jody and her activities to be on the safe side."

"I'm going to take a leave from my job," Jody said. "I don't want anything to interfere with a safe delivery."

Elias stepped forward and hugged them.

"Congratulations. You do what you have to and we're here if you need us."

"Thanks, Dad. Now, we're going home to grow a baby."

"Call me if you need anything," Maribel said. "I'm not that far away."

"Thanks, Maribel." Jody looked at Chase. "I'll meet you at my house."

Chase nodded.

After she left, he said to his parents, "I'll call Grandma and Grandpa and tell them and the boys. I don't want them to hear it from someone else. I'll try to get out there soon, and, Dad, sorry, it looks like I won't be able to help you anymore. I'll have to stick close to Jody in case anything happens."

"Don't you worry about it."

Chase walked out feeling better than he had in a long time. He went to Ivy's grave and sat on the bench for a few minutes. He wasn't sure why he was here, but he knew he had to come to help him deal with everything. "You're going to have a baby brother or a baby sister. He or she will never replace you. You will always have a special place in my heart. Love you, sweet baby girl."

He got in his truck and drove away, ready to embrace the months ahead and eager for that second chance Jody talked about.

CHAPTER EIGHTEEN

JODY TOOK A leave of absence from her job and followed Paige's instructions to the letter. Chase was right there with her. The more involved he became with the baby, and with her, the more hope she had for the future. Even she could see he was losing that hardness he'd developed over the loss of Ivy.

She had a box of children's books she'd bought when she was pregnant with Ivy. Chase got them out of the attic and started reading to the baby. He'd found out that it was good to read or talk to your child so they would know your voice, so both of them read to her stomach daily. She slept in her room and he slept in the spare room.

It was now June, and they talked about the remodel of Chase's house and decided to go ahead with it. They would now need a baby's room, so the plans would have to be altered. They had to knock out walls and add on to it to get everything they wanted.

Every evening they walked. Paige had said it would be the best exercise for Jody. They walked all over town and he was there to make sure she didn't overdo it. He went with her to the doctor. He went with her to the grocery store. He never left her side. She could see him changing right before her eyes. Every time he smiled at her, they grew closer and closer, and she didn't feel his resentment anymore. One night as they were sitting on the sofa and Chase was reading to the baby, a thought occurred to her.

"I have an idea. Don't object until you hear me out."

"I hope you're not thinking of going back to work. It's too much stress."

"I was thinking about our parents and what we put them through. I guess I can see their side now that I'm pregnant. If this is a girl—" she patted her stomach "—I would be devastated to miss her wedding. I just…"

He had his head resting in her lap, reading to the baby. He sat up. "Don't get upset."

"I just feel so bad about it."

"Don't, please."

"I think we should get married again in a church, just like they wanted, not only for them, but for us and the baby, too." She picked up his hand and threaded her fingers through his. "Chase Rebel, will you marry me?"

He stared at their hands and she held her breath. *Please, don't say no. Please.*

He picked up her other hand and twisted the engagement ring she refused to take off, even when it looked like they would never be together again. "I guess it's time to put the matching wedding bands on."

"Oh, Chase. We were grabbing at life before like spoiled teenagers. I want us to get married as mature adults who are about to be parents. And two adults who are as deeply in love as when they first met."

She was pushing him, but she needed a full commitment. She needed to know that he loved her and would always love her.

Chase sat up straight, his hands clasped between his knees. "I was lost for a while and couldn't find my way back to where I was. You hurt me deeply. I didn't understand how you could keep a child from me. Then Erin told me everything that happened and everything that you went through because you thought I was with someone else. Then I blamed myself for not being there for you. That's a lot of guilt to deal with, but through it all, I couldn't forget you. It's just like Grandpa said. You never get over that first love."

"So you forgive me?" She waited for his words because she knew it would define her whole life, their whole future.

He looked at her, his eyes dark. "If you'll forgive me."

"Oh, Chase." She wrapped her arms around him and they sat for a long time just holding each other. Slowly Chase began to talk and they shared everything, their thoughts, their feelings, their hopes and dreams. They would trust each other from that day forward. If she lived to be a hundred, she would never forget this moment when they forgave each other for the pain.

THEY DIDN'T MAKE a big thing out of the wedding. She invited Maribel and her mother over and told them they had two weeks to plan a wedding and they had to make all the decisions. Both mothers were thrilled by this prospect and promised to make sure everything was simple and stress-free.

Her mom would stop by every now and then to give her an update. The bridesmaid's color would be blush, she was told. Her mother had a notebook for all the wedding information.

"There's only one bridesmaid and that makes it easy. Since Martha Kate, Bailey Rose and Annie are singing, I'm ordering dresses for them, too. They're summer sleeveless dresses. The front is fitted and the skirt is short and flirty. Eden, Gracie, Olivia and Emily will read Scripture and wear the same dresses, too."

"You're doing a great job, Mom. I love the dress. Is Erin wearing it, too?"

"Same color, but the skirt is longer. It's more mature."

"Are you letting Maribel do anything?"

"Of course. We went shopping yesterday and got our outfits. I'm going to blow your dad's mind in antique pink. It's off-the-shoulder sequined lace with a fitted bodice and a slit up the side."

"Did my mom pick out anything?" Chase asked.

"You wait and see," Peyton said. "You will not recognize your mother in a beaded mesh pink champagne gown. Miss Kate picked out a salmon pink mid-sheath dress and beaded jacket. Everyone will look gorgeous." Peyton picked up the notebook.

"Now, what else do I need to tell you? I'm trying to fit all the Rebel cousins into the wedding and there are a lot of them. The girls are either singing or reading, and the boys will light candles across the church from John to Logan Mac. JR, Tre and JW are ushers. I just can't find a spot for Eli." She glanced at Chase. "Do you think he'd mind being a flower boy?"

Chase chuckled. "You'll have to ask Eli."

"I'll check with Maribel. She might want to change something. I'd better go. I have to meet her in fifteen minutes." She leaned over and kissed Jody. "Take care of yourself, baby."

"Peyton," Chase called before she went out the door. "Could you talk my mom out of catering the wedding? I want her to enjoy the day."

"Already done."

"What?"

"I told her there was no way she could cater the wedding and actually see the wedding going on. She would miss half of it. She thought about it and agreed. She doesn't want to miss a second. We've already booked a caterer, so it's a done deal.

See, I can work magic." She winked at him as she went out the door.

"I've never seen her so happy," Jody said. "It's like she's drinking bubbly champagne all the time. I can see now how important my wedding was to my parents. I'm trying not to feel guilty…"

Chase sat down beside her and gathered her into his arms. "No stress. We're doing it right this time, so smile at me."

She leaned her head back and smiled. "We're so lucky to have this second chance."

"Yes, we are, and I don't think I will ever forget it."

"Me, neither."

Chase laid his head in her lap and began to sing. "Hush, little baby, don't you cry. Mommy and Daddy's gonna buy you a teddy bear, and if that teddy bear don't sing…"

"That's not how it goes." She laughed and reached down and kissed him. They were happy and she prayed this happiness would last forever.

All too soon the wedding date arrived. Jody was calm and rested and couldn't wait to see what her mother and Maribel had put together. Erin drove her to the church and helped her get dressed in a small dressing room. She'd wanted to wear the same silk-and-lace dress she'd gotten married in the first time, but it was too tight around the middle. Thankfully her magical mother had found a seamstress to fix it.

The wedding went off as smoothly as their mothers had planned. Even Eli agreed to be the flower boy. Before the wedding, she took a peek inside the church. The beautiful white flowers and candles took her breath away. There were even big white bows and flowers on the end of each pew. It was breathtaking. A fairy-tale wedding.

When Annie played the piano and sang "Beautiful in White," the words got to her and a tear slipped out. Chase wiped it away with his thumb and she knew everything was going to be all right.

The fun part came at the end when they were getting ready to walk back down the aisle. Martha Kate said, "This one is for Gramma," and she broke into "Can't Help Falling in Love" by Elvis Presley. Everyone started clapping and smiling. Jody knew her gramma was watching.

They went to the reception from there, which was at the church activity center. Their mothers had outdone themselves again with the decorations. Linens and flowers were on every table and the meal was served, not a buffet. Everything was perfect. They didn't stay long at the dance. She danced the first dance with Chase to "Bless the Broken Road" and Maribel danced with Chase to "My Wish." Then Jody danced with her dad to "I Loved Her First." Her dad teared up and so did she, and she was so glad that they had made peace with each other. "I love you, Daddy," she said as the song ended.

"I love you, too, baby girl, for now and always."

After that she danced with Elias, and as she looked into his face, she knew she was looking at Chase in twenty years. Since Elias had cut his hair and shaved, he looked even more like him. Next she danced with Grandpa and that was it for her for the evening. She sat with Chase on the sidelines and watched as their parents took the floor, but first Elias stepped up to the microphone. "God bless Chase and Jody. May their two families be bound together forever. Now we're going to show you how it's done."

Everyone clapped as the two couples

sailed around the floor. "Our parents look so young," Jody said.

"Mom was barely eighteen when she had me and tonight she looks eighteen and happy. I'm happy we gave her this chance to have fun. No one deserves it more than her."

Jody's arm was looped through his and she squeezed his arm. She could hear in his voice how much he loved his mother. For so long it had been just the two of them and she had done a wonderful job raising Chase.

People came over to say hi and wish them well, and she and Chase watched everyone have fun. Eli was wearing Maribel out because he wanted to dance. He stepped on her shoes, her dress, and finally she took them over to a little girl in a blue dress who was dancing by herself. Maribel introduced them and walked away. The girl was doing all the latest moves with her arms and legs, dancing around Eli. He stared at her with a frown.

Jody whispered to Chase. "Eli doesn't know what to do."

Chase got up and wove his way through the dancers to make it to Eli. He leaned over and spoke in his ear. Jody didn't know what he said, but he pointed to JR and Tre, who were dancing with Gracie and Annie.

Eli gave a thumbs-up sign.

Chase made his way back to Jody and watched as Eli got into the dance, pointing his finger, hopping up and down and twisting. It wasn't exactly the way it was supposed to be done, but Eli was having fun. He didn't bother his mother anymore. She spent the night dancing with her husband and the rest of the family.

Jody rested her head on Chase's shoulder. "Ready to go home?"

"I want to stay and continue to enjoy this, but we better go home. I'm getting a little tired."

He kissed her cheek and then stepped up to the microphone and thanked everyone for coming and asked that everyone pray for them in the coming months. Then her dad took the microphone and invited everyone to stay and enjoy themselves, dancing, eating and drinking. And he warned everyone about too much beer. He got booed.

Jody walked out holding on to Chase's arm. Erin and Zane followed them. Zane said to Chase, "Good luck, my friend." They all hugged and Chase and Jody got in the truck and went home.

"It was perfect," Jody said.

"Yes," Chase agreed.

He helped her out of her wedding dress and she went to bed, but not for long. It was too lonely. "Chase?"

He came running in his underwear. "What? What's wrong?"

"I'm not sleeping alone on my wedding night."

Chase crawled in beside her. "Go to sleep." And she did, resting comfortably in his arms. But she could still hear the music and feel the happiness. It was a wedding of forgiveness, hope and love. And they needed that for the days ahead.

THE MONTHS PASSED QUICKLY, and before they knew it, the heat of the summer gave way to September and the kids went back to school. Hay season was over except for a couple of fields that might get a third cutting. Chase graduated from college. At the beginning of August the twins had their eleventh birthday, and toward the end of August Eli turned seven. He got a very limited phone and was excited until two days later when his mother threatened to take it away from him. He was annoying everybody by calling every few minutes. Now he had rules.

It was good they had events to take their minds off the pregnancy for a little while. One night Chase was reading to the baby with his head in Jody's lap and he felt something against his cheek. It took him a second to realize what it was. Was the baby kicking? He sat up quickly and put his hands on Jody's stomach.

"What are you doing?"

"The baby is kicking. I felt it."

"I was waiting to see if it would do it again." She placed her hands over Chase's.

"Come on, little baby. Kick for Daddy."

"Oh! It's kicking!" Jody shouted. "It already knows your voice."

Chase had chills all over and he couldn't take his hands from Jody's rounded stomach. It reminded him this was his child, their baby, and he couldn't wait to find out what it was.

They were supposed to find out the sex of the baby in July, but Paige had a doctor's conference. They didn't want anyone else to do it. They had an appointment today. It was a nail-biter.

He watched as Paige's assistant got Jody ready for the ultrasound. "The doctor will be right with you," the girl said as she went out.

"Are you nervous?" Chase asked Jody.

She reached for his hand and he held it tight. "A little bit. I just want it to be born and to be healthy."

He kissed her. "I know. I'm right here."

Paige came into the room in her white doctor's coat over scrubs. "Are you ready?"

"Yes," Jody replied. "We can't wait to know what we're having."

"Well, let's find out." Paige began the ultrasound and an image popped up on the screen. Paige stepped back so Chase could look.

"You can see the baby?" Chase asked. "I see nothing but a bunch of swirling lines."

"Come here," Paige instructed. "See, this—" she pointed with a pencil "—is your baby. Here's the head, both arms and legs."

"Oh, man," Chase said as the image came into view. "It's a baby. Our baby." He glanced at Paige. "And?"

"It's a girl!"

"A girl," Chase echoed. "A little girl. Oh, man." He ran his hand through his hair and his knees buckled. He had to clutch the wall.

Paige grabbed him. "Are you okay?"

"It's…it's…" He ran around the bed to

Jody. "We're having a girl. Isn't she the most beautiful sight?"

"Yes," Jody replied, wrapping her arms around him. She stroked his face. "Are you okay?"

"I didn't know how I would feel if it was a girl because of Ivy. But I feel fine. This baby is the cherry on the cake, so to speak. And I love her and her mother so much."

Paige's voice drew them apart. "I need to talk to you for a minute before you leave."

"What do you think that's about?" Chase asked as he helped Jody get dressed.

"I don't know. Let's go see."

Hand in hand, they walked to Paige's office and took their seats.

"Is everything okay?" Chase asked.

"Yes," Paige replied. "Everything is fine with this baby, but I wanted to talk to you about Ivy. I finally got your records from Austin and I saw some things I didn't like."

"Like what?" Jody asked.

"Your blood pressure. Your blood pressure has been normal every time I've seen you, but when I look at these records, your blood pressure started going up in the second trimester. Did the doctor ever address that?"

"He said my blood pressure was a little high and he might have to give me something, but he never did and we never discussed it again."

Paige placed a piece of paper in front of them. "These are the dates you saw the doctor and what your blood pressure was. You can see it go steadily up until Ivy was stillborn. It's the highest the last time you saw the doctor. In my personal opinion, I think your high blood pressure slowly cut off blood supply to Ivy. It should have been caught, and I contacted the doctor in Austin, but he has since retired. When I tried to contact him personally, I was told he was in hospice care and dying with cancer."

"I don't care," Chase said. "He should be cited for negligence in Jody's care, and the hospital, as well."

"I'm filing a complaint against the doctor and the hospital in hopes that this never happens again. That's about all we can do." She looked directly at Chase. "I'll take care of filing the negligent claims. I want you to take Jody's blood pressure three times a day and keep a record of it and bring that information in when you come to your next visit. If it goes up, I want you to bring Jody in or call me." She scribbled something on a piece of paper. "Here's my private number."

"You bet."

"You can pick up an upper-arm blood pressure kit at any drugstore. It's simple to use and you shouldn't have any problems."

"You can count on me."

Jody kept sitting there as if she was stunned. "Jody—"

"My high blood pressure killed Ivy?"

Paige got up and went to Jody. "I don't know for sure. No one ever will, but I wanted you to know in case we have to deal with it in this pregnancy."

"It can be dealt with?"

"Yes. I'd have to put you on some medication to control it. Now, I want you to put it out of your mind and concentrate on this baby. This healthy, strong baby."

Jody rubbed her stomach. "And she is healthy?"

"Yes, and I'm going to make sure she stays that way." She put her arms around Jody and hugged her. "I want you to stay strong. We're going to make sure you carry this baby to term."

"Thanks, Paige. We appreciate everything you're doing."

"You're very welcome." She went back to her desk. "I have to say, my family thoroughly enjoyed the wedding. Olivia and Emily danced the night away. Jude got tired and he made them dance with their cousins. The Rebel cousins had the time of their lives. It was a fun night and I'm so happy you had the chance to do it over so we all could be there."

They walked out of the office, smiling. It had been a magical night, but thoughts of Ivy now intruded on those memories. They got into the truck and Chase stared at Jody.

"What?"

"You're thinking about Ivy and how it's your fault. Please don't do that. If it's your fault, it's my fault, too. I should've been there to help you through the pregnancy. I should have tracked you down and made you listen to me."

"It's hard not to think and see every mistake I ever made."

"Don't do it. Let's think about this baby and a name. We have to name her."

"I was thinking about something with both our mothers' names, but I can't come up with anything that sounds good."

"Are you kidding? This baby will be like

a wishbone between them anyway. Let's go neutral so they don't fight so much over her."

Jody sat up straight. "Oh, Chase."

"What?"

"We forgot to call our parents the moment we found out the sex of the baby."

"Oh, man." He pulled out his phone. "Okay, I'm sending *It's a girl* to Mom, Dad, Grandpa, Grandma, JR, Tre, Zane and, of course, Eli."

"I've got Mom, Dad, JW, Hardy and Erin. Let's send it at the same time."

They pushed Send and within thirty seconds most of Horseshoe knew they were having a girl. Their phones lit up immediately with congratulations from everyone. They stared at each other and laughed.

"That's the fastest response to a gender reveal in the West," Chase joked.

"We're so lucky to have a supportive family. I wish I could've seen that when I was a teenager." Things would've been so much easier if she had, but that wasn't how life worked. She had to learn from her mistakes, and Jody had learned from a big one. Always trust her parents. They were much older and wiser and she should have listened.

"We do now and that's what counts."

And she would need their support now.

Deep down, she knew she wouldn't survive losing a second child. Her stomach cramped at the thought and she glanced at Chase. She needed his support the most. Happiness was just within their grasp.

CHAPTER NINETEEN

THE DAYS SEEMED to drag as they reached the end of the second trimester. Chase took Jody's blood pressure and wrote it in a tablet every day, three times a day. It fluctuated only a number or two, nothing severe. He prayed things stayed that way. While he checked on the house, Peyton stayed with Jody. He didn't want to leave her alone until after the birth and maybe not then.

He took Eli to deposit his pennies once again and then he wanted to visit Jody so he could talk to the baby. Eli got right against Jody's stomach and said, "I'm your uncle, that's what Mama said, and my name is Eli. What's your name?"

"She can't talk back to you, Eli," Chase reminded him.

"But she has to have a name."

"We don't know what it is right now. Just call her baby."

"'Kay. Your belly is big." Eli looked up at Jody.

Chase groaned.

The remark didn't faze Jody. "Yes, it is. The baby takes up a lot of room."

"Is she gonna be big?"

"We won't know until she's born."

"I'm glad I'm not mad at you anymore 'cause I don't want to walk in your shoes."

"What?" Jody was totally confused.

Chase got to his feet. "It's time to go, buddy. I heard Mom drive up."

"I wanna stay with the baby."

Chase let his mother handle that and it didn't take her long. "You can't stay. Your dad is looking for you and you have chores to do."

"Ah, Mama."

"Jody needs to rest."

She held up a finger as he started to protest. "Not one more word."

As they left, Jody said, "I hope our baby has some of Eli's personality."

"I think he's one of a kind."

"What did he mean by walking in my shoes?"

He told her what his mother had said. "Your mother and I are getting along very well." Chase was pleased about that. His mother had this need to always do everything for everyone and he could tell she'd backed off a little to let them have time to themselves.

HE WAS SURPRISED when Eli's teacher called him and asked him to come for a visit. He immediately called his mother to find out what it was about. She was clueless. So he prepared himself for whatever. Or whatever trouble Eli was in.

He met the teacher at noon on her lunch hour in Eli's classroom. They shook hands and the first thing he noticed was that she was young. Maybe twenty-three.

"I'm Amy Greene."

"I'm Chase Rebel. Not sure why you're contacting me instead of my parents."

"Eli told me something I'm not sure is true, and when I said I would talk to his mother, he said to talk to his big brother because he takes care of all his business."

"Business? He's seven years old."

The girl threw back her long dark hair and smiled. "Hilarious, isn't it?"

"You could say that." The girl was flirting with him and he had to get out of there as soon as possible. Nothing was going to shake his marriage this time.

"Eli said you played football. Should I know you?"

"Probably not. I'm retired now. What is it you wanted to talk about?"

"There's no rush. I'm trying to place you 'cause my dad watches football all the time."

Eli came running in. "Chase, did you tell her?"

"What's this about, Eli?"

"I told her I was saving money to buy gifts for kids who won't get anything for Christmas and she didn't believe me. I told her you take care of my business."

"Yes, I heard." He turned to the teacher. "Eli has been saving pennies all spring and summer, and he's deposited them into the bank."

"I'm sorry, Eli. I've just never heard of a kid doing this before. I'm sure the principal could help you with this."

"Thank you," Chase replied.

Eli ran to some kids who walked into the classroom and Chase moved toward the door, but before he could go through it, Miss Greene stopped him. "If you're not doing anything later, maybe we could get a drink."

"Sorry, but no, thanks. Later I'll be rubbing my pregnant wife's feet."

"Oh, whoops. I didn't know you were married."

He held up his ring finger. "Forever kind of married." As he walked out, he thought the girl must not be from around here or she would've heard about him and Jody. They had teachers come in from a lot of small towns.

He took the time to speak to the principal and get everything set up like Eli wanted. The lady at the bank had already told the principal and he thought it was a wonderful thing Eli was doing.

Chase went home and told his wife about the young teacher. He'd learned quickly about the mood swings his mom had told him about and he wasn't quite sure how she was going to react. Today she laughed and put her feet in his lap. "My feet could use a rubbing."

FALL BROUGHT COOLER temperatures and football. Chase and Jody went to a couple of high school games and got into the spirit of the holidays. Chase watched NFL games as much as he could, but he didn't miss playing the game. His life was occupied with other, more important things. They had Thanksgiving lunch with the Rebels and ate supper with her parents. It worked out fine. That night Chase put up the Christmas tree and she decorated it with Gramma's ornaments, some of which were Elvis-themed. Then they sat in front of it and sang Christmas songs.

Jody clapped her hands, singing, "All I want for Christmas is you…" They went on to sing "Jingle Bells," "Rockin' Around the Christmas Tree," "Away in a Manger" and "Rudolph the Red-Nosed Reindeer." They couldn't remember all the words, but they sang anyway.

Chase sat on the floor, his legs outstretched and Jody sitting between them. His hands were on her stomach as the baby kicked and kicked. The more they sang, the more she kicked. Jody turned her head to look at Chase.

"What?"

"I'm so happy, but I can't help being afraid."

"We don't have much more time. Two more months and the baby will be here and we can all stop worrying."

AT THE BEGINNING of December, the square was all dressed up and ready for Christmas. Wreaths with bright green and red bows decorated every window of the courthouse and a big one greeted everyone at the front door. Poinsettias lined the staircase inside and sat on every desk. Red-and-green-plaid bows adorned every streetlight, and every business on the square had a Santa, a tree or a wreath in their windows. It was certainly Christmas. The big tree was sitting on the square, just waiting to be lit on Christmas Eve. Everyone was in a festive mood and "Merry Christmas!" echoed everywhere.

Jody decided their living room didn't look festive enough and thought of something else she wanted to put out. Namely the nativity scene her gramma had had as a child. The figures were made of wood and hand-painted, nestled around a baby on a wood tray.

"It's old and I have to be very careful with it," Jody said as she placed it on the coffee table. A snow globe was beside it and she picked it up and shook it. "Now it's snowing. It's so—"

He looked up as she held her hand to her head.

LINDA WARREN

"What's wrong?"

"I'm dizzy."

He guided her to the sofa and ran for the blood pressure monitor and took her blood pressure. "Oh…it's up. We have to get to the hospital. Don't panic. Stay calm."

"No, Chase. It can't be happening now."

Chase thought of the fastest way to get there. He pulled out his phone and called Wyatt. He came right to the point. "Jody's blood pressure just shot up and we need to get to the hospital quickly."

Within seconds the sheriff's car roared into the driveway. Chase carried Jody out and they got into the back seat. The sheriff pulled away with the siren blaring all the way to Temple. Wyatt called the ER to let them know he was coming in with a pregnant woman. Chase, in the meantime, was on the phone to Paige. They met in the emergency room.

Chase and Wyatt stood outside as they rushed Jody into the ER. Paige was waiting for her.

Wyatt patted him on the back. "She'll be okay. Take a deep breath."

Up until that moment he hadn't realized he wasn't breathing. His lungs were tight. He let out a long breath and rushed in to find Jody. They tried to keep him out until Paige said, "Let him in."

Jody reached out for him and he took her hand, gripping it tightly. The baby was on a monitor and he could see her moving around. "The baby's okay?"

"Yes, she is," Paige said, "and so is her mother. We got her blood pressure down with medication. I'm going to keep her overnight and monitor her blood pressure to make sure the medication keeps it down."

"I'll go tell her father."

"Meet us in room 326."

"Is she okay?" Wyatt asked as soon as Chase stepped out of the ER.

"Yeah," Chase replied. "They're going to keep her overnight to monitor her blood pressure."

Wyatt grabbed him in a big hug. "Are you okay?"

Chase returned the hug, needing to lean on someone else for a change. "Yeah, I'm good now that Jody and the baby are okay."

"I'm sorry I ever doubted you, Chase. You're a good husband to Jody and I should've listened years ago. You're welcome in our home anytime, day or night."

"Thank you, sir. Now I have to go to Jody."

"And I have to call Peyton."

"Thanks for the ride, Sheriff," Chase called as he headed for the elevator.

Wyatt smiled.

Chase called his mother on his way up in the elevator. He wondered if there would ever come a day when something happened and they didn't call their parents. As a grown man, he could only think that would be a bad thing. A support system was everything.

Chase went into the room and Paige was there checking monitors on Jody, who was asleep.

"I gave her something to keep her calm," Paige said. "She was really agitated."

Jody looked so pale lying in the bed and he kissed her cheek just to touch her and to make sure she was okay.

"I want her to rest," Paige was saying. "The machine will take her blood pressure and it will start beeping if it goes up and the nurse will be alerted. You need to get some rest, too. I'll call for a cot."

Chase got comfortable in the recliner and went to sleep. He really didn't need the cot.

Paige came in again around midnight and he was surprised to see her.

"Are you still here?"

"I just wanted to make sure the medication was working and it is. She can go home in the morning, but please keep taking the blood pressure and you know what to do if it goes up. Everything should be good now."

THE NEXT MORNING, they went home very cautious and very grateful. Their parents were waiting for them, even Elias. That was how they spent the next two weeks, with their parents coming and going, watching out for them. Jody received a Christmas card from Heather, who was now living in an apartment close to campus. She was doing well and the news lifted Jody's spirits.

She tried to occupy her time by putting wedding pictures in an album for her parents and Chase's. It would be their Christmas gift, along with a gift card to a nice restaurant. The biggest gift would be the little bundle in her tummy, and every day Jody prayed for another day to give this baby a chance.

IT WAS TIME for Eli to donate his money to the Children's Christmas Fund. Maribel had taken over the chore of helping Eli because Chase couldn't leave Jody. They stopped by the house before they went to the bank.

"Chase, you don't have to worry," Eli said. "Mama's helping me."

"I'm sorry, buddy."

"It's okay. You helped me raise lots of money, and now Mama is going to take me to the bank and then to see the principal. They're gonna take my picture for the newspaper. Grandpa told me to be sure to smile."

Eli gave him a silly grin and Chase hugged him. "You did good, buddy."

"Since I'm on the committee to buy the gifts, I took it upon myself to visit with the families," Maribel said. "Two families are new here and out of work. Between them, there are five kids who wouldn't have received a gift for Christmas if it weren't for Eli. We thought about what else we could do for them. I was able to hire one of the ladies at the diner and Anamarie hired the other one at The Bake Shop. One of the men is a mechanic and I got Bubba to hire him. The other man we hired on Rebel Ranch to cut firewood and other things that need to be done."

"Oh, Maribel, that's wonderful," Jody said.

"A church and the grocery store have taken them food so they'll have plenty for Christmas."

"Come on, Mama," Eli said. "We have to go."

After they had left, Chase watched Jody as she worked on Christmas ornaments.

"You made one for Ivy and one for this baby. Ivy has her name on hers. What's on this one's ornament?"

"Well, you were very close to your nana and I was very close to my gramma." She held up the ornament. "This is what I came up with. How do you like it?"

He stared at the name. "I love it and I love her mother."

"Oh, Chase."

CHRISTMAS EVE WAS a night of excitement as everyone milled around the square, visiting. Since it was chilly outside, Chase made sure that Jody was bundled up really warm in a red turtleneck, pull-up maternity jeans and boots. Her long blond hair was down her back as he liked it best. Her jacket wouldn't fit around her stomach, but she wore it un-zipped.

The square was full of people drinking coffee or hot chocolate and eating kolacky and cookies. Everyone was enjoying the holiday.

All the Rebels were there and later they would be at Grandma's house, which was his dad's house, for Christmas.

He shook hands until he thought his arm would fall off. Cole, the chief deputy, was there with his wife, two kids and his grandpa. His best friend, Bo Goodnight, was also there. He worked SWAT in Austin. Bo and Cole had been friends forever. Bo pushed a double stroller.

"I didn't know you had another child," Chase said, squatting by the babies in the stroller.

"Two boys, eleven months apart," Bo said with a laugh. "I have a daughter running around here somewhere. She assures me that she's grown."

"They're adorable," Jody said, smiling at the babies.

"Congratulations on your baby," Bo said.

"Thank you. We're trying to get through Christmas."

They moved on to visit with friends from

high school, and everybody who lived here seemed to be on the square tonight. Martha Kate, Bailey Rose, Annie, Gracie, Olivia and Emily sat up on the courthouse steps and started singing Christmas songs.

It stopped for a moment as the mayor gave a speech and the city lights were turned down. They flipped a switch and the Christmas tree lights came on.

Everyone clapped as the lights shone brightly toward the sky. They turned the streetlights back on and all the kids ran forward to put ornaments on the tree and Martha Kate and her group started singing again.

Some of the kids were too small to put the ornaments on the tree, so their parents held them up and helped them. Chase reached into his pocket for the two small ornaments Jody had made.

"Put them up high," Jody said. And he did, as far as he could reach. Then he put his arms around Jody and they swayed together as Annie sang "Blue Christmas."

"Chase."

"Hmm?"

"My water just broke!" Jody cried. "It's too soon. It's just like last time."

"Shh, stay calm." He looked at her jeans and saw she was all wet in front. He didn't have time to waste. "Wyatt!" he shouted.

Wyatt strolled over, shaking hands with people.

"Get the car. Jody's water just broke."

So many things happened that it was hard for Chase to think. The baby was coming too early.

The sheriff's car jumped the curb and Chase got into the back seat with Jody. His mother threw a blanket and towels in as Peyton got into the back seat with them.

His dad took the keys away from Wyatt. "You're shaking. I got this."

Wyatt ran around to the passenger side and his dad slipped into the driver's seat. Within seconds they were off with the siren blaring. Peyton helped him get towels beneath Jody, as well as a blanket over her.

"Just hang on."

"It hurts," Jody cried.

Peyton stroked her face. "Take a deep breath. Mama's here."

Wyatt reached for Jody's hand. "Hold on, sweetheart. We're almost there."

Jody let out a scream and at the end of that scream was Chase's name. "I'm right here." He reached for her hand and she gripped his tightly.

"The baby's coming. I can feel it. It's too early." She let out another scream and Wyatt and Peyton were having a hard time controlling their emotions. "Is she breathing, Chase? Is she breathing?"

"Calm down, Jody. I can't tell if she's breathing, but your stomach is moving. Just hold on. We're driving into the ER."

His dad came to a screeching halt in the ER doorway. A stretcher met them and Jody was loaded onto it.

She had a death grip on his hand and he followed her into the ER. He was vaguely aware that his mother had driven up behind them.

"Chase," Paige said. "You might want to step outside."

"No!" Jody screamed.

"I'm not going anywhere," he said with grit in his voice.

They cut Jody's jeans off, her sweater, too. She'd lost her boots in the car.

Paige did a thorough exam. "We have a problem. The baby's breech."

"What?" Chase said, the blood draining from his face.

"She's coming butt first instead of head-first. Let's get her to the OR."

"What?"

"First I'm going to try to turn the baby, but if that doesn't work, I'll have to do a C-section."

"Chase!"

He looked into Jody's worried eyes. Her face was red and blotchy and he wished he could take her pain away. This was hell. "It's going to be okay. I'm right here."

"Is the baby okay?" Chase looked at Paige because he didn't want to lie to Jody.

Paige nodded. "Yes. Now we have to make sure she stays that way."

"Let's go," Paige said, and everyone went into action, pushing the stretcher to the OR. Chase paused for a second to talk to their parents and told them what was going on.

"Oh, no, my poor baby," Peyton wailed.

Maribel put her arm around Peyton. "You have to be strong for Jody. Let's sit for a minute and say a prayer."

Wyatt stood there, pale and unmoving.

"Wyatt," Peyton called.

"Why is this happening to my kid? She doesn't deserve this."

Elias put his arm around the sheriff's broad shoulders and Chase left them to deal with it in their own way. And he had to do the same.

When he got to the OR, two orderlies stopped him. He shook his head. "Oh, no. This isn't going to play. I'm going in there even if I have to go through you. My name is Chase Rebel and I played wide receiver and went through linebackers a lot stronger than you, so you're not keeping me out."

Paige came to the door. "Chase, this is going to be very painful for Jody and it would be much better if you waited out here."

"No. I have to be with her. I need to be with her and I hope you understand that."

"You Rebel men are so stubborn. Come in, but you have to be very, very quiet. Do you understand?"

"Yes, ma'am."

"Just be very aware. If I can't turn the baby, we're going to put her to sleep and operate."

Chase watched as Paige's team got Jody ready. Monitors were everywhere and an IV was in her arm. Another doctor was in the room and three nurses. Paige got on the table between Jody's legs and began to push on Jody's stomach.

Jody screamed and he clenched his fists. Paige kept working with the baby and Jody started to cry. He reached down and kissed her. She was mildly sedated.

With tears streaming down her face, Jody said, "Sing to her, Chase. Sing to…her."

Paige continued her assault on Jody's stomach and slowly Chase began to sing. "Hush, little baby, don't be afraid. Mommy and Daddy's gonna buy you a rocking chair, and if that chair don't rock, Daddy's gonna buy…"

"Keep singing," Paige shouted. "She's turning. She's turning! Keep singing. Keep singing!"

Chase found his voice and kept on singing, making up words because he couldn't remember the original. Finally Paige jumped up from the stretcher.

"She's in the birth canal and will deliver any minute. Chase, if you want to catch your child, you'll have to come around here."

"Go," Jody urged.

"Now, Jody, I need you to push. I mean really push hard."

Jody pushed and screamed and cried until Chase could see the head. "She's coming." The baby came out in a rush of blood and water right into his hands. For a moment he was paralyzed as he stared at his little girl, who was the most beautiful sight he'd ever seen.

Paige cut the umbilical cord. "Put her on Jody's chest."

He gently laid their baby on her chest and walked around to Jody. "She's here."

The nurse had a vacuum or something and was cleaning her mouth and wiping her eyes. The baby let out a scream to let everyone know she was very much alive. Jody started to cry again and she smiled and wrapped her arms around her child.

"I have to let our parents know. They're worried sick outside."

He stuck his head out the door and was surprised to see the waiting room full of Rebels. "She's here. Grandparents, you're up."

He didn't have to tell Peyton twice. She rushed past him to Jody, and she and Wyatt stopped and stared at the baby in her arms.

"Oh, heavens. She's so tiny." Peyton took her from Jody and handed her to Wyatt. His hands shook as he held his granddaughter and tears welled in his eyes. His mother took her from Wyatt, and she and his dad oohed and aahed over her.

The nurse took the baby out of his mother's arms. "I have to clean her up, but I will bring her back."

"Chase, go with her," Jody mumbled weakly. "Don't let her out of your sight."

"I won't."

He watched as they weighed his daughter and measured her and did several other things and then dressed her in a onesie with a Santa hat. Before the nurse put the hat on, she put a red bow around the curls on the top of her head.

Chase watched in awe. The baby was perfect. Ten fingers. Ten toes. And the most beautiful face he had ever seen. She looked like Jody.

The nurse laid her in a rolling crib and he pushed the baby back to Jody. He stopped in the family waiting area outside Jody's door to let everyone see her, especially Grandpa and Grandma. But Eli pushed his way through. He wanted to meet his niece.

"She's so tiny. What's her name?"

"Let's go ask Jody."

Chase took the baby in, placing her in Jody's arms. "Everyone wants to know her name."

"I've asked a thousand times and you always say you don't know. Well, it's time to know," Peyton said.

"Chase and I thought and thought about it and couldn't come up with anything. Chase was crazy about his nana and I loved my gramma. Both their middle names just happen to be Lillian."

Jody cuddled the baby close. "So, everyone, I'd like you to meet Lily. Lily Rebel."

"It's perfect," Peyton cried. "I wonder what she'll call me."

"She's calling me Nana," Maribel said.

"Why do you get Nana?"

"I just do."

While their parents bickered back and forth, Chase gently stroked Jody's wet hair and reached down and kissed her. "I love you now and forever."

She smiled, her eyes bright. "I love you, too. Right now I'm hurting so bad, but I'm the happiest person in the world. You're my first love, my only love."

They'd finally put the past behind them. Chase knew there would be ups and downs, but they were more mature now and trusted each other. He scooped the baby out of Jody's arms. He would love this little girl and her mother for a lifetime and beyond.

EPILOGUE

One year later—Christmas morning

LITTLE FINGERS TOUCHED Chase's cheek. "Da-da-da-da, tree."

He opened one eye and stared into the big brown eyes of his daughter.

Jody raised her head from his chest. "Is that Lily?"

"Yes. She's standing by my side of the bed and saying something about a tree."

"How did she get out of her bed?"

"I was wondering the same thing." He reached down and pulled Lily into the bed with them. She giggled and snuggled beneath the covers for a second.

"Oh, somebody stinks." Jody picked her up and carried her to the baby bed.

"No." Lily wiggled in defense. "Tree. No, Ma-ma-ma-ma, tree."

"She's so excited. Do you think she knows?"

"We've been talking about it for two weeks or more. Yes, she knows it's Christmas and her birthday."

Jody finished snapping up her Christmas pj's and set her on the floor.

"Tree." She started to run, but Jody caught her. "Wait. We have to put on our Santa hats." With the hat firmly in place, Lily made a dash for the living room.

Chase wrapped his arms around Jody. "Merry Christmas."

"Merry Christmas." She leaned against him. "I'm not sure I'm awake."

"Da-da-da, tree." Lily pointed to the decorated Christmas tree.

"Okay, we're coming." They walked slowly into the living room and sank down by the sofa.

Jody looked around the tree. "There's a bow way over here. Some paper is torn off this package and an ornament is on the coffee table. She's been up without us knowing it."

"Oh, man, that's scary."

Lily squatted at the tree, touching packages, knowing she wasn't supposed to open them until Christmas. Or at least that was what they kept telling her.

"Okay, precious, open your presents."

Lily stared at him.

"Show her," Jody suggested. "It's her first Christmas. She doesn't know what to do." Chase reached for a small gift-wrapped package and tore into it. Lily giggled and finished pulling off the paper.

"She's doing everything so early," Jody said in a forlorn voice. "She sat up early, crawled early and walked before her nine-month birthday. Now she's talking, saying words and understanding us. It's too early, Chase. I want her to stay a baby a little longer. You know what they say?"

"No, I don't, and I'm afraid to ask."

"She's getting out of the way for another one."

Chase sat up straight. "Are you kidding me? You want to go through that again? No! Lily is our family. That's it. We're not going through that pain again."

"If it's a boy, I'd like to name him Carson, after my dad." Jody kept on as if he hadn't spoken.

"What about my dad?"

"His last name would be Rebel. I think that covers it."

For the next thirty minutes they opened

presents and then picked up the trash and had breakfast. Jody had made Lily a big cupcake, and she put a candle in it and set it in front of Lily in her high chair. They sang "Happy Birthday" and Lily clapped, smiling.

"Whose birthday is it?" Chase asked.

"Me." She poked herself in the chest.

"How old are you?" Jody asked.

Lily held up one finger.

"Yes, you are," Jody said and lit the candle.

Lily blew and blew until it went out. Then she stuck her face in the big cupcake, licking all she could into her mouth with her tongue.

Chase laughed. Jody laughed. They were mesmerized by the actions of their child.

The year had gone by so quickly and at times Chase just wanted to stop time and enjoy his daughter, but he knew that was unrealistic as each day she grew more and more. Jody didn't go back to work for six months, and he took the coaching job and didn't start until mid-August. So they had a lot of time with Lily, much to each grandma's chagrin. They were really glad when Jody and Chase went back to work so they could keep Lily.

Sometimes his dad would come and pick up Lily from the diner and take her to the ranch so Grandpa and Grandma could visit for a while. Lily had them all wrapped around her little finger, especially Eli. He loved his niece.

Last night they went to the lighting of the Christmas tree on the square and talked about how different it was from last year. Lily, Katie and Lizzie, Rico and Anamarie's daughter, sat on the courthouse steps together. They were a threesome, holding hands and wiggling their butts to the music. From the square, they went to Grandma's house to celebrate Christmas.

After breakfast Chase lay on the sofa just to get a thirty-minute nap. Soon Jody joined him and Lily crawled up next to Jody and they all went to sleep. It was eleven o'clock when Chase woke up.

"Jody, wake up. It's eleven o'clock and we have to be at your parents' by noon for Christmas dinner."

"Oh, no." Jody jumped up, holding on to Lily. "I'll take a shower and give Lily a bath. Don't worry. We'll make it."

And they did, right at the tone of twelve o'clock. Wyatt and Peyton were standing at the door. He got Lily out and set her on her feet and she went running to them. They needn't have worried what Lily was going to call them. She had her own names for them.

"Gam-ma, Gam-pa." Wyatt grabbed her before Peyton could.

"Gampa wants to show you something." They all followed Wyatt outside to a swing he'd put in a tree—a baby swing with a safety belt. Wyatt pushed her until lunch was on the table, and then Lily, not wanting to get out, cried. Chase took her and she cried for a little while on his shoulder.

They had a good lunch and then they rushed home to get ready for the party. Lily's first birthday party. Of course, his mom was making pizzas, and all they had to do was supply the drinks and snacks.

Zane and Erin were among the first to arrive. Katie shot into the house with a gift in her hands. She gave it to Lily and then they hugged so tight they fell down giggling. They would grow up to be best friends, just like their parents.

His uncles and cousins started arriving. When he saw his mom's SUV drive up to the curb, he let Lily out the front door and she ran to them. "Pop-pa, Na-na."

His dad caught Lily and threw her into

the air. She giggled and spit all over him and he didn't mind. JR helped Grandpa get out of the vehicle and Chase wondered why the other boys weren't getting out.

With Lily in his arms, his dad said, "We need to talk about Lily's birthday."

"Why?"

A mixed-breed Jack Russell terrier bounded out of the SUV and sat on his haunches next to his dad's feet. A dog, without asking permission.

"Well, I guess the dog's out of the bag."

"We got her a dog," Maribel said. "If you don't want her, we'll take her."

Lily squirmed to get down to the dog. "Dog." Then she hugged it.

"Her name is Cuddles."

Eli got out of the car with a dog bed and some food. "Look, Lily, this is her bed."

Lily sat in the dog bed and the dog got in the bed with her.

"So?" They waited for his answer.

He looked at Jody. "I think it's great. I had a dog when I was little and I can't imagine my childhood without Dolittle. Of course it's okay."

And the party went on. Some of the guys played poker and others played football with

Chase. As he threw the ball, he realized his arm had fully healed, but he still had no interest in going back to the NFL. He had everything he wanted right here.

Lily fell asleep on Grandpa's shoulder. Chase lifted her away and she woke up, as did Grandpa.

"Where you taking her?"

"To put her to bed."

"Oh, yeah. It's past my bedtime, too." Grandpa got to his feet and reached for his cane.

Chase kissed his daughter. "Tell Grandpa good-night."

Lily leaned over and kissed the old man. "Pa."

Grandpa patted her back. "She's the sweetest thing God ever created." He looked at Chase. "Didn't I tell you not to give up?"

Chase grinned, putting an arm around his great-grandfather.

Chase was grateful Grandpa got to meet Lily and he prayed the man had more time to get to know her. But it wasn't a given and he cherished each day.

Soon the last person trailed out the door. They'd had a full, wonderful holiday and they were happy to go to bed. As soon as the light went out, Lily woke up.

"Da-da-da-da."

He got up and sang to her, but as soon as he walked away, she popped back up. "She's exhausted and can't go to sleep."

"Let me have her." Jody got up and took Lily and sat in the rocking chair. Cuddles was right there if she needed any help.

"What's wrong with Mommy's baby?"

Lily rubbed her eyes.

"Yes, I know you're tired." Jody began to rock and sing a song Gramma used to sing to her. "When the moonlight shines over the water, searching for the sweet Lily that sleeps there beneath the willow. Sweet Lily. Close your eyes, my sweet Lily."

Lily was a daddy's girl. She followed him everywhere, and if he got out of her sight, she would cry. But if she was hungry, sleepy or tired, she wanted her mommy. It took two people and a family to raise a child and Lily got the best of both worlds. They would always adore her, love her and steer her in the right direction.

Jody got up and brought Lily to her bed and tucked her in. "She's out." She removed the red bow from Lily's hair. "I wonder if she'll ever know how much we love her."

He turned Jody into the circle of his arms. "I wonder if her mother will ever know how much I love her."

"Yes, every day." She wrapped her arms around his neck and they shared a deep kiss.

They had been tested, and now all they had to do was step into the future, as many Rebels had before them. They had fought for their happy-ever-after and now it was theirs.

* * * * *

Get 4 FREE REWARDS!

We'll send you 2 FREE Books plus 2 FREE Mystery Gifts.

The Sheriff's Promise
RENEE RYAN

To Protect His Children
LINDA GOODNIGHT

Love Inspired books feature uplifting stories where faith helps guide you through life's challenges and discover the promise of a new beginning.

FREE Value Over **$20**

YES! Please send me 2 FREE Love Inspired Romance novels and my 2 FREE mystery gifts (gifts are worth about $10 retail). After receiving them, if I don't wish to receive any more books, I can return the shipping statement marked "cancel." If I don't cancel, I will receive 6 brand-new novels every month and be billed just $5.24 each for the regular-print edition or $5.99 each for the larger-print edition in the U.S., or $5.74 each for the regular-print edition or $6.24 each for the larger-print edition in Canada. That's a savings of at least 13% off the cover price. It's quite a bargain! Shipping and handling is just 50¢ per book in the U.S. and $1.25 per book in Canada.* I understand that accepting the 2 free books and gifts places me under no obligation to buy anything. I can always return a shipment and cancel at any time. The free books and gifts are mine to keep no matter what I decide.

Choose one: ☐ **Love Inspired Romance Regular-Print** (105/305 IDN GNWC)   ☐ **Love Inspired Romance Larger-Print** (122/322 IDN GNWC)

Name (please print)

Address   Apt. #

City   State/Province   Zip/Postal Code

Email: Please check this box ☐ if you would like to receive newsletters and promotional emails from Harlequin Enterprises ULC and its affiliates. You can unsubscribe anytime.

Mail to the Harlequin Reader Service:
IN U.S.A.: P.O. Box 1341, Buffalo, NY 14240-8531
IN CANADA: P.O. Box 603, Fort Erie, Ontario L2A 5X3

Want to try 2 free books from another series! Call 1-800-873-8635 or visit www.ReaderService.com.

LIR21R2

Visit ReaderService.com Today!

As a valued member of the Harlequin Reader Service, you'll find these benefits and more at ReaderService.com:

- Try 2 free books from any series
- Access risk-free special offers
- View your account history & manage payments
- Browse the latest Bonus Bucks catalog

Don't miss out!

If you want to stay up-to-date on the latest at the Harlequin Reader Service and enjoy more content, make sure you've signed up for our monthly News & Notes email newsletter. Sign up online at ReaderService.com or by calling Customer Service at 1-800-873-8635.

RS20